"The witty, improbably propulsive rom-com you didn't know you were waiting for—and just the sparkling, slightly sinister love letter to New York City that New York City deserves. An effervescent delight."
—ELIF BATUMAN, author of *Either/Or*

"Crosley skillfully crafts these stories so each relationship feels full and unique, as if each could have made a book of its own. And yet *Cult Classic* moves swiftly, cutting quick . . . A spirited, sometimes delightfully mean-spirited, occasionally weird trip through urban life and love in the twenty-first century."
—CAROLYN KELLOGG, *The Boston Globe*

"While *Cult Classic* is a meditation on love, . . . it offers a refreshingly realistic, nonprecious attitude toward modern romance."
—CADY LANG, *Time*

"*Cult Classic* makes an uproarious time of romantic carnage. Sloane Crosley captures the brutal mirror of past love, the slow creep of ambivalence into dread, and the sense that a detour can easily become a life."
—RAVEN LEILANI, author of *Luster*

"One of the funniest writers in the business . . .
The pleasure is as much in Crosley's sharp, chatty style
as it is in the narrative arc."
—JAMES TARMY, *Bloomberg Businessweek*

"Lola's wit and savvy make her a genial narrator, but it's her
emotional honesty that makes her a strong one. Crosley's writing
is as funny as ever, with a great line or clever observation on
nearly every page . . . Her fascinating conceits—entertaining and
compelling in their own right—are the engines of the narrative, but
her insights into contemporary life are the fuel."
—JONATHAN RUSSELL CLARK, *Los Angeles Times*

"*Cult Classic* is a sharp, witty *Slaves of New York* meets Natasha
Lyonne's *Russian Doll* guide to the trickiest of all scrapes:
the obstacle course that is romance in Manhattan. True to form,
Crosley's writing is dripping with both style and substance,
enough to last you all summer."
—ERIK MAZA, *Town & Country*

"*Cult Classic* is easily the funniest fiction I've read this year.
Crosley brings the same offbeat humor she utilized to acclaim in
her nonfiction to this novel that defies easy categorization.
Riotously funny, suspenseful, weird, and insightful, it's a unicorn
of a book that's a perfect summer read."
—DAVID VOGEL, *BuzzFeed News*

Praise for *Cult Classic*

❖

"Addictive . . . [*Cult Classic*] is like your favorite rom-com meets *Eternal Sunshine of the Spotless Mind*, with a light soupçon of *Ghostbusters* . . . Crosley casts a spell with lightning wit, devilish dialogue, and walloping truths about how little reason there is to anything resembling love."

—Annie Bostrom, *Booklist* (starred review)

"In Crosley's sharp and funny prose we get real insight into love and relationships, turning the who's-behind-it suspense into a meditation on what it means to be in love and hope for happy endings . . . I'll read anything Sloane Crosley writes, of course, but *Cult Classic* is for everyone."

—Emily Firetog, *Literary Hub*

"I love a secret society, and I love a wry narrator alive to the mysteries and absurdities of the world. Set in a Manhattan that feels accurate down to the molecule, *Cult Classic* is unbelievably smart on modern love and start-up mystics alike. Sloane Crosley can do it all."

—Robin Sloan,
author of *Mr. Penumbra's 24-Hour Bookstore*

"*Cult Classic* is aimed with deadly accuracy at those unfortunate enough to have dated only during the twenty-first century. It's witty—of course, because Sloane Crosley wrote it—and razor-sharp, and very clever, ditto, but it's more romantic and redemptive than one had any right to expect. It's so good. I couldn't stop reading it."

—Nick Hornby, author of *High Fidelity*

SLOANE CROSLEY
❖
Cult Classic

Sloane Crosley is the author of the novel *The Clasp* and three essay collections: *Look Alive Out There* and the *New York Times* bestsellers *I Was Told There'd Be Cake* and *How Did You Get This Number*. A two-time finalist for the Thurber Prize for American Humor and a contributing editor at *Vanity Fair*, she lives in New York City.

CULT CLASSIC

MCD ⊛ PICADOR FARRAR, STRAUS AND GIROUX NEW YORK

CULT CLASSIC

SLOANE CROSLEY

MCD
Picador
120 Broadway, New York 10271

Copyright © 2022 by Sloane Crosley
All rights reserved
Printed in the United States of America
Originally published in 2022 by MCD / Farrar, Straus and Giroux
First paperback edition, 2023

Title-page illustration by June Park.

The Library of Congress has cataloged the MCD hardcover edition
as follows:
Names: Crosley, Sloane, author.
Title: Cult classic / Sloane Crosley.
Description: First edition. | New York : MCD / Farrar, Straus and
    Giroux, 2022.
Identifiers: LCCN 2021059966 | ISBN 9780374603397 (hardcover)
Classification: LCC PS3603.R673 C85 2022 | DDC 813/.6—dc23
LC record available at https://lccn.loc.gov/2021059966

Paperback ISBN: 978-1-250-86717-9

Designed by Abby Kagan

Our books may be purchased in bulk for promotional, educational,
or business use. Please contact your local bookseller or the Macmillan
Corporate and Premium Sales Department at 1-800-221-7945,
extension 5442, or by email at MacmillanSpecialMarkets@macmillan.com.

Picador® is a U.S. registered trademark and is used by Macmillan Publishing
Group, LLC, under license from Pan Books Limited.

For book club information, please email marketing@picadorusa.com.

mcdbooks.com • Follow us on Twitter, Facebook, and Instagram at @mcdbooks
picadorusa.com • Instagram: @picador • Twitter and Facebook: @picadorusa

1   3   5   7   9   10   8   6   4   2

For the men. For some of the men.

The only place outside Heaven where you can be perfectly safe from all the dangers and perturbations of love is Hell.   —C. S. LEWIS

Hell is other people.   —SARTRE

CULT CLASSIC

PROLOGUE

There exists a contest among the dead. Each week they enter a lottery. They hold slips of paper between the dusty tendons of their fingers and creep up to a hat that's been placed on a small table in their respective town squares. They drop the slips of paper inside the hat, extending and releasing like carnival cranes. The hats are then collected by a particularly ghoulish bureaucratic employee, their contents dumped inside a spinning ball, the location of which is kept secret. Back at home, the dead turn on their screens or plug in their phones or their AM/FM radios (depending on when they died). Then they wait. There was some debate, at first, over whether to broadcast the lottery live. The concern had to do with time zones. In the afterlife, your day and night are the same as they were on Earth. It seemed unfair that every dead Japanese person who'd ever lived would be sleeping when the results were announced. But selecting a time was better than selecting no time.

What the dead win is the chance to walk among the living for exactly three minutes. Very little can be accomplished in three minutes (aside from murder, ask around) but three is all they get. This explains why every ghost sighting in history has taken about the same amount of time. Ghosts don't go on road trips. They don't wait in line with you at the supermarket or watch television over your shoulder. Astoundingly, some try to stretch their time. These are the kinds of ghosts who, when they used to be people, sauntered into dressing rooms and tried on pants at a pace that suggested an unfamiliarity with pants. They get summoned back quickly. On top of which, they have their pads of paper revoked for all eternity. It's a devastating blow. But this is how much it means to them, this opportunity to stare at a cracked ceiling, to wash their hands or set the table or tidy their rooms. They miss it so much, the chance to participate in the mundane, it consumes them beyond reason.

This is the story Clive Glenn's mother used to tell him whenever he'd complain of boredom.

I think about this story a lot these days, which is strange, since Clive has given me plenty to think about since. It's more successful as an anecdote than a lesson, but part of the story had stuck with Clive, maybe the wrong part. Being a kid is like this. Your parents pack you a suitcase full of pedagogical messaging and by the time you're grown, it turns out most of the items were perishable anyway. You have to start over, pack your own bag. I remember the day I heard Clive talk so earnestly about this parallel ghost world, expecting him to laugh it off. But he wasn't laughing, he was confessing. That's the first time I can recall thinking something was off with him. Way off. For all our surface similarities, there was a whole layer of one-eyed sea creatures on Clive's ocean floor.

It was a Friday afternoon. We were sitting around the conference room table, perched on the edges of ergonomic chairs, plastic bowls of half-eaten salad warmed by the midtown sun. A centerpiece of untouched delivery napkins. We assumed Clive was turning his mother's wacky parenting into lunchtime fodder, but no—he was floating the idea. Did we think it was possible that the dead operate like this? That this is how planes of existence are organized and maintained? Look beyond what you know, beyond "science," and just ask yourself what's possible.

But we were not capable of asking, never mind answering. We were young and poor, eating lunch at the office so we didn't have to pay for it ourselves. We scrounged for segues. Vadis had an aunt who'd hired an exorcist once. Zach had a toaster oven that would turn itself on in the middle of the night. That was pretty weird. Clive excused himself to make a call.

I'd hoped that was the end of it. But as we were leaving an editorial meeting the next day, Clive held me back to tell me about the time he'd seen a ghost in the building. Our magazine had occupied the same space for more than a decade. Before us was a branding agency, before them, the ad men, before them, a Berlitz language center, before them, a Pan Am call center. Really, it could've been anyone haunting the halls. It wasn't a figure, he clarified, so much as "a shadow that moved with its own intent." Could I believe some poor schmuck had used its break from eternal damnation to watch the light on our copy machine plead for a refill? I shook my head. What I could not believe was that we were having this conversation.

The shadow, he went on, unprompted, was a reminder to appreciate whatever lies beyond our way of thinking, a world made no less logical by our lack of understanding and no less valid by our skepticism.

"Mysticism," he concluded, "is as rational as math for those living inside it."

I blinked, waiting for him to say something else. He didn't.

"Are you kidding me with this shit?"

Now seems like a good time to mention that the magazine in question, where Clive was editor in chief for eleven years and I was his deputy editor for nine, was called *Modern Psychology*. This was a scientific periodical, the oldest and most prestigious in the nation, if not the world. We were the gate-keepers for the profession, the legitimizers of research, the debunkers of myth. I was not trained for this kind of talk, certainly not from my mentor, a man animated by logic and brown liquor. I felt betrayed by his sincerity regarding the occult, and he, in turn, felt betrayed by my judgment. It wasn't long before he began shutting me out, confiding in me less, whispering into the phone, missing work without telling me why. Our coworkers hadn't gotten the memo. Whenever they needed a stamp of approval, they asked me if I knew where Clive had gone. Or when he'd be back. I was the one to ask. But I never knew.

This was before the magazine folded, before the print-media world evaporated, before we began new lives.

And now? Well, now nothing, Clive. Now you're dead.

I hate to be the one to tell you this, but life on Earth has proceeded at pace without you. All your scheming did not alter the human experience as we know it. No one's emotions can be purchased or cured from the outside. People are not your puppets. If it's any consolation, *I* am not the same. Not after everything you did to me. I no longer believe in coincidences, for one thing. I often feel as if someone is waiting for me as I round certain corners, a feeling strong enough to set me walking in the opposite direction. I have difficulty relaxing in crowds, which is hardly exceptional, but solitude can be fraught in the same way. When I fall asleep, a force not entirely benign passes behind my eyelids. Like I can hear the mechanics of a curtain being drawn.

And if it helps, I'm sorry. That one is tough to admit, considering all the time I spent feeling wronged by you, but I suppose death is the ultimate lubricant for truth. You were my friend once and I'm sorry I didn't try to understand you better when I could have. I fell for the projection and forgot the person. I wish I'd listened to you that day in the conference room. What you were trying to tell us is that, like ghosts, each of us would sacrifice anything—money, sanity, security—for a chance to go back in time, to make sense of our choices, of the unholy mess that is ourselves. So if it helps, Clive, I think you are out there right now, writing your name on a slip of paper, patiently waiting your turn. I really do. If it helps, I know you can fucking hear me.

1

Our dinner was winding down in Chinatown when I got up to get cigarettes. This was more about giving myself something to do than satisfying a craving, unless you count the desire to take a break from other people as a craving. I don't smoke, not officially. A significant portion of my friends would express surprise to see me smoking at all. I also never smoke the whole thing, opting to leave a trail of crushed paper flutes in my wake. I sometimes wonder how this aborted indulgence reads to the naked eye, aside from registering as litter. I fantasize about other people's fantasies, about cars that arrive earlier than expected, sweeping me off to some glamorous event. Sometimes I go darker. I think of kidnappings, of vans, of men in ski masks tossing me behind a steel partition. The traces of saliva on the filter—this is how the identifications will be made. Alas, the unlikelihood of being yanked off the street in downtown Manhattan kind of declaws the idea. But it beats vaping.

"What kind?" asked Vadis, tearing herself away from Zach too easily.

Her face was flush. She put an elbow on the table, triggering a little earthquake in her wineglass. Gold bangles slid down her arm, chasing after each other until they became one. Zach reached for his phone in an attempt to claim his own distractions.

"The ones with the nicotine in them."

"Oh," she said, somehow disappointed.

What kind. What a meaningless question. Cigarettes are not seasonal and Vadis didn't smoke. Though she'd always been brimming with meaningless questions, asking what time meetings to which she wasn't invited began, if I knew a long-dead psychiatrist's contact information, if B. F. Skinner had pets, if "we" had an angle on this emotional intelligence feature, if I had any double-sided tape. Who, in the history of the world, has ever had any double-sided tape? Then she'd sigh over my desk after I told her I couldn't help her, drumming those aristocratic fingers on my monitor as if her standing there would produce a better answer. The longer she stood, the more insulting her presence became. This was Vadis's way of suggesting she knew other people's minds better than they did.

"I once read this article in *Harper's*," said Zach, eyes still fixed on his screen, "about people who did all sorts of crazy shit on Ambien. They woke up in the corner of the room or boiled their underwear. This one woman, she buttered her cigarettes and ate them."

"*Harper's* published this?" I asked.

"Somewhere," he said. "Cautionary tale."

"That's not a story about cigarettes," Vadis corrected him, combing her hands through her hair, "it's a story about Ambien."

"Or butter," I offered.

"It's a story about the confluence of desire."

"Don't say desire," she scolded him.

"An orgy of vices then."

She looked at him hard.

"Really don't say 'orgy.'"

"The woman probably crushed up the pills and rolled the cigarettes in them," Zach muttered.

"What?!" Vadis hissed.

"Like Mexican corn."

"No one knows what you're talking about."

"Lola knows."

"You guys can leave me out of this if you want," I said.

How did these people wind up being my people? I'd had other friends before them, had I not? It was hard to remember. After *Modern Psychology* folded, it was as if a starting pistol had been fired and we scattered to separate corners of the professional universe. Vadis went to a "bedding and lifestyle" company run by a socialite (the arbitrary delineation between "bedding" and "lifestyle" amused us all), running their events and producing their content (blog posts with headlines like "Thread Count On Me" and "Bath Bombs to Detonate Calm"). Her work complaints centered around her flighty, impetuous, presumptive boss, traits I associated with Vadis herself. It was therefore difficult to tell if the socialite was a real problem or if Vadis was unaccustomed to engaging her mirror.

Zach wound up overseeing the editorial page of a headhunting agency. The idea was that if *Modern Psychology*, the world's preeminent psychology periodical, had seen fit to employ Zach, he must be a people person. He must have insight into the needs of people. When they fired him, they cited a personality conflict. The fact that it took them six months to come to this conclusion was alarming. Generally speaking, being fired would've been a badge of honor for Zach. Alas, to be an unemployed headhunter was to be the butt of a joke that even he did not find funny. Disillusioned with corporate America and "the hoi polloi corruption of media," he went the practical route rather than settle for some "foggy facsimile" of culture. He entered the gig economy, delivering medical supplies, building bookshelves, drilling holes in the walls of useless liberal arts graduates, picking up dog medication for old ladies. He would've preferred to report to the dogs.

Of Clive's protégés, only I stayed the course. Or the closest to the course. I wound up running the arts and culture vertical of a site called *Radio New York*, the pet project of a venture capitalist who mostly left us alone. I farmed out bite-size nostalgia in the mode of lists of popular books and movies and podcasts, or assigned essays on popular books or movies or podcasts or think pieces responding to widely circulated essays on popular books or movies or podcasts. The Lloyd Dobler nightmare for the new millennium. *Radio New York* stifled every voice and clipped every word count. The culture of quotas and reviews was difficult for some (me) and a given for others (anyone under the age of thirty-five). But at least the specter of media decay felt different than it had at *Modern Psychology*, where the end of the magazine felt greater than itself. In the new media landscape, reduction was baked into the deal. Like going to work as a stunt double. Probably nothing bad will happen to you immediately but probably something bad will happen to you eventually.

"Is there any of that spicy cauliflower thing left?" asked Vadis, looking down the length of the table.

The table had been demonstrably cleared, all dishes replaced by dessert menus.

"I worry about you sometimes," said Zach.

"Worry about yourself," she said, patting him on the cheek.

He jerked his head back in a halfhearted way that suggested that cheek would go unwashed. I touched my jacket on the back of my chair. It was a thin army jacket, flammable, more for style than utility. I told myself I would leave it as self-imposed collateral.

In the beginning, these dinners were a lifeline to the past. The brainchild of Clive Glenn, our erstwhile king, they came with the air of leadership, no matter how neutered. Which is what we wanted and what we had lost. There was a time when we'd spent every moment with one another, arguing over articles like "Arguing Productively with Your Coworkers." We were shipwrecked from newsstands, kept alive by doctors' offices that allowed us to claim a staggering 17.5 pairs of eyes per copy. We were not invited to the cool parties (except, sometimes, Vadis) or the all-day Twitter wars (except, often, Zach) or the televised panels (except, toward the end, Clive). But we had low health insurance deductibles and we could stand the sight of one another.

Alas, even we were not spared from the shifting American attention span. Advertisers had clued in to the futility of the magazine ad, even in a targeted publication like ours. Print ads are like "tossing wet pasta down a well," said the rep for one account, a mixed metaphor that kept us amused—*It puts the pasta down the well or else it gets the hose again*—as we switched from monthly to bimonthly, from bimonthly to quarterly, from quarterly to online only, from online only to newsletter, from newsletter to dust.

Only Clive was somehow bolstered by this entire experience. Not unscathed, not like me, placed with some media host family until he found his forever home. *Bolstered.* Even when his name still crowned the masthead, he'd begun to step away from the drier aspects of running a magazine and morphing into a full-blown psych guru. He wrote the introduction to an anthology about psychic pain. He invented a DSM drinking game that he played at intimate dinner parties with celebrities who posted videos of the experience on their private social media accounts. When the videos leaked, he issued an apology for his insensitivity that landed him on NPR. He got his own talk show for a while, which was something. Tote bags appeared with the silhouette of his face on them. His speaking fees skyrocketed. But even Clive, with his Brain-Wise™ meditation kits and fancy friends, even Clive—well, I just never got the sense that any of us were as happy apart as we'd been together.

Which is why, counterintuitive as it sounds, I dreaded these dinners.

We were flaunting our former selves to our current ones. We'd become too disconnected, too leery of bridging the gap, too likely to run down a list of conversational categories as if detailing a car. *How's the family? The job? The apartment hunt?* As if making deeper inquiries would open up a sinkhole of sadness from which we'd never escape. Once, at an Indian restaurant, I watched Zach sullenly picking cubes of cheese out of his saag paneer. I don't know why he ordered it. He was in a self-flagellating relationship with dairy. I asked him if he had any fun summer plans.

"Lola," he said, twisting his face, "are you 'making conversation' with me?"

We hated asking these questions. Besides, I knew all the answers already. For instance, I knew *all* about Clive's apartment hunt. He'd gutted a place in my ever-gentrifying neighborhood, a duplex penthouse with heated bathroom floors and two terraces, one of which got caught in the fold of the design magazine spread about the renovations. The building was a complex for childless men who divorced early and without consequence, men who would be young at fifty. Clive had a live-in girlfriend now, a giraffe of a person named Chantal with thighs so thin, birds probably flew into them. But he was still a poster child for New York divorcees, for inoffensive fine art and impressing women half his age by boiling linguine. Sometimes I'd see him on the subway platform and hide. I was not proud of this. But I was never in the right frame of mind to deal with Clive.

And yet the temptation was always there, to grab a stranger, point, and whisper: "Ask me anything about that man over there."

"Is Lola leaving us?" Clive barked from his end of the table.

He hiccuped but seemed delighted by it, like a baby. No one made it out of these dinners sober. Perhaps because they took place on Friday nights. Or perhaps it was because Clive never took care of the check and was impervious to all suggestions that he should. Zach's theory was that being cheap made Clive feel like he was running for office. *Gather 'round, ye townspeople, and watch the multimillionaire eat a hot dog!* Mine was that it was a show of respect, like we were all on the same playing field now that he couldn't fire us. Vadis's was that we were overthinking it: Rich people stay rich by not spending money; she should know (she was being grossly underpaid by the bedding socialite). Whatever the reason, we always split the bill, which meant cutting off our noses to spite our wallets and ordering as many cocktails as possible.

"How could you?" Clive asked, feigning a wound.

"Because I'm not interested in spending time with you."

"Liar," he bellowed, and slapped the table.

Even drunk and sloppy, a Viking demanding mead, the man was alluring. Maybe not to me, not anymore, but certainly to the Chantals of the world. See the sharp cheekbones to which his youth had clung like a cliffhanger. See the sparkly eyes of indeterminate color lurking below the swoosh of hair that flaunted its bounty. See the chin scar from a childhood bike accident in a town with no plastic surgeons.

"Where are you going?" he mouthed, more sincerely this time.

I pressed two fingers against my lips and moved them away. I could tell he wanted to sneak out with me, the conversational equivalent of eating a hot dog. But he couldn't risk being spotted smoking by some wellness fanatic with a platform. Plus, his desire to hold court was too strong. To leave would be to acknowledge the conversation would continue without him there to moderate it.

A long bar area connected the entrance to the dining room in the back. Patrons attempted to shift their stools even though they were nailed to the ground. They nursed cocktails with spears of dark cherries and citrus rinds. Mirrored shelving made the rows of booze seem infinite. I felt a sense of pride, imagining a foreigner stumbling into this place, noting that all the world's swank looks more or less the same. It was mid-May, the season formerly known as "spring," but the restaurant had yet to take down the velvet curtains that circled the entrance. Passing through them felt like walking onto a stage.

I was unfamiliar with this section of Chinatown, as much as anyone can be unfamiliar with an island on which one resides. The area a few blocks over was experiencing a mini-resurgence in the form of vegan provisions and upscale boutiques manned by Parsons students (the prices could be guessed by multiplying hanger distance and overhead). This was perplexing to me, as there was nothing to resurge. The neighborhood had been fashionable for years. Whatever businesses opened now did not arise from cheap rents or a triangulation of community and so ladling on layers of practiced nonchalance made it feel as if people with no sense of history had planted a flag in a neighborhood where the denizens had been drinking natural wine since 2005.

All this cool I wanted to avoid. All this cool made me tired.

So I made a left, toward Houston, into a less self-consciously trendy zone. There were remnants of a street fair, racks of stiff leather jackets spilling out onto the street. I passed an art gallery with no art, a dive bar with no sign, and buzzers with no names. Eventually, I spotted the telltale yellow of an electric awning. This was a high-class bodega; the kind with enough energy bars to set the mind to calculating how long the body could last if trapped inside. I waited behind an elderly man as he selected lotto numbers and a pack of Merits. The hem of his pants dragged along the floor as the cashier suffered him patiently. Atop the register was a wide-eyed plastic cat, its paw moving up and down in silent protest.

When it was my turn, I felt compelled to be extra sane. I forwent matches in a tone that suggested I was giving up my inheritance.

"I'll take a lighter, too," I said. "Please."

The cashier slid one across the plastic counter. I gave the metal wheel a quick roll.

"Don't light that in your pocket," he warned.

"I wouldn't dream of it."

Actually, I would dream of it and often did. I worried that I'd be mindlessly playing with a lighter in my pocket and set myself on fire. I thought about it so much, it was a miracle it never happened.

I walked back along the same side of the street, packing the cigarettes against my palm. I got a disproportionate kick out of pleasant interactions with strangers. I suspect it's because these were the kinds of interactions I wished I could see performed by every man I'd ever dated. Or vice versa. So many of my past relationships devolved into fights on public transport or long chains of undignified texts and I'd think: If only I could see you, flipping through your mail. Or booking airline tickets. And if only you could see me, wishing the driver a good night. Or either of us, reciting our social security numbers to prove we are ourselves. Where did these seductively functional people go when sex got in the way?

It was then that I spotted my ex-boyfriend Amos.

Amos was standing outside the restaurant with a taller friend. The two of them shared a square of sidewalk, the friend running his thumb under the strap of a messenger bag to relieve the weight. I could tell they'd just come from inside. Larger forces had protected us from seeing each other, but larger forces had done all they could. When I left and came back, they'd washed their hands of me.

This was not a place I would've expected Amos to have heard of, forget patronize. When we were together, he was dismissive of the "fetishized expense" of Manhattan. Manhattan was soulless, gentrified, once for the very young and the very rich, now only for the very rich and the very soulless. Reduced to a high-end strip mall, all the city's personality was in the past, all its pride delusional. I was too tired to mount a defense—tired, probably, from having to schlep to Bed-Stuy to see my boyfriend. Dropping our near-identical rents or the pilates studios of his neighborhood into conversational evidence bags didn't seem worth it. Besides, what Amos never understood was that with each pronouncement of my home as a dead zone, he made me feel better about living here. The eye of a hurricane may be inaccessible, but it's still the eye.

Toward the end of our relationship, I felt a reactionary love for all the things Amos hated. Not just Manhattan, but streaming services, nature videos, expensive toiletries, pop music, smartphones, beaches, throw pillows, bottled water, alternative milks, kitchen gadgets (a strawberry destemmer—who knew!), and cats. So completely did I commit to these things (was this the first time anyone adopted a kitten out of spite?), I convinced myself they were more indicative of who I was than the deeper things Amos and I had in common. I became resentful of the books and politics and niche references that had brought us together, as if they had betrayed me by leading me into the arms of a man who diagnosed Clive as a charlatan and my friends as "morally impoverished."

Our relationship never would have lasted for the two years it did were it not for Kit. Amos had a twenty-something cousin named Kit, a Hollywood starlet with a penchant for filters and quotations. But she was a blood relation, which made her tolerable to Amos, which, in turn, made him tolerable to me. When Kit was filming in New York, the three of us went out to dinner. She ordered food as if she and the waiter were working on a project together. She recounted stories from Amos's childhood and demanded our conversion from tequila to mezcal.

"You're such a good proselytizer," Amos told her, "too bad you're Jewish."

Kit flicked the straw wrapper she'd been balling into Amos's face and he cackled. She unlocked a less captious Amos. He refrained from deriding the Hollywood industrial complex in front of her. When the bill came, Kit grabbed it like it was nothing. I'd never seen someone take a check like that, without momentarily losing track of what they were saying. Amos didn't flinch. Whereas whenever I grabbed the bill, we had weird sex afterward.

After we broke up, I found myself watching the multi-cam sitcom on which Kit appeared, searching for his jawline in hers. I wasn't trying to torture myself, though I did manage to do that, only to search for evidence that Amos had been real, that I had kept this person's contact lens solution in my medicine cabinet. I often felt like this after breakups, no matter who had cut the cord—that fresh shock that life does not end from a single blow. A comforting concept in the long term, a jarring one in the short term. Resiliency is overrated. To get hit by a truck and ride the subway the next morning is not commendable, it's insane. But thanks to Kit, I could postpone this mourning process indefinitely. I watched her show so religiously, my interest in it took on a life independent of Amos. At the magazine, Zach and I shared a cubicle wall, so I foisted plot summations on him, despite his having zero interest in hearing about a sitcom meant for teenagers. I read the recaps, scrolling for Kit's name to see if any of them had isolated her performance. I closed out of these articles if I sensed Clive or Vadis behind me.

When the show was canceled, I felt a second wave of remorse about Amos that felt a lot like the first wave. Details that should've cycled through my memory long ago came rushing back in—the holes in his clothing, the scratches in his records, the disability that prevented him from wringing out a kitchen sponge. I remembered the layout of his apartment too well. This included the musty sofa on which he explained that monogamy was a vestigial construct gifted to us by the Puritans. It wasn't me, I had to understand. Except that it was me because there was only one of me.

We sat there, like guests of the furniture. I told him that I did not like the way he was talking about this, as if he had some kind of affliction that required him to put his penis in multiple people. I said that I could forgive someone, even him, for cheating, but I could not forgive someone, even him, for plotting to cheat.

"Why do you have to call it 'cheating'?" he asked in that redoubtable tone of his.

"Call it whatever you want," I said. "Pancake. I am not going to sit here while you pancake every woman you meet."

"*Every* woman is unlikely," he said, scoffing.

The breakup was about six years ago. Kit's show was canceled two years ago. As I approached, I worried this discrepancy in mourning would be palpable. I also happened to have on the same shirt I'd worn the night we broke up, as if I'd been walking around in a mausoleum the shape of Amos Adler, breathing stale Amos Adler air. I reminded myself of the full life I had now. I had a steady job that I didn't completely hate. Old, good friends. Ten fingers, ten toes. I had wiped all the sleep from my eyes before noon. Also, I'd been having sex.

More important, the sex I'd been having was with my fiancé. My fiancé to whom I was engaged to be married, a person I'd swindled into a lifetime of mutual tolerance.

Here was a man who would never pancake on me (though I sometimes worried this was more a failure of imagination) or disappear for weeks, breaking the silence with a three-thousand-word screed or, better yet, the insistence that there had been no silence. May our gaslights illuminate the bridges we burn! Here was a man whose snobberies were logical (buy the more expensive concert tickets, vote early, make your own coffee). Here was a man who asked me about my day because he wanted answers, not credit. A man who intuitively sensed the relevance of my summer camp stories. A man who let me refer to him as "Boots," a nickname that began during a conversation about parents who give their babies nonsense names in utero. Never mind the implication he was the *child* of our relationship. He didn't care. Because here was a man who did not think of himself as woefully untapped by the world, who was not driven to an existential crisis by an unread literary journal. Here was a calm, nonjudgmental soul who knew of Amos Adler only because I'd mentioned him once, in passing.

"Famous Amos?" Boots asked, mulling it over. "Like the cookie?"

"More or less," I said, balling up the old sweatshirt of Amos's that had inspired this exchange.

"I've never known an Amos."

I wanted to add "me neither," but I knew I had to end this conversation.

When we first got together, Boots and I made an agreement never to speak about our exes unless absolutely necessary. Say, one of them died in a freak accident and one of us was tapped to deliver the eulogy. Or one of them was elected prime minister of a small country. It was his suggestion that we move into the future with only each other. He'd been scarred by a girlfriend who was obsessed with her ex. It was exhausting and scary, trying to predict her triggers. She "carried around hatboxes of baggage, like a cartoon of a woman with steamer trunks behind her."

"And a poodle!"

"What poodle?"

"Nothing, go on . . ."

"Well anyway, I guess my baggage is baggage."

And so I agreed to this arrangement, even though I thought this policy was too strict, not to mention robbing us of imagery that could be pocketed for sex. But I was the one who stood to benefit: Boots had been in two serious relationships, college girlfriend and scary girlfriend included. We were never going to be seated at a table with someone who required an explanation. I, on the other hand, had nothing but explanations. Some of us get smaller denominations from the romance ATM than others. In addition to the flings, I'd had about fifteen five-month relationships, not to mention the six- and nine-month relationships, not to mention the ones that came to life in the night like haunted toaster ovens: *You up?*

I had tried to explore the why of it. Thanks to *Modern Psychology*, I had access to the most complete therapist database on the planet. My parents were still happily married. No one had abandoned me, beaten me, or withheld their love. Was I enamored by disinterest and disinterested in affection, set on giving my heart to people who didn't deserve it? See-sawing between desperate and inscrutable like a deranged child? Was I trying to find replicas of my father and then smashing those replicas? Had Cupid's bastard brother snuck into my bedroom and whispered in my ear, "My child, never commit"? I'd begun to suspect that my search for an inciting incident *was* the inciting incident. But before I could get to the bottom of it, I met Boots, who made it all stop, who could not unbreak me but who could protect me from the narrative of the broken.

The night we got engaged (along the Brooklyn Heights Promenade, the lights of the city winking in approval), we were in a cab going over the Manhattan Bridge. I was drunk by then, flirting with nausea in the backseat. I cracked the window and looked down my left arm, following it to its natural conclusion.

"Whose finger is that?" I asked.

"Who put that there?" Boots laughed, teasing me, declaring me wasted.

But I was not talking about the ring. I was so drunk, I was talking about my actual finger.

Boots had asked my parents for my hand, if it *was* my hand, in marriage. This conversation was easy to imagine, one of them screaming at the other to pick up the kitchen phone. They are not tough people. A phone call is all that would be required to sell the house and pay off the terrorists. Or marry off their daughter. But he and I had not discussed marriage, not seriously, only implicitly, in the way we kept filling up the calendar, facing holidays head-on. So while the question did not come out of left field, it was no fastball to home base.

I knew I'd spend no small amount of time, working it out in my head, wondering if I'd be just as disturbed by him *not* getting permission. I often felt my prime years to figure out if I subscribed to the concept of marriage were when I was a child, back when all of life was hypothetical. As an adult, it's hard to come down on a common institution to which you have no anecdotal access. It smacks of sour grapes. Boots had come along at a time when any reasonable person would've assumed I had an educated stance. If I wanted to take the political route, marriage was confinement, a raw deal. People hoped for transformation but too often got lobotomization. Idealization hardened into disappointment. But life is not lived in politics, it's lived in days.

And so I was content, sitting in the back of that cab with nothing to look at but the profile of Boots's head, the city rising up beyond him. Even if I was only ever borrowing someone else's certainty, it would become mine eventually. I could let the idea roost. I decided right there and then that if there was ever anything so terribly wrong with me, it was only that I was a woman who'd spent her youth in New York and never left.

To make this moment exponentially worse, Amos had, in fact, become a famous Amos. Time bends differently for each of us, but it had bent so favorably in Amos's direction, it was clear any post-breakup curses had backfired. He'd written two novels and, last I heard, was compiling a collection of his poetry. The first novel was long and pretentious and inspired the kind of critical ire so extreme, you couldn't argue he was doing something right by getting a rise out of people. The second was equally long and pretentious but about a Palestinian child who, while playing one day, wanders into a dilapidated house. He opens a kitchen cabinet and stumbles upon a Hamas-built tunnel that he crawls inside, but instead of popping out in Israel, he winds up in an alternate reality where there's no such thing as war. It was on the bestseller list for four weeks, popular enough to amend the consensus about Amos's first novel, which went from "unreadable" to "dense." Suddenly, Amos was not a poet who'd tried his hand at fiction, but a novelist who'd dabbled in poetry.

The taller man with the messenger bag was probably his new editor. This person must have selected the venue and expensed the meal. He spotted me first. Amos clocked the break in his audience's attention and followed the taller man's gaze. He smiled and rocked back on his heels.

"Hi there," I said, hugging him to buy myself time away from his face.

"Lola," he half-whispered.

"I feel like calling you 'Stranger.'"

"Go ahead," he said, chin moving against my shoulder.

"Hello, Stranger."

By the time we detached, he had this beatific look on his face. Here was someone who'd mourned well, whose memory was flushed of unpleasantness.

"Are you coming or going?"

"Neither," I said, holding up the pack of cigarettes, "coming back."

Amos smoked more than I did, or at least he used to.

"How *are* you?" he asked, as if having administered a truth serum.

"Just, you know, meandering the mean streets of Chinatown. You?"

"Oh, it's far too much to sum up in a sentence."

I had to refrain from flicking the lighter in my pocket.

"It's good to see you," he continued. "Are you still editing?"

"Are you still pissing standing up?"

"What?"

"Nothing," I said, waving at the air. "Yes, of course I'm still editing. I'm at *Radio New York*."

"The tech thing?"

"It's not a 'tech thing,' it's just funded that way. I'm a little disappointed you don't know where I work."

"Or am I just pretending not to know?"

"Now there's a question. Clive and Vadis and all them are in there."

"You're kidding," Amos said, looking over his shoulder as if their faces would be pressed against the glass. "I didn't see them."

"Well, that's probably okay."

"I never had a problem with those guys."

"Clive's toned it down," I said, "since he found inner peace and a billion dollars. And Vadis's not, I don't know—"

"Barking at interns?"

"No, no barking. She's gypsy chic now."

"I'll pretend to know what that means. But man, how did I miss seeing you?"

Should we just fuck on this pavement square and get it over with? Amos was shorter than most of the guys I'd been with. "Napoleonic sexy," as Vadis dubbed him after a digital slideshow. Amos looking pained on a panel. Amos looking pained at a party. Amos looking pained on a dock in Maine. A real-estate broker who was not Amos at all. Success had unlocked his grooming. He'd always been a fancy person trapped in a starving artist's body. It was the jawline, destined for good suits and clearly defined from the neck like a Pez dispenser.

I offered my hand to the tall man, feeling Amos's eyes trained on my breasts.

"We've met," he said, taking my hand, "a couple of times. Roger."

I was sorry Roger didn't have his own ex-girlfriend to screw on his own pavement square, but there was no need to punish me for it.

"Of course," I said, shaking my head. "Are you guys working together?"

"As in, is he my author?"

No, as in on a construction site.

"Yes, as in that."

"I wish," Roger said.

"He wishes," Amos confirmed, as if some fantastic joke had passed between them.

"So why aren't you? I'm not sure if you're aware, but Amos is a very brilliant writer. I'm sure he has another book or six in him."

"Well, I wouldn't want to mess with Jeannine."

"Jeannine Bonner," I said, just to prove that some people's names were worth remembering.

"Jeannine is *very* proprietary," said Amos, as if it were a burden to be claimed by a legendary editor, to be conversant in her personality.

Roger removed his glasses and began cleaning them on his shirt. He was at least five years junior to Amos and me, as many as eight. I got a whiff of a roommate. Laminate flooring. Roach traps.

"I hope you didn't pay for dinner," I said, "since Amos is the property of another woman."

"More like the other way around," tittered Roger.

"By which you mean that Amos makes women his property? Is that a thing we're admitting in public now?"

"Can you believe we used to date?" Amos asked, and then to me: "Are we getting a drink or what? Roger has to go home so he can wake up to a screaming baby."

Roger released a theatrical sigh. My eyes zipped down to his left hand as my brain confirmed the improbable calculus— yes, his left was my right and there was a gold band on it. The roach traps vanished, replaced by soft toys and frozen breast milk. I could feel Death stringing cobwebs along the walls of my uterus like Christmas garlands.

"I need my jacket," I announced.

I left with the understanding that Roger would have absented himself by the time I returned. It was helpful to have a buffer, but I did not enjoy this version of myself made uneasy by a young family.

Inside, my jacket was waiting, zombie-like over my chair.

"We went through your pockets," said Vadis.

"Anything good?"

"Nothing. A pen. It's broken."

"Keep your coat off," instructed Clive, stretching his arms. "Stay awhile."

A waitress was flipping the chairs upside down, slamming wood against wood.

"Nope," I said, "I'm leaving you all."

"Booo," said Zach, who was now drunk enough to express emotion.

Alcohol knocked the intellectual out of him. He would not like knowing that Amos Adler was outside. Amos was a more successful, more confident version of Zach. They were the same species. Same politics, same takes. This was the primary source of Zach's distaste, a conclusion so obvious, he never reached it. Instead, he spent years analyzing why Amos

Adler "sucked so hard." I kissed them all in the vicinity of their faces, but when I got to Vadis, I whispered: Amos. Outside.

"What?!" she hissed, with a sharp "t."

She twisted in her chair, as if taking in more of my body would reveal further truths. If there was further truth to be had, it was that I was shocked Vadis would remember Amos. She had inverse retention skills when it came to men. The more firmly planted someone was in my life, the more likely she was to give that person a dismissive nickname or forget his name altogether. One night, I told her that the reason she made up names for these men was so they could never be real. Because if they weren't real, they couldn't take me away from her. I don't think I meant a word of it. But this is how you speak when you're in a bathroom stall in your twenties, high on cocaine, and testing the depths of your friendships.

When I went ahead and got engaged to someone with the nickname of an unborn baby, it was like I did Vadis's job for her.

"Amos," Vadis stage-whispered, looking toward the door. "I can't believe it."

Then she turned abruptly and shouted: "Clive!"

"What?!" he shouted back. "Jesus."

"Vadis," I said, putting my hand on her shoulder, "don't."

"Nothing!" she said, before turning back to me. "How did he get here?"

"Well, to be fair, how did any of us get here?"

"Obviously. Right. It's just . . . Okay. Have fun. Report back. Be careful."

"Of Amos? I'll let you know if he stabs me in the neck with a quill pen."

"Just, you know, in general. Take notes."

She tapped at her temple as if turning on a button.

"Okay," I said, patting her on the head, "you're weird. Cute, but weird."

I left quickly, feeling pressure to get back outside. I was sure the reality of seeing each other felt just as tenuous to Amos. He could just vanish. But when I stepped back through the curtain, there he was.

"Where to?"

I was disappointed by his reliance on me to pick a place. During the years of not speaking, I'd superimposed a new person on Amos, composed of all the things I liked about him as well as an eradication of all the things I didn't like. In this case, an inability to select venues.

"Give me a second."

I removed my phone and began rapidly scrolling through my texts. I'd gone on a date with Boots to a perfect bar around here, but I could never remember the name. It felt less like a betrayal to take Amos to the bar than it did an insurance policy that I'd be reminded of my relationship, of who had become responsible for my healthy associations. I held the phone close to my face, putting a spotlight where Amos was already looking.

"And when you're done," he said, "you can tell me about this."

I let him hold my arm up by my engagement ring. My hand went limp in his, a napkin in its napkin ring. Which is about how big the ring suddenly seemed. The ring had belonged to Boots's grandmother. Why my generation assumes that entire generations before us had taste when only a few of us have taste now is a mystery. The diamond is cloudy and pear-shaped. It's fixed in a setting that brings to mind the word *prongs*. I learned the hard way to turn it around every time I put on a sweater.

"It's dual-acting," Boots decided, "a shiv and a ring in one!"

He had a way of putting a positive spin on everything. It's one of the things that first attracted me to him. I did not need another poet, arguing that depression was the only reasonable side effect of intelligence. The downside was that when the subway smelled or the food was inedible or the hotel room was too loud, Boots would be the last person to call the manager. You can't make lemonade out of everything, I posited, some lemons are meant to be tossed. On our fourth date, I broke my ankle and Boots refused to ask the emergency room nurse for pain medication.

"She already said she'd bring it," he assured me.

"But that was thirty minutes ago."

We didn't know each other well enough for me to use him as my personal pit bull, and a trip to the emergency room was a premature stress test. But even then, I knew I had this man on my hands who would sit with me for as long as it took, one who brought me flowers and stripped his tone of disappointment when he saw me light a cigarette afterward.

"I didn't know you smoked."

"I don't," I said, forgetting that I was supposed to be trying to impress him.

The filter pulled at my skin as I yanked it away and threw it on the ground.

"I also didn't know you littered."

So what if he was being serious? And so what if he would not harass the nurse? Or allow himself to be overcharged for the wrong flowers?

It was just a ring. But sometimes, when people complimented it, I tacked on a disparaging comment. I worried that the ring broadcast how disconnected I felt from Boots of late, how secretly full of misgivings, none of which I felt I could share with him. The ring was dangerous in this way. But the ugliness of the thing was one of our private jokes.

I pulled my arm away from Amos. He cleared his throat. "What?"

"I didn't say anything," he said, hands in the air.

I had not hidden my relationship. In fact, where was my thanks for not shoehorning it into the conversation? I'd done nothing wrong except, perhaps, to lay the groundwork for wrongdoing. My only crime was relying too heavily on Amos. I knew he would notice the ring and, once he did, we'd be safe. Amos was intolerable on the surface but good deep down. Whereas I was starting to worry I was the reverse.

We sat at a shellacked block of wood beneath a canopy of Christmas lights that never got taken down. New York was perpetually waiting for the cold, steeling itself for gray skies and sleet. I pawed for hooks beneath the bar and put my foot onto Amos's stool so that my leg hovered between his. We clinked glasses. Then he asked me why I wasn't in love with Boots.

"Good morning," I said, swallowing beer foam. "You never did like to preheat the oven."

"Neither did you. Answer the question."

"I *do* love him," I stressed.

Amos winced. That "do" was pretty damning. But all I wanted was to feel the brush of Amos's fingertips on my kneecap, to rent some of our old electricity. Of course I loved

Boots. We'd been together for two years—over two, by his count. But admitting I was not being held captive in a loveless cage was a buzz kill.

"Were you ever *in* love with him?" Amos asked.

"Define *love*," I said, tossing chum in the water, "define *ever*."

Amos rolled his eyes.

"You're asking if I've ever had a six-hour phone call with him? Or driven upstate in the middle of the night to tell him I'm sorry only to get into a second fight and lock him out on the porch with the raccoons? No, I have not."

"Glad it's just me."

"I never said it was just you."

"Clever girl," Amos said, taking a sip of his drink.

"That's what they call the dinosaurs in the movies right before they shoot them."

"You're still quick."

"Fuck you. We're the same age. Don't talk to me like I have dementia."

Amos sighed into his lap, exposing the flesh beneath his collar. I played out a reality in which we had never broken up, in which he had only ever wanted to see *me*, only wanted to put his penis inside *me*. Would he kiss me right now or would we be annoyed at the sight of each other? Just because something ends prematurely doesn't mean it won't end eventually. Usually that's exactly what it means.

A wiry gentleman in a short-sleeved button-down emerged from the bathroom, removed a book from his backpack, and began reading and drinking Fernet. He looked like a grad student. Amos and I watched him do these things, taken by the mutual distraction. He wanted to know what the man was reading. I wanted to know why some grown men wear backpacks. At their best, they suggest an insolent outdoorsiness; at their worst, a lifetime of student loans.

"I know what you think of me," Amos said, twisting back around.

"This should be good."

"But we wanted the same things, Lola. I wanted a real relationship with both of us sitting in the same room, eating takeout, not fucking."

"You wanted to sleep with half of North America."

I knocked the outside of my knee against the inside of his.

"Yeah, but that wasn't the only reason we broke up."

"Amos. I'm not sure 'extra reasons' is kind at this juncture."

"I'm of the belief that our kind of love, the six-hour-phone-call kind, melds into the other kind of love. And the second kind is more important. Agreed. But for whatever reason, we only had the intense kind. I couldn't reach the second kind on your timeline."

"We dated for years. Literally. Years."

"It's no one's fault."

"Is it not mostly your fault, though?"

The man at the end of the bar read with his elbows spread out in front of him, as if we were in a library with a liquor license. Perhaps my generation made not enough of selecting jewelry but too much of selecting a partner. Perhaps the internet had spoiled us more than we suspected and we already suspected quite a bit. Why *couldn't* I just mate with this guy at the end of the bar? Why couldn't we be happy? What difference would it make?

"I'm saying every relationship needs both kinds of love to go the distance," Amos said, trying to catch my eye. "A galvanizing agent."

"Like acid to the face."

"What will you remember when you and this dude are seventy?"

"And by 'this dude,' you mean my *fiancé*?"

"You have to remember the passion. You'll have decades to go back and forth and swim all the laps you want, but everyone needs to start by pushing off the side of the pool. Really shoving off."

I slugged the rest of my beer.

"Love is not a race, Amos. Or a competition. This is your problem. It's why you refuse to 'swim laps' with one woman."

"I'm not talking about racing, I'm talking about not drowning."

"And you know all this because of your vast experience with monogamy?"

"I take offense to the accusation that I'm unevolved, especially coming from you. The idea that you have to have had a long relationship to know what makes a good relationship is a lie propagated by society to make men settle down and women settle. It's also a capitalist boondoggle to get the masses to pay higher insurance premiums. What kind of failure of imagination does the world think I have? Why assume I have no idea what it might be like? I've never drunk my own piss, for example, but I'm pretty sure I know what it tastes like."

"Because you've drunk other people's piss?"

"Don't be clever."

"Five seconds ago, you liked that I was clever."

"My point is I couldn't see into the future. You wanted someone to have an archetypical life with you and it wasn't gonna be me, and great, maybe now you have it."

"Fuck off."

"It wouldn't bother you if it wasn't true."

"Oh, so we've never heard of slander, I guess."

The man at the end of the bar looked up from his book. The bartender turned on the music, the kind of droopy tune that makes you want to cry on trains. I had not noticed the silence before. What would have been a welcome part of the atmosphere when we arrived now made me feel estranged from the moment, as if I'd been enjoying the wrong thing. Like when you're already halfway done with your pasta and the waiter comes over and offers to grate cheese over it.

Amos saw his opening.

"Just tell me about him, then."

I knew it was wrong to talk about Boots with Amos, like feeding a beloved cat to a lion. So I decided to tell Amos a safe story.

"We met at a surprise party, actually. My friend who I was meeting there was adamant that I arrive early so when I thought I saw the birthday boy crossing the street with me, I darted out of the crosswalk and nearly got hit by a bus. Like I felt the wind of the bus. I could even see a couple of the passengers, all shaken by a potential suicide. And out of nowhere, the guy rushes over, yanks me toward him, and escorts me out of the street."

"The birthday boy?"

"No, different guy. You all start to look the same after a while, you know that? Anyway, we were both so high on adrenaline, we couldn't stop laughing the whole night. Then he asked me out. Now one of our jokes is about that time I flung myself into traffic to avoid him."

"You were in shock."

"No, I wasn't."

"Why isn't the joke that he saved your life?"

"I don't know, Amos," I said, folding my fingers together. "Maybe we're both waiting for the day I turn around and say, 'That's right, asshole, I *did* fling myself into traffic to avoid you.' I'm joking."

"Are you?"

"*Am I?*" I mimicked him. "Should the day come when you manage to face-plant yourself into a relationship, you'll find there are certain fragile truths every couple has. Sometimes I'm uncomfortable with the power, knowing I could break us up if I wanted. Other times, I want to blow it up just because it's there. But then the feeling passes."

"That's bleak."

"To you, it is. But I'm not like you. I don't need to escape every room I'm in."

"But you are like me. You *think* you want monogamy, but you probably don't if you dated me."

"You're faulting me for liking you now?"

"All I'm saying is you can't just will yourself into being satisfied with this guy."

"Watch me," I said, trying to burn a hole in his face.

"If it were me, the party would have been our first date and it never would have ended."

"Oh, yes it would have," I said, laughing. "The date would have lasted one week, but the whole relationship would have lasted one month."

"Yeah," he said, "you're right."

"I know I'm right."

"It wouldn't have lasted."

"This is what I'm saying."

"Because if I were this dude, I would have left you by now."

Before I could say anything, Amos excused himself to pee. On the bathroom door was a black and gold sticker in the shape of a man. I felt a rage rise up all the way to my eyeballs, thinking of how naturally Amos associated himself with that sticker, thinking of him aligning himself with every powerful, brilliant, thoughtful man who has gone through that door as well as every stupid, entitled, and cruel one, effortlessly merging with a class of people for whom the world was built.

I took my phone out, opening the virtual cuckoo clocks, trying to be somewhere else. I was confronted with a slideshow of a female friend's dead houseplants, meant to symbolize inadequacy within reason. Amos didn't have a clue what it was like to be a woman in New York, unsure if she's with the right person. Even if I did want to up and leave Boots, dating was not a taste I'd acquired. The older a woman got, the more diligent she had to become about not burdening men with the gory details of her past, lest she scare them off. That was the name of the game: Don't Scare the Men. Those who encouraged you to indulge in your impulse to share, largely did so to expedite a decision. They knew they were on trial too, but our courtrooms had more lenient judges. These men quizzed you about every hurt and humiliation until you were so flattered by the inquiry, you forgot that quizzes are made to be failed. This process was made worse by the garb of flirtation.

Vadis called it the "millennial music rider."

"Just tell them the worst thing that's ever happened to you and get it over with."

"What is this, the McCarthy hearings? I'm not naming names."

"It's your own name, dummy. Your own trauma."

"What if the answer is 'this conversation'?"

"Well, maybe don't say that."

Whereas with every last man I knew, even Zach, the full trajectory of their lives became more appealing with age. Every gash added up to something intricate and alluring. Heartache was something that happened to them, not something they made happen. Feminism failed us on this point. Women are meant to emerge into each chapter as if from cocoons, divine creatures with a smattering of flaws. Just look at what drivel comes out in the wash: slideshows of dead houseplants.

By the time Amos returned, the man with the book had left. More people had arrived, seeming to have come here with the express purpose of discussing an absentee friend's social infractions. Amos had a hangdog look on his face, the look of someone who'd recently confronted a bar bathroom mirror. He was wearing a button-down shirt that gaped at his stomach, exposing a keyhole of belly.

"We can stop talking about this if it upsets you," he offered.

"Good," I said, "but not because it upsets me. Because it will cannibalize everything and I'll wake up tomorrow feeling like I don't know anything about you. Tell me about your life."

"I have no life."

"Tell me about the new book, then."

"I'm sick of hearing myself talk about the book. All I do is summarize my own opinions as if I read them somewhere. It's hard to talk about the thing you're supposed to love when you don't feel connected to it anymore. Maybe you can advise me."

"My advice would be to trust the process."

"Tell me what's good about him."

"*Amos.*"

"Tell me his name."

"No."

"I'm going to find out eventually."

"So you can find out eventually."

"Do I know him?"

"No."

"Then tell me his name."

"Amos."

"Come on."

"I don't want to hear you say his name!"

The bartender looked at us, waiting to see if there was more where that came from. It was at once the most protective thing I'd said about Boots and the most revealing thing I'd said about my leftover feelings for Amos. I pulled at the edge of my cocktail napkin until it broke apart.

"He's considerate. People love him. He's weirdly tall. You'd hate him."

"What's weird?"

"Like six-three."

"That's not weird."

"He's a good listener. With some people you can see the little kid inside them, raising their hands in the air while the teacher is talking. He's not like that. He's smart without being esoteric. I've never looked at him and had to ask what he's thinking."

"Is that maybe because he isn't thinking anything?"

"He went to Brown."

"Gross."

"He's from Illinois. He blows glass."

"He must be great at going down on you."

"He makes sculptures, if you must know. But he also runs his own business, selling glassware to restaurants."

"An Ivy League educated Willy Loman."

"I don't know why I'm defending him to you. He does Per Se."

"He does what per se?"

"The restaurant."

"Oh. Thomas Keller 'does' Per Se. You should be engaged to him."

Amos sincerely expected to wake one day to the news that I'd married a famous person. Or a diplomat. To him, the definition of a compliment was "to set apart." When we were falling in love, he'd enumerate the ways in which I was not like other women, listing traits such as intelligence and sanity—leaving me with the choice of rejecting the compliment or betraying my entire gender.

He fished a tissue out of his bag, a canvas satchel with leather trim. I must have been ogling the bag.

"My cousin gave this to me," he said. "She got it in a 'gifting suite.'"

Kit. I desperately wanted to ask about her. For years, I'd fantasized about her doing the same. *What ever happened to Lola, Amos? She's the only one I ever liked.* But before I could nudge him down this conversational rabbit hole, he announced that it was getting late. We should go. An hour ago, I'd harbored fantasies of Amos pushing me against a wall. Now my head pounded, my eyes burned, and a squeal that did not belong inside a human body came from Amos's stomach.

"Hospital?" I asked, furrowing my brows.

"Roger convinced me to split the General Tso soufflé," he lamented, touching his stomach. "It's grumbling chaos in there."

"You should give restaurant blurbs."

I got up from the stool and grabbed my coat.

"It's a self-inflicted punishment," he said. "I chose that place."

I froze, arms partially sleeved.

"You picked an actual location?"

"Sort of. Roger is in Baby Land so I asked Jeannine. Do you ever get paralyzed whenever anyone asks you to pick a restaurant, like you've never left the house?"

Amos had a way of presenting quotidian problems as karmic ailments. A MetroCard with insufficient fare was just his luck. Spam was an act of personal oppression.

"This is going to sound nuts," he said, "but I had crazy déjà vu right when you walked up. Did you know they figured it out, déjà vu? It's your brain temporarily processing present tense as past tense, like swallowing something down the wrong pipe. You should write about it for *Modern Psychology*."

"I don't work there, I'm not a writer, and it doesn't exist."

"Oh. Right. Well, it wasn't *déjà vu* déjà vu. It was more like clairvoyance. Like my lizard brain knew I should keep standing there. I think I was waiting for you."

"Amos, that's the sweetest thing you've ever said to me."

There were few cars when we got out on the street. The air was thick, as if someone had put a lid on the city. I heard the beep of a garbage truck and panicked, thinking it must be 3 a.m. But this was a regular truck backing up and it was only midnight. There was nothing wrong with staying out, drinking with another man, even one I used to date. I lost track of time. This was an emotional one-night stand, not an emotional affair. Still, I felt guilty for not checking in with Boots.

Amos reached into my jacket pocket and removed one of my cigarettes. It was intimate, having him fish around in there.

"Lola, can I offer you another piece of advice?" he asked, lighting the cigarette.

I could hear the crackle of the paper, like water being poured over thirsty dirt.

"Was there a first piece of advice I missed?"

"It's more of an observation."

"Ah, the gentleman has more of a comment."

"What I loved most about you was your decisiveness."

"One of us had to look up movie times."

"I don't mean with me. I mean you decide things and go do them. You decide to live on this shithole island, you live on this shithole island. You decide to skip work and go to a museum, you don't hem and haw until it's too inconvenient to go. You're not afraid to *move*. You decide to quit your job, you quit your job."

"I was laid off when the magazine folded."

"Oh," he said, blowing smoke upward. "Really?"

I nodded.

"Well, my point still stands. You of all people, I mean, get married or don't get married but indecision doesn't suit you. Opinionated *and* indecisive is lethal."

"What indecision? Why do you keep poking at this?"

"Because I've met you. And even if we both live to a hundred and even if I never speak to you again, that means we will have known each other for like ten percent of our lives. That's a lot. But it's none of my business."

"Oh, *now* it's none of your business?"

He looked around, momentarily confused about where he was.

"Once more to the subway!" he yelled. "God, isn't Shakespeare great? You don't even need a verb to get anywhere."

"Amos, your charms are wasted on this city's interns."

"Spoken like someone who's never banged an intern."

I hugged him tightly. His body felt foreign in my arms.

"I have the weirdest feeling I won't ever see you again," I said.

"I was kidding. We know hundreds of people in common."

"That's true, but I didn't see you for years."

"Well," he said, pulling away, "now the seal has been broken."

I nodded but felt an unexpected sense of loss. Amos used to have a quote from an obscure philosopher taped above his desk: "Every goodbye is a little mourning just as every orgasm is a little death." He gave me his new phone number, typing it into my phone, as if I were too drunk to do it (was I too drunk to do it?). I was happy to have the number, not so I could contact Amos but so I would not be caught off guard if he contacted me. But by the time I got home, I realized I'd deleted it when I meant to save it.

2

There was a 24-hour diner across the street from our apartment called the North Star Canteen. Instead of being spelled out, the star was an electronic star shape, an asterisk, which sent the eye searching for a correction that wasn't there. No matter how late it got, our apartment had a dawn-like glow. It would not have occurred to either of us to ask a broker to come see it at midnight. Though when your apartment is filled with hundreds of glass pieces, there are advantages to being able to see where you're going.

In addition to the industrial-size rolls of bubble wrap leaning like thugs against the wall, there was a narrow hallway that led from the living room to the bedroom, covered with shelves of glassware. They were stuck to the wall like mushrooms on a tree trunk. We told ourselves it was all so high and undustable to keep the cat from knocking everything over. Really it was to keep ourselves from knocking everything over. Hand-blown candlesticks, mouth-blown bowls, sake cups, cake stands. The longest shelf was home to Boots's bespoke creations, most of which were excluded from his website because they included flaws. These were little sculptures twisted like Medusa's hair or melted to resemble gobs of candle wax, afflicted with seed bubbles and fractures. They had bumps like outie bellybuttons from where they'd been cut from the rod or straw marks from where the glass had cooled in a disappointing way. There was a set of Russian nesting dolls, cleverly colored with the darkest in the middle. But apparently the gradation wasn't quite right. So much of glass blowing was in the home stretch of it, in how it settled.

I loved how discerning he was in this department.

I kissed the cat on the head, my little spite tabby, all grown up. I'd named her Rocket. It didn't suit her, even as a kitten. She sunbathed all day long, like a suicidal slug. She was unflaggingly lazy, her greatest physical feat being the skyward extension of her back paw for easier access to her own anus.

Boots was allergic to cats, which meant spending his life in a constant state of near-tears, but he'd gotten used to it. He'd gotten used to being outnumbered by finicky females who functioned on their own terms, who couldn't help but capitalize on his stoicism. But he did install heavy blackout shades in the bedroom. Even he, for whom discomfort was a foreign concept, agreed that something *must* be done about the light.

"All we need is death metal in our ears," he'd said.

Boots was already in bed by the time I creaked over the floorboards.

"How was dinner?" he asked, groggily.

He was curled up, facing the wall. This man belonged in a California king, not a sagging queen abutting a heating pipe. There was something ridiculous about it, like a bear riding a tricycle. I was suddenly very drunk and needed to touch something solid. I pulled back the duvet and felt for his back in the dark, my fingertips pausing at birthmarks. I often found myself in conversation with the terrain of his skin. I had a whole relationship with the freckles on his shoulder, these mute witnesses to a childhood I'd never see. I told him Vadis said hello even though she had not.

"Hi, Vadis. What time is it?"

"It's almost one."

"Oh, really? I went down hard. Can you do that forever?"

I brushed my fingers along his arm, fondling his shoulder, stroking the occasional burn scar. Hairless strips that were pink in the light.

"I gotta go to San Francisco for a couple weeks," he announced, "starting Monday."

"What's in San Francisco?"

"Weed. Facebook."

"Ha-ha."

"Massive amounts of homeless people due to a broken mental health system?"

"Less ha-ha?"

"There's a restaurant group that wants me to do their stemware. And their salad plates, which are also glass, which is stupid for about a hundred reasons, but it's a significant contract if I get it. They own a couple of spots in Vegas."

"San Francisco," I said, making a noise like I did not believe San Francisco existed.

I stared at his head, submerged in what little light had edged in around the shades, moving my fingers up his skull and feeling his hair fall back into place. He emitted a little moan of pleasure but was too tired to do anything about it. For this, I was grateful. On the one hand, seeing Amos was an aphrodisiac. On the other hand, I'd begun stockpiling the times Boots didn't want to have sex to make myself feel better about the times I didn't want to have sex. A respectful order of things had been established in a way that felt closer to baking a cake (add wet ingredients to dry, heat and cover) than sex. Our days of throwing ingredients into a pan had passed too quickly. As for fucking? Can we not embarrass ourselves by drawing attention to this recital of desire? Not when "that feels good" passes for dirty talk. We mostly used the word when we weren't doing it. The other night, I caught myself calling him "hard" in a tone that would not have been out of place in a conversation about mineral water.

"Why so late?" he asked.

"We got drinks after."

"Was it fun?"

"The funnest," I whispered, "and now nothing in this world will ever be so fun again."

"Okay," he said. "Night, baby."

It was never *bad* with Boots was the thing, but I wondered what kind of bar this was for a marriage: a low one or an elevated one? Sometimes, when I pictured our lives together, it felt like settling in the very best way, like a picnic blanket that falls into a manageable shape on the first try. Other times, I imagined we were siblings who'd been assigned to the same bed on a family trip. No snoring, no kicking. That's all that was required. This allowed me to remold him in my mind as some combination of every man I'd ever known. A testosterone hydra. If he knew about this heavy lifting or, worse, those times I had to pretend to be a prostitute, and not in a fun way, in order to have sex, it would devastate him.

I knew Boots had his concerns too, but he would not take the crucial step of realizing it was *I* who was making him concerned. He chalked up our moments of disconnect to a mutual fear of the same gods. His hesitation manifested itself logistically, in the discomforts of compromise: How will we intertwine our families? What will potential babies do to our potential sleep? What will we do if one of us develops a gambling addiction and we have to move into an RV and live off fried crickets and malt liquor?

My worries were more abstract yet more pernicious. I worried about the betrayal of memory. I worried my former love life was a bomb waiting to go off or, worse, that it would *never* go off. That I would wake one day, having buried the past so well I'd find myself unrecognizable, having moved to a city I hated, slowly losing touch with my friends, then with the culture at large, until the only books I read were the ones I read about in nail salons, the only art I knew was presented to me through my phone, and the only plays I saw were the ones that had been adapted for the screen. And I'd have to pretend there was nothing wrong with this because there *was* nothing wrong with this. Not for that version of me. But is this what all my romantic dramas and career had been for, their natural conclusion? A life of palliative television? If I ever felt restless, Boots would have to be enough. And if he wasn't? I'd punish him with resentment. I would've preferred not to worry so much. But I had no choice: I was worrying for two.

I closed my eyes and let my mind go fuzzy at the edges. Soon I was in an Olympic-size swimming pool, doing laps. Men filled the bleachers. I knew them all but I couldn't make out their faces. Some were cheering, some were jeering, some were ignoring me entirely. I wanted to get out of the pool but I had to dive down to retrieve some treasure and was not allowed to come up until I found it. Finally, I spotted it, flopping around by one of the filters. It was my mother's diaphragm from the '70s, which I have never seen in real life but knew on sight in the dream. Translucent bits of tissue clung to it, floating by their bloody threads. I laughed so hard, I woke up coughing.

The cat had developed this habit of pacing around my desk chair, waiting for me to pick her up. She was perfectly capable of jumping up herself, but all it took was a couple instances of elevator service and this was what she demanded henceforth. Boots had indulged this behavior, which was fine for him (if not his eyeballs—he'd once tried to pet her with oven mitts and she wasn't having it). He wasn't the one who worked from home half the week, editing quotes for redundancy. Sometimes I found it to be a rewarding game, trying to trick our audience into thinking *Radio New York* had a fresh take on the world. But a science website we were not.

Every hour, the cat meowed and pretended to walk away, stopping close enough for me to grab her. Then she'd squeak as if this whole process weren't her idea.

We were engaged in this dance the next morning when my phone lit up. I was in the midst of reading a first draft of an article on ad-hoc "rage rooms." Several commercial loft spaces had figured out a way to make money between corporate inhabitants. The rooms charged people $75 each to smash up television sets and mirrors but offered no face shields or gloves. It was a lawsuit waiting to happen. Or a trend piece. Whichever came first. Rage rooms were more expensive than escape rooms because, as one proprietor told our reporter, "you can't unsmash stuff."

The text I received was from a college friend, Eliza Baxter, asking if I wanted to have dinner. Eliza and I had not been close during college, but after graduation we decided that if only we'd been mature enough to look beyond our surface differences, we would've been great friends. She moved to Cincinnati shortly after this realization and so now our friendship was composed of supportive social media behavior and the rare dinner occasioned by her law firm sending her here.

Yes, I texted her back, *IN. Where are you staying/restaurant requests?*

I scanned our refrigerator door, knowing that behind it lay a week-old container of garlic sauce and a carton of brown rice (a healthy idea whose time had never come). Boots would not mind making a meal out of this.

Bronxville!!! Long story don't ask—she went on to tell the story anyway—*Jordan's mom is having a "breakdown" so staying up here for two nights one of which I've bargained to have to myself yr so lucky*

FUN, I wrote.

know where I want to go please hold . . .

When I clicked on the link, I brought my face close to the phone and then took it away again, playing an invisible trombone. I felt like I was being interrogated. Yes, officer, this is the spot. This is the mirrored bar and fancy cocktails. This is the Szechuan bisque, the sweet-and-sour leeks, the General Tso soufflé.

Can we go anywhere else I was just there

She sent back a frowning emoji. Forlorn. Round. Yellow. The woman was never in town. She was stuck comforting a mother-in-law who despised Eliza for idiosyncrasies like not being Jewish.

Jordan's friend is the sous chef!!

Being forced to return to the same restaurant two nights in a row was a first world problem if there ever was one. Too often New Yorkers treated experiences as vaccinations. They went to the Whitney every two years, Coney Island every five, the ballet every twenty. I did not want to be one of those people. Besides, nobody said I was required to order the General Tso soufflé, to post videos of its salty plateau folding in on itself.

Boots had never even heard of Eliza, which was part of a developing problem. It used to be that the introduction of new people was a thread that led to tales of summer adventures or first jobs—anecdotes of import, the kind that emerge in green card interviews and lend subsidiary definition to any relationship. But after a while, a Rubicon had been crossed. We were on symbolic ground. Recently, one of his friends mentioned a desire to go fishing in the Grand Canyon. I said it was as beautiful as advertised, but there were surprisingly few fish there. Boots shot me a distrustful look, as if I'd intentionally duped him into believing I was someone who'd never been to the Grand Canyon. He was older than me by several years. Even Johnny Two-Chicks over here, with his few relationships, should appreciate the difficulty of intravenousing a lifetime of formative experiences into someone else's bloodstream. Vadis and Clive had come the closest to fluency in my life, but only because I'd spent nine hours a day with them for as many years.

Perhaps if, like Boots, I'd been gifted with a dormitory full of bright, uncomplicated people, I wouldn't have needed to look farther afield. But as it was, the temperamental discrepancy between our friends was the size of the aforementioned canyon. We would be at some civilized picnic in

Prospect Park with these tucked-in citizens who traded in good-natured ribbing and I'd receive a series of texts from Vadis about how the DJ she'd stopped fucking had broken into her apartment and defecated on her (open) laptop. Eventually, my guilt over not adoring his friends burned off like a fog. No more farro salad, please. No more mass emails that began with "gang." No more quantifiable drug use and convenient politics. No more yapping about the past as replacement therapy for the present.

I treaded carefully while contextualizing Eliza's existence. I drew her connection to people Boots had met while minimizing her personal significance, swallowing the niggling resentment I felt over doing this. I was not ashamed of Boots—if anything, I took pride in my proximity to such a likable human being—but I could not talk about him in front of him, which should've been the kind of Girls Night Out logic he was accustomed to from his friends.

"It's not that I don't want you to meet her," I explained, "it's just that I never see her. Next time she comes, we'll have her over."

Our kitchen table was covered by a broken burner and cardboard boxes. Boots was in the midst of repairing the burner and the boxes were for his pieces, some of which had actually been selling these days. Four in the last month after zero in the last six. This was a healthy turn of events for us both.

"It's fine," he said, remaining upbeat. "I'll just be here, watching all the shows without you."

"So low."

"When do you think you're coming back?"

He looked like he might cry but this was a function of the cat.

"Just curious," he added, "it's not like I'm waiting by the phone."

He picked up his phone and tossed it onto a chair across the room.

The hostess decided against my familiarity as she removed a menu from her stand. Who goes to the same restaurant two nights in a row? No one, I telegraphed, let's stick with that. In a different place, in a different neighborhood, repeat patronage would be perceived as a positive. But this place was too trendy. She probably ate this food for free after hours and was sick of it. She escorted me to Eliza, who was already in a booth in the corner, shielded from the din of the room. Spindly orchids hung from the ceiling, reaching down with their crooked joints.

"Do you think those are real?" Eliza asked.

Her manicure was the same shade as the petals.

"I know they're real."

"Fancytown," she said, whistling.

Within minutes, Eliza was describing a distant universe. In this universe, her husband was putting pressure on her to have a second kid. I already knew this because of her tweets. New mothers were required to post *all* debates pertaining to the plights of motherhood as well as *all* articles about the conditions in places like Bhutan, stories that unsubtly boomeranged to the fact that they too had done something frightening and painful. Granted, they had done it on clean sheets and with lots of drugs, but they had entered into a universal sisterhood. Though I somehow doubted the mothers they pitied devoted any time searching for ways to hitch their virtue to the Elizas of the world.

Eliza's offline universe was filled with local library drama, choking hazards, high fevers, faulty pelvic floors, gasoline-splattered shoes, and property disputes. The closest I'd ever come to a property dispute was the time we caught our neighbor kicking our wayward welcome mat away from her door.

"Are you guys thinking of getting pregnant?"

"I don't know. We'll have to flip for it."

"Be serious, you're thirty-eight."

"I know. I can count."

"Don't take it out on me," she said, squeezing the words through her hyperaligned teeth.

"Take what out on who?"

Maybe I'd *never* connected with Eliza. Maybe we simply reminded each other of being young and any bond we felt was rooted in our respective narcissism and that's why our odd-couple bit was collapsing like a soufflé.

Halfway through the meal, her sous chef friend appeared with an order of chèvre fritters. He had to get back into the kitchen, he explained, but first he wanted to hug Eliza. He was younger than I expected, for a friend of her husband's. He wore a puka shell necklace and had ringlet hair and enormous vacant eyes, the kind that looked as if they were staring into the middle distance. *Modern Psychology* once printed that staring into the middle distance meant you were having a minor stroke, our copy editor having taken it upon himself to drop the words "urban legend has it that." That was a bad week.

"How's your food tasting?" he asked, hiding an anxious grin.

This question has always made me feel as if I'm being

poisoned but Eliza had nothing but reassuring smiles for him. He seemed desperate for her approval.

"Brody's like Jordan's little brother," she explained, after he disappeared. "He had a really hard time just existing before he went to culinary school."

"Drugs?"

"No, that's Brody. The *hammock* kid."

She waited for me to be blown back in my seat.

"You know this story," she insisted. "It's a cautionary tale."

"Against what?" I asked, amused. "Nap marks?"

Convinced of my ignorance, Eliza recounted the story. When Brody was a kid, his mother married a wealthy man. They flew up to the guy's lake house on his plane, and Brody was left to bond with his toddler while their respective parents had sex and boiled lobsters. One morning, the toddler shook Brody awake because he wanted to go play on the hammock.

"Oh . . . *no.*"

Eliza continued: So Brody walked the toddler outside and they played a game where Brody spun the kid around like a cocoon and let go. The kid insisted on going faster and spinning more. Eventually, Brody wound the netting too tight. The boy couldn't hang on. He hit his head on the corner of a rock and "that was that."

"It's the worst story of all time," Eliza said. "You probably knew it somewhere in the back of your head."

"No pun intended."

"You're evil."

"Tragedy makes me nervous."

"It's become one of those things like how people remove the doors from old refrigerators before putting them out on the sidewalk. Except now there are safety warnings on hammocks. Because of Brody. *That* Brody."

"Do you get sent to jail when something like that happens?"

"Lola, he was a child. He got sent to therapy. God, you're so punishing."

"What's that supposed to mean?"

Eliza shrugged, as if she'd picked the word out of a hat and was now fishing around for another one.

"Judgmental? Not all the time. Unforgiving, maybe. Always searching for fault."

"It feels like I'm always searching for a *lack* of fault."

"Yeah, that's judgment."

"Well, it doesn't feel like it. It feels like something I should get credit for."

Our waiter passed by and asked if we were "still picking." We shook our heads. Suddenly everyone in the restaurant seemed lucky to me. They'd seemed lucky before, to be laughing and gesticulating over thirty-dollar entrees, but now they seemed lucky to have never committed involuntary manslaughter. The defenselessness of our species was all out of proportion with the amount of ways we manufactured harm.

"I have to pee," Eliza announced, shimmying out of the booth.

I checked my phone while she was gone. I wanted to see if the story was famous enough to be procured using only the words *Brody* and *hammock*. But before I could, I saw two text boxes. One was from Boots (a photo of Rocket sprawled out on her back, accompanied by his commentary: "slut"). The second was an automated box, offering me nearby Wi-Fi networks. Most were gibberish or strings of numbers, but one jumped out: "Willis Klee's Phone."

It was possible, I supposed, that there were multiple Willis Klees in the world, in the country, even in the city. But how many, I wondered, had left a stick of incense on the window-sill of a bed-and-breakfast in Carmel, California, during the summer of 2011 and nearly burned it down? How many had then accompanied me to an abortion clinic a month later, shaking his knee in the waiting room, a cup of ice chips in his hand?

Not that many.

My eyes darted around the room. I saw nothing. Then, atop the staircase that led to the restrooms, arose Willis. He looked like a mirage. Not in the way Amos had looked like a mirage, like he could disappear, but in the way Willis Klee had never looked real. There was no getting around it: Willis was the most physically attractive man I'd ever been with, a real boon in the "keep the baby" column. But I was too young to have a baby (at the "where would I *put* a baby?" age) and Willis was too cartoonish to be a dad, at least in my estimation. If asked about fatherhood, he would talk about how exciting it would be to teach his son to throw a football and ride a bike. I resented how reality-free this fantasy was. If I were to express excitement about having a little girl because then I could have someone to dress up, I would be deemed unfit to breed.

The decade gap from when I last saw Willis to now had not eroded his beauty. It had only made him more passable as a human man as I watched him weave between tables, tucking his hair behind his ears, a familiar tic. He did it when he was preparing to be falsely modest about something.

Ours was more of an experiment than a relationship. We met at a crowded bar on Vadis's birthday, both of us angling to order a drink. Willis, consummate gentleman, tried to make room for me. He was not doing so to hit on me, but only because I had the correct anatomy to trigger chivalry. In the congestion, the only feature I could properly examine was his hands. There, on his pointer finger, was a clunky gold ring.

It looked too unscathed to be a family crest. I assumed it was a collegiate ring. Back then, Vadis was still selecting bars with twenty beers on tap, populated by men who *would* be wearing their collegiate rings, who had already stretched their emotional bandwidth as far as it would go by listening to Wilco.

I thanked Willis for carving out space. That's when he actually looked at me. I felt startled to the point of embarrassed by his face. That Superman-goes-into-the-phone-booth face. That nose at which all the marble sculptures of Greece and Italy were aiming.

"Hi!" he chirped, extending his hand over the short distance, "I'm Willis."

"Lola," I said, keeping my hand to myself.

How certifiable does a person have to be to lead with his name?

"It's like a Dial commercial in here," he said. "You know, aren't you glad you use Dial?"

"Don't you wish everybody did?"

Ah, so we were roughly the same age. Same commercials, same cartoons, same hazy memory of historical events. Oh, what nature had done with two specimens of the same species! It was as if a stopwatch had been clicked in our respective delivery rooms and Willis went one way, very fast, and I went the other, very slowly.

Willis beamed, a goofy smile that caught the bartender's attention even though it was not aimed at the bartender. It was not aimed at anyone, for Willis, mindbogglingly, seemed to have no conception of his own appeal. I couldn't understand this. Surely he had empirical evidence of the world treating him differently. Only later did I realize that it was not a lack of evidence but a *glut* of it that created a bubble around Willis. Any breaks in the universe's abject affection were deemed glitches and dismissed. The effect was the same as in a confident person, but the math was wonky. It's a form of mental illness to assume everyone who stabs you meant to hug you.

I ordered a Corona and Willis followed suit, shoving the lime down the neck of his bottle with farm-like precision. He looked shocked when I asked him where he was from. I looked shocked that he looked shocked.

"Iowa," he gave in, drawing a box with his finger.

"Ah."

It crossed my mind that I was dealing with a missionary and would need to extricate myself from the conversation.

"Actually," he corrected himself, "more this."

He drew another box, creating a squiggle down the side.

"And is that your college ring?"

I gestured at his hand with my bottle.

"Oh, no," he said, tucking his hair behind his ears. "This is my Olympic ring."

"For what?"

"For the Olympics?"

"You're shitting me."

I yanked his hand toward me. Sure enough, there were the five circles stamped on top and flames etched on the side. I held it until the circles left an indentation in my skin, until it occurred to me that I was holding a stranger's hand. Having had no record of athlete infatuation and marginal athletic ability myself, I was surprised by how much I wanted Willis's glory to rub off on me. Perhaps because it was indelible, the kind of achievement that no one could ever malign as over-rated. New York was a field of tall poppies, awaiting a be-heading. But here, pushing up through the concrete, was an undebunkable success. Not only was Willis a long jumper—a niche profession, even by Olympic standards—but he was the best long jumper in the world. It all made sense now: He talked like Captain America because he *was* Captain America.

Willis was in town to present an award at the New York Athletic Club. He told me the name of the award as if it were very obvious but referred to the Hilton Garden Inn, where he was staying, by its Christian name. He also referred to subway lines by their colors instead of their letters. At his request, I detailed the characteristics of all the neighborhoods in Manhattan and Brooklyn and attempted to define a burrata as "a turducken but cheese." I would like to say that it was Willis's curiosity that kept me by his side long after Vadis had moved on to the next bar. But I had no deeper connection to this person. For once, I wanted nothing from a man but to see him naked. If I wanted a second thing, it was the novelty of him seeing an average woman naked.

There were segments of Willis's body that I had noticed only in passing on other men. The thighs, for example. I had always considered them to be a transient area, a highway connecting the ass to the knees. And the back, peppered with extra muscles that visibly shifted when he did. I had no extra muscles. But I did fit through the door of his hotel room. Willis seemed taken with this fact, gawking at me in a way that began to feel vaguely insulting. In order to medal in an Olympic sport, you have to think of your body as special, that all your hard work will pay off because it's being poured into a genetically superior container. When you operate in an echelon of minor physical differences, trafficking in seconds and millimeters, you assume that civilians who play no sports at all are lucky to stand upright. Hence Willis's delight upon finding that my knees didn't crack, that my hip bones protruded when I lay on my back.

"I thought you'd have a librarian's body," he said, stroking my side.

"I guess you're not one of those guys who has hot librarian fantasies."

"Are there guys who fantasize about librarians?"

The next morning, I woke to the groaning of the electronic keypad in the door. Willis had gone down to the lobby and returned with two coffees in cups with bold graphics on the side.

"This is me, bringing you coffee," he said, shaking his head.

Despite having traveled the world thrice over, leaping over sand pits from Seoul to Salzburg, Willis had negligible dating experience. No prom, no drama, no bad decisions. Now he was in a race to catch up with the rest of the world. There was something newborn about the way he moved through it. Bringing a girl coffee in a hotel room was a scene out of the movies.

I thanked Willis and sipped. He also sipped, looking around the room, smiling at the walls. Then his face grew slack as he told me he had a confession to make. It was true, he said, that he was in town for the awards ceremony but it was also true that he would be moving here. Permanently. He'd always wanted to live in New York and he had always wanted to go to college. So he decided to kill two birds with one NYU course catalog.

"I just want to be the best possible version of myself," he said, the admission of a professional athlete.

"Of course you do. Your body is your temple, mine is my garbage disposal."

"But your mind is your temple and, without an education, mine is going to be my garbage disposal."

"Fair point."

He asked me if I was busy that night. I probably should have said yes and let this be the easiest one-night stand of my life. Willis was a person, not a safari animal. But I thought: Men date women far more beautiful than they all the time, women with whom they see no future. They don't avoid it. They brag about it.

"Sure," I said, "I'd love to go."

"Awesome! The invitation says 'cocktail attire.' Your guess is as good as mine about what *that* means."

And so we went to the ceremony, where I felt like human margarine as I washed my hands next to champion volleyball players in the ladies' room. The towel dispenser responded to the wave of their hands like it feared them. We complimented one another on our earrings.

During the cocktail hour, I jumped whenever Willis put his hand on my shoulder. I was unused to the angle of it.

"How are you telling people we met?" I asked.

Somehow I considered him in training for perpetuity, which would mean no alcohol, no bars.

"I'm telling them we just started dating," he said, kissing my forehead.

To my credit, Willis was on safari too. The idea of an editor-as-sex-object was a new challenge for him. We tried to meld into each other's life, curious to see if we could be one of those theoretically incongruous couples that makes sense in practice. As if we could prescribe ourselves to each other. He wrote an op-ed about gender inequality in athletic brand sponsorships. I took up running. But no one was interested in publishing the op-ed and I got winded after two miles. All told, our safari lasted five months. The only reason it lasted that long was because Willis was accustomed to contorting himself to make things work physically and I was used to doing the same mentally. This is the lesson we taught each other: Sometimes practice only makes more practice.

Then came the abortion and that put real a damper on things.

Eventually, Willis moved back to Iowa, where he married a health coach. One shudders to imagine the collection of statement mugs in that house. Last I'd checked, he'd become the father of twin girls. And this I barely knew. Willis, oblivious to the wants and needs of ex-girlfriends, used social media for taking pictures of the family dog. In ten years, I'd seen only one photo of the wife and it was taken from behind, her biceps curled, wearing a T-shirt that read: "Don't need a permit for these guns!" I imagined him telling her about me. Because *they* probably didn't make some nonsense pact. And because, unlike Amos's cousin Kit, who'd probably never given me another thought, Willis would almost have to tell his wife about me. I imagined him talking about the day he found out I was pregnant, about the strained conversation. But I never imagined him telling the story wistfully or even morally—only as a hurdle he had to overcome. Those words exactly.

Willis sat at a table occupied by two older men in identical neckties. One of them had half a name tag stuck to his blazer. It made me happy to think of Willis as having a career outside the centimeter of sand that had made him a champion. He used to keep a framed picture of himself from his winning moment on a shelf beside a velvet case containing his medal. This shelf struck me as morbid, putting me in mind of plastic trophies being picked over by detectives in the bedroom of a teenage girl. In the picture, Willis's muscles are flexed and an ambitious vein protrudes from his neck. He looks like a giant ligament. In the foreground is a tsunami of sand. Looking at that picture, I knew, as deeply as you can know something about yourself, that I would never feel that level of dedication to anything. But when Willis looked at it, he saw his last definitive moment. Every moment after would be colored by a conflicting desperation to move forward and a petrifaction of being forgotten.

"What are you staring at?"

Eliza was back from the bathroom, lips glossier than when she left.

I gestured at her to sit before Willis spotted her, but then I remembered they'd never met. Only Vadis had met Willis. Even Clive had only ever heard of him. ("You slept with a child," he joked, with casual cruelty. "You should be arrested for statutory rape.") But of course everyone but Boots *knew* about him. Whereas I somehow doubted Willis was running around Iowa, bragging about that time he dated an associate editor with hip bones. Boots was aware of the abortion, but only the age at which I'd had it. No further detail. Our nondisclosure pact was practically built for Willis. No man enjoys hearing the words *ex-boyfriend* and *Olympian* in the same sentence.

"That's the javelin thrower?" Eliza asked.

"Long jumper."

"Go say hello."

"I can't," I said, shaking my head.

"What? Why?"

When I lost my taste for Willis's cocktail of guilelessness and naïveté, I lost it quickly. This is how it is with most relationships. So many of the things that attracted you come to repel you and sooner or later you find yourself going out the same door you came in. But I did not go gentle. I began trashing Willis's career plans under the guise of saving him from harsher criticism from the outside world. As if I, personally, had dug him up and thawed him out. I became resentful of his prettiness, of the ease it afforded him. I leaped on him if he'd never heard of a historical figure or film director with whom I myself had only a passing familiarity. At one point, he bought me a notepad with "You Got This!" printed across each page.

"Thanks," I said. "I'll write my suicide note on it."

Then, the final frontier: sex. My period came earlier and stayed later. I ate large quantities of takeout, passed out before 11 p.m., left for the office at 8 a.m., had arid conversations in between. My attempts to push through were halfhearted and cruel—I'd slide my hand beneath his boxers, get one gander at his goofy grin, and take the hand back out. And, because I was apparently committed to behaving like a garbage person, I decided my lack of sex drive was an *honorable* thing, a testament to my depth.

I did not want to say hello to someone who'd seen me behave like that.

And then, just like that, it was out of my hands.

Brody came bursting out of the kitchen, falling over himself to thank Eliza for coming. As if one of us had kicked him in the shins, he collapsed into her arms and started weeping. Shoulder-bobbing, jaw-stretching, face-crumpling, throat-closing weeping. He insisted that it was nothing, just a thing that happened when he got triggered. What in this restaurant had triggered him to think about the time he'd spun a boy to death was anyone's guess. The orchids?

"It's the guilt," Brody said between gulps of breath, "exiting my body."

Eliza folded him up in her arms. She was great at this. A natural. She should have that second kid. Half the restaurant turned to look, including Willis, who spotted me in the process. I waved, he pointed at the bar.

"Holy cow!" he exclaimed, shaking his hands above his head. "Lola!"

"Hi!" I squealed.

In small doses, Willis's enthusiasm was contagious. How many boyfriends had I had who weren't over our relationship before it began, who weren't consumed with how it would end? He hugged me, crushing my nose against his torso.

"What's going on with that?" He nodded over my shoulder.

"Oh," I said, grateful for the mutual focal point. "It's my friend's husband's friend. He works here."

There was nowhere for us to go with that information.

"He's the hammock kid."

"What's a hammock kid?"

"No, *the* hammock kid. You know, the kid who spun his stepbrother to death in a hammock and now that's why there are all these warnings on hammocks."

I knew Willis to be in possession of a hammock. Multiple pictures of the stupid dog in the stupid hammock when all the people want is the goddamn wife.

"Yikes!"

"Yeah. What are you doing here?"

"Here in this restaurant? I read about it somewhere."

"No, in New York."

"I'm here for a conference. We just moved to Fort Worth."

"Got it," I said, even though I could detect no connection between the two facts.

"I'm in sports marketing now. They only send three people from the company each year. I'm here to prove that the accounts guy knows what it means to be an athlete."

He patted his stomach through his shirt.

"It's kind of stupid that they trot me out for these things," he mused, tucking his hair behind his ears. "But duty calls!"

"And how are the twins?"

"Oh, *well*," he said, not flinching at the idea I possessed information he hadn't shared. "Since you asked, I'm obligated to do this."

He scrolled through pictures of baby girls. They were formal portraits, the girls wearing pink bows tied around their bald heads. Or else they were asleep in their cribs and the photos were of the nursery itself—a girlish explosion of matching mobiles, rose-patterned wallpaper, and monogrammed piggy banks. The last photo was of one of the girls, naked, propped up on Willis's old sofa with his gold medal around her neck. There was a time when I had sat on that same sofa, wearing the same outfit. I gave Willis his phone back.

"New York always reminds me of you," he said.

"I'm not sure I'm prepared to represent a whole city."

"We came in to see the tree last Christmas and it was butt cold. And I thought of how cold you must be in your apartment because you refused to take out your air-conditioning unit between seasons."

"It's not worth it."

"It is."

"Agree to disagree."

"Agree to freeze your ass off!"

Behind me, Brody had spread himself out in the booth, head down as if he were searching for something in the folds of the leather. Eliza was stroking his arm with a mixture of vibrancy and pity.

I told Willis about my new job, about the magazine folding. He only registered it as an updated LinkedIn profile, not the death of a way of life. He always said that everyone in New York identified too much with their careers. This was a stunning piece of hypocrisy, coming from an Olympian, the kind of blanket statement that made for a champion athlete but a strangely unfeeling civilian. Willis never saw "what the big deal was" in any given scenario, no matter how significant. A swastika on an advertisement, rendered in sharpie, was "just one idiot." Global warming was "something the Earth was gonna do eventually." I suspected that if Rocket died, he'd be the first to tell me it was an opportunity to get a kitten.

There were perks to this worldview. Willis knew the answers to his own questions before he asked them. Like Boots, he was not tortured. Unlike Boots, he used words like *goals*. Though I will give him this: Willis had a healthier grip on the confines of his own mortality than most of my peers, even if I didn't agree with his rationale. Marriage, children, home ownership? Real. Jobs, boyfriends, landlords? Fake. This is why some people got engaged in the first place, to step off the fake list and onto the real one. And I had joined their ranks. I had turned another human being into a talisman against social grief. So I lifted my left hand and fanned my fingers in a way I had never done before, not even to the mirror.

"Ahh!" Willis said, lifting me up off the ground.

I squirmed to get back down. I had a full stomach and I also did not like how thrilled he was. I was only aiming for

71

placation, to wipe that anthropological look off his face. When this first started happening with men, I was flattered. Clearly, my siren song was so loud, having a wife of their own was not enough of a deterrent. They needed me to be off-limits as well. It did not take me long to realize their relief had nothing to do with some long-suppressed desire to sleep with me. As a single woman, I made them uncomfortable. How hard it must have been for them to place me in their firmament of friends prior to me being part of a couple. Occasionally, they'd pump me for dating stories in the name of vicarious living, but they only missed their old lives, not my current one. On some level, I must have sensed this difficulty because I made constant efforts to demonstrate my wholeness, my effervescence. Feel the breeze, boys. As it turned out, all my efforts were for naught. Their current relief belied old pity. I mourned for all the time I'd wasted, concealing bouts of bitterness or depression, minimizing the impact of disappointments. I may as well have been smashing stemware against the fireplace.

Eliza was trying to catch my eye. Brody was still in the booth. The last train to Bronxville left in an hour.

"Tell me everything," said Willis.

"What? Oh. He's an architect," I lied.

After all this time, I still wanted to seem otherworldly to Willis. Superior somehow. I immediately regretted it.

"He must be really smart."

"Oh, I don't . . . I don't care about that as much as I used to."

"Why wouldn't you care about being smart?"

"Well, I probably care about it even more in one sense. You get older, you want the people you're with to know just as much about the world as you do so that you can make your jokes and send your links. Or women do. We don't, you know, get off on teaching other grown-ups. But being smart isn't the only quality."

"You've always been such a thoughtful person."

I stared into his Captain America eyes, which were obscured by his cheeks because he was smiling. His assessment of me as thoughtful filled me with sadness. I didn't deserve it, not when I didn't care about his opinion when it mattered.

"Listen," I said, "this may be weird, but now that you're in front of me, I just wanted to say sorry I was so shitty to you."

Willis screwed up his eyes.

"You weren't shitty to me, not ever."

"Willis. I was. Constantly."

"Aww," he said, ruffling my hair, as I stood there, stock-still, letting him. "You were just being yourself."

I studied his face. Was it possible he'd dismissed my egregious behavior as the customs of a different world? *In New York, we browbeat our men, mock their gifts, and tell them their ideas are sophomoric.* Willis had applied the platitudes of hero videos to his personal life. He had rewritten history so that all his struggles were necessary in order to get him to the finish line—to his wife, to his girls, to his dog. I was a human sandpit.

"But, well," I said, studying the ceiling, "I'm sorry about the abortion. Not, like, sorry *for* you. Not for the act. Just, you know, in general."

"If you're determined to apologize for something, apologize for never taking your air-conditioning unit out."

"I'm serious."

"It was a long time ago," he said, shutting the conversation down. "Another life."

It was not another life for me, it was still my life. All mine. I sometimes thought about what our child would have looked like and if it would have hated me by now. What if it had gotten Mommy's muscle mass and Daddy's brains? But after Willis and I split, he had not thought about any of those things. He had pulled up the anchor. All this time, I thought I had turned him into cocktail fodder when I was the cocktail fodder. There was no life experience too big to fit into Willis's tidy box, including that one time we semi-killed a semi-baby. His wife probably had her own box. Maybe a sorority hazing gone wrong. Maybe a whole rape that she thought of as a "date rape" if she thought of it at all. *Just one idiot.*

One of the tie-wearing men at Willis's table waved in his direction.

"Duty calls," he said again. "The call of duty. So cool to see you, Lola."

Willis smiled broadly, skipping back to his life. Then he turned around and practically shouted across the restaurant:

"What are the chances?!"

People looked up from their meals.

"I don't know!" I shouted back.

What *were* the chances? Or the odds?

Modern Psychology had once devoted the back page to "luck language." The same event could happen to four different people and one would deem it a coup, another kismet, another ironic, another auspicious. A coup signified chaos, kismet signified fate, irony signified order, auspicious signified faith. Meanwhile, odds were quantifiable but chances were not. Chances were abstract and "for" whereas odds were concrete and "against." Hopeful people, of which Willis was one, used "chances" in the same spots where skeptical people used "odds." I was an odds person.

Eliza approached with my bag in hand. She had the look of a mother who'd been forced to change diapers while her husband played solitaire on the toilet. But I was not the one who insisted we come to the restaurant with the unhinged kid in the kitchen.

"Why did you pick this place?"

"I told you."

She seemed exasperated with me as she pulled her hair back, an elastic in her teeth.

"I mean, how long has Brody been working here? Was he working here the last time you came to visit?"

"Yeah, I think so. Hopefully, he'll still be working here after that spectacle tonight."

That spectacle. Crying in public. I looked at our now vacant table.

"Is he okay?"

"I mean, no. I don't think he's ever meant to be *okay.*"

"It's late, I'm sorry. Are you ready?"

"You're the one who's been glued to the floor of this place."

3

In order to explain the coincidence to Boots, I would have to reveal that I had not told him about Amos. Which would be making a big deal out of a medium deal. This is why the pact was in place. The bones of the concept were solid. No one has the power to control how an ex blooms in one's partner's imagination. Every breakup becomes the wrong size in the retelling. You can keep your food from touching all you want, it all winds up in the same place. Besides, there were maybe five people in the world who had met both Amos and Willis, who would understand the peculiarity of the past forty-eight hours. And then one of them invited herself over.

Vadis was in the neighborhood because she had a Victorian lampshade in need of repair and, unbeknownst to me, our apartment is in the lampshade district.

"Row," she corrected herself, panting into the phone as she cut through street traffic. "It's more of a row."

"I feel like I would have noticed."

"They're not *storefronts*," she said, disgusted at my

ignorance. "They're ateliers that specialize in refurbishing lampshades."

"Only you."

"Well, no, not only me or they wouldn't be in business. Anyway, I'm here."

The buzzer rang. Boots poked his head out of the bathroom, letting a front of steam into the apartment. His hair was plastered to his head, a streak of shaving cream on his cheek.

"Vadis," I said, leaning on the buzzer.

"Who drops by unannounced? Is she Mr. Rogers?"

"Was that the premise of Mr. Rogers?"

"You know what I mean."

I leaned on the buzzer once more, letting her through the second door. Boots scrambled for a shirt. He and Vadis got along so long as I was there to translate. I'd let them gang up on me, tease me about inconsequential things like how long it took me to leave the house or my low alcohol tolerance or how attached I was to little things, like matchbooks and birthday cards. These were easy sacrifices for the sight of my best friend and my fiancé enjoying each other's company. But whenever I walked in on just the two of them talking, it was like watching a daisy and a stapler trying to hold down a conversation.

Vadis came flying through the apartment with a bushel of pussy willows. The ailing lampshade had already been dropped off at the lampshade hospital and she'd gone on a pussy-willow-buying rampage.

"I live in the flower district, too?"

"You need to leave the house more," she chided.

Vadis lived the kind of ultra-rural life that, because it took place in New York, was considered hip. She owned a car. She composted. She knew the name of her butcher. She had a butcher.

"You're wet," she announced, hugging Boots with her free arm.

"You're observant," he said.

He put her pussy willows in a jug on the floor.

"Like a bull in a glass shop," he murmured.

I could sense his pride in a bad joke setting in. I gave him a simpering smile to keep it from going airborne once more.

"Why are you taking a shower?" she asked, sniffing around him in circles. "Have you killed a man?"

"Because I came from the gym and I'm going to get a beer with my friends. Is this satisfactory to you?"

"Oh," she said, "well, that's reasonable. Lola, you have a man who goes to the gym and drinks beer. It's like a catalog. Hold on to this one."

Deciding this comment was within an acceptable range of sarcasm, Boots gave her a "ha" and retreated into our bedroom. Vadis and I sat on the sofa, where she launched into a story about a guy she'd started sleeping with who was insisting on *day dates*. I posited that if I were dating Vadis and being siloed into sex, I, too, would inquire about music festivals and walks in the park.

"Maybe," she said, having lost all interest in her own quandary.

Courtship for her was a simple affair. Vadis: I like your shirt. Suitor: I like your bone structure. Anyone who wanted more was deemed a nuisance and dismissed.

She yawned and complained her jaw hurt.

"From giving head!" she shouted over her shoulder.

"Why do you have to do that? He doesn't care who you blow."

"Maybe that's why."

Rocket examined the pussy willows with great interest. Vadis slid out a branch and gave it to her, a gift she accepted with shock followed by reckless abandon. Boots emerged, holding a single shoe, staring down at a pile of shoes by the door.

"Where's your friend?" he said to the shoe. "Ah-ha!"

When the door shut behind him, the cat darted into the bedroom to reclaim the bed and I could feel Vadis's presence unfurl in the apartment.

"I like what you haven't done with the place."

"Wine?" I offered.

"Yes, please. Is it white?"

"It's red."

"Either way."

I cracked the cork so that half of it got jammed in the neck of the bottle. The only way out was down, so I drowned it with a chopstick.

"Watch out for shards," I said, handing her a glass.

We were silent for a moment, curled up on the sofa. Vadis scraped at her nail polish with her teeth. She told me she was bored of her love life, that it wasn't part of her the way it was part of me. She said she envied me my string of boyfriends. Not in the way married people envied it, but the reverse. To Vadis, *I* was a relationship person, the conventional one. Then she began grilling me about Amos. Where had we gone? Did he give me a reason for being at the restaurant? I told her we had a drink, that we fought but not really. What else was there to say? The world did not spin off its axis. She strummed those long fingers on the back of my sofa.

"There is one weird thing," I said.

She sat up straight as a rod.

"I wound up at the same spot last night and guess who was there?"

"Morgan Freeman?"

"Was that just on the tip of your tongue?"

She shrugged.

"Willis Klee."

She snarfed her wine onto the sofa cushions and it dribbled down her peasant blouse like a dainty nosebleed.

"Vadis!"

"Sorry. *Willis* Willis?!"

"You remember Willis? Ten points for you."

"I listen."

"Yeah but no, you don't."

She got up, wet some paper towel over the sink, and began blotting her chest. The water hit a spoon and splashed everywhere.

"Olympians I will always remember."

It's not that Vadis was an unkind person but she could never be confused for a curious person. Wanting to encourage this behavior, I told her about my conversation with Willis. I had not told her about the abortion when I had it. We weren't as close then; she'd just started working at the magazine before her party, the one where I'd met Willis. But now Vadis hung on every detail, desperate for as much of a transcript as I could reproduce. When I was through, she sank back into the sofa as if she'd been tossed there.

"As you know," she announced, "I don't believe in coincidences."

"Did I know that?"

"I believe you were meant to run into both of them."

"And now I have."

I used her knee as support as I got up to retrieve the wine.

"And how does that make you feel?"

I spun around. She was patting her shirt, waiting for a response.

"I don't know. I feel like time passed and certain boats came by and I didn't get on board. Or else I wanted to be on a boat but was pushed overboard and so, sure, that makes me reflect on the seaworthiness of the boat I'm in now and it's just all very nautical."

"You have so much difficulty letting go of the past," she decided, wheels turning. "Like, more than anyone I know. Like with the matchbooks."

"People keep matchbooks, it's a decorative choice."

"Everything gets stuck in the craw of the consciousness with you."

"Did you knock yourself on the head on the way here?"

"It's like the Cranberries said: Do you have to let it linger? Do you have to, do you have to, do you have to—?"

"No?"

"No. Let's go out. It'll help."

"I don't need help."

"It's nice out."

I checked my bare wrist. I wanted to be here when Boots got back. I was practicing equilibrium, maintaining a balance between putting him first and putting my own whims first. Most couples seemed more self-regulating than we were. They knew when it was okay to be absent the day their other half returned from a trip and when it wasn't, they referred to each other as "halves" without vomiting into their hands. They knew when it was okay to stay out all night with an ex-boyfriend and when it wasn't. We never knew. So I erred on the side of obligation. Which was doing no one in our relationship any favors.

Vadis's pussy willows drew stares on the subway platform. She put her arms through the straps that held them together. Strangers assigned cultural meaning to the bundle of twigs and their transporter and were uncharacteristically under-standing when the pussy willows got caught in the subway doors. Uncharacteristically understanding when they got popped in the eye. One woman offered to give Vadis a seat but we stood, our bodies swaying. It took me a minute to notice how quiet she was being.

"Everything okay?" I asked.

"Of course."

"Just because you've never just dropped by the apartment before."

"I believe in spontaneity."

"Got it," I said. "Yes to spontaneity, no to coincidences."

I stared at the heads of strangers, the silver hairs at the part lines of women entering middle age, the things they could not see in the mirror. On the other side of the window was gradating darkness, the occasional graffiti tag.

"Are we on the express?"

I hated the feeling of being whisked at high speeds to the wrong place. Then I remembered I didn't know where we were going.

"Don't take me somewhere cool," I chided her. "I'm not dressed for it."

We emerged onto Canal Street, determined to get off it. Or at least I was. The view from Varick, looking east, was like approaching a town in the Old West. The humble parks and 99-cent pizza places ended abruptly when the lofts and factories sprang up, giving the skyline the air of a Potemkin village. My tolerance for this strip of town had weakened with age. The billboards that blocked the sky, the way the sidewalk seemed to offer you up to traffic like an animal sacrifice, the souvenir shops guarded by mechanical frogs treading in their troughs. Boots and I had once spent an ill-advised weekend looking at apartments around here, despite not being ready to move in, mentally, emotionally, or certainly financially. We wanted to see what was out there. For "fun." So we toured a place on Canal and Mott. The trick with this part of Canal, the broker explained, was that it was "secretly SoHo."

"If I was SoHo," Boots mused, "I wouldn't keep it a secret."

The apartment had a skylight, floors segmented with area rugs, and a little bedroom in the back that fit a queen-size bed if one forwent nightstands. There was also a dining table that looked like it belonged in a barn. It would not be there for new residents, but it would leave the suggestion of dinner parties in its wake. We could never afford a place like this, but I wasn't desperate to make it work anyway. I'd feel trapped. Just the thought of double-parking a moving van on Canal made my chest seize.

"If you don't like something, you don't like it," said Boots, walking ahead of me down the endless stairs. "But for the record, I could live anywhere with you."

In addition to the pussy willows, Vadis was in the market for snow globes. The bedding scion for whom she did her bidding was throwing an intimate dinner for sixty, and Vadis had been sent to procure snow globes for each table setting.

"This is the surprise? An errand? It's very weird to me that this is your job now."

"I hated journalism," she said, as if the opposite of journalism was buying party favors.

"But what do snow globes have to do with bedding?"

"They remind people of sleep."

"You know what else reminds people of sleep? Klonopin."

We entered a narrow shop where a saleswoman followed us around as if we were picking out our wedding china. A middle-aged man in clear-framed glasses leaned on the glass behind the register, filling out a crossword in pen. I flipped a globe and watched the city turn upside down. Chunky snow settled into the well. When I flipped it over again, the snow collapsed onto the buildings. The globes with the glitter were more flurry-like. Their reflective flecks swirled around a Statue of Liberty sporting sunglasses and a bikini, an outfit that defied the logic of the globe's own making.

"Do you have any of these ones but bigger?" asked Vadis.

The man behind the counter didn't look up from his crossword. The saleswoman was at Vadis's side, answering for him.

"What you see," she translated.

Vadis gave her a look like she knew better, like she was just here to price things out. She waited for a better answer but the woman wouldn't budge. Then a bell chimed and she walked away to greet a new customer.

"Ready?" Vadis asked me, texting as she spoke.

Outside, the air was saturated with the smell of decaying garbage. Two cab drivers were parked at a light, berating each other out their windows while their passengers texted through the disruption. I smiled. Uber drivers didn't yell at each other, they couldn't.

"On to the next one?" I asked Vadis.

We had not walked four steps before I noticed her staring at me. Her eyes were a kind of accidental blue, the color of sink water after washing something navy in it.

"What?"

"Do you feel weird, being around here? Or different?"

"I mean, I'm hungry."

Eating out multiple nights in a row was bad for the wallet, bad for the metabolism, but I needed to shove bread into my face. Wine on an empty stomach had become pathetically damaging. Vadis surveyed the landscape and began ruminating on restaurants as if she could see through the buildings. I bent down and stretched my legs. Then, on the way back up, I screamed. I surprised myself with the sound of it.

"Jesus Christ," Vadis said, rubbing her ear.

I squatted and tugged at her sleeve, forcing her to squat with me.

"What are we doing?"

Was it possible to hallucinate after two glasses of wine? Is anyone's tolerance so low? Running past the fruit carts was Dave Egan. I'd gone on a handful of dates with Dave more than a decade ago. Part of me wanted to be rewarded for recognizing him at all; he was such a brief interlude. Though he didn't look markedly different. Perhaps on account of all the incessant jogging.

Dave was in the market for a type, not a person. What Dave needed was a hearty sex maniac who could play blackjack and fix a carburetor, someone with no neurosis or limitations, someone with no nerve endings except for the ones in her clitoris. He needed a certain kind of guy disguised as a certain kind of girl, someone to make him feel like he'd finally gotten everything his thirteen-year-old self had wanted. If I'd known Willis when I knew Dave, I imagine Dave would've worshipped Willis. The more Dave forced me to say no (No, I really have no interest in polar bear plunges. No, I really have never driven stick or used a butt plug), the more he accused me of digging my heels into the soft padding of my "comfort zone," the more I revolted.

"This is New York," I explained. "Everything is outside everyone's comfort zone. Why push it?"

By date five, I found myself claiming to be riddled with physical quirks, sensitive organs, pulled muscles, intractable habits—a disagreeable child who barely used her legs. And still I thought: This could work? That's what really stuck with me about Dave, not Dave himself but how I felt that if only I'd been more *game*, more apt to commit, he'd have pledged his loyalty to me. If I really wanted to be over and done with dating, to have a life like Eliza's, all I had to do was flick the switch. But I didn't even know where my switch *was*.

Dave was one of the few blond men I'd ever been with, an Aryan slate that belied his Jewish heritage. On the last of our encounters, I suggested that he would have survived the Holocaust, passing for gentile, whereas I wouldn't have. Unfortunately, this comment harmonized a little too well with the "I'm weak" advisories I'd been issuing. All I meant was: One humid day in Warsaw and the jig would be up. But Dave took my implication to be that the Jews who died in the Holocaust did so because they were too frail to survive, because they didn't want to go kayaking in the Hudson. He draped his arm around me and told me he would've *gladly* snuck me out of a camp. Or brought me "scraps of food." I smiled weakly at this, which he took as an invitation to elaborate.

"I would've forged your papers," he went on, "gotten you out of there . . . for a price, of course."

I pushed it out of my mind as we walked into a movie theater and shook our popcorn. But there was a shift when we had sex that night and neither of us dared speak of why: He was playing prison guard. I did not suspect nice-guy Dave Egan harbored secret desires to make Holocaust victims fuck him in exchange for their lives. It was not so much the fantasy that bothered me, as his lack of understanding that he was having it. Even more bothersome was his inability to unhook his jaws from an off-color joke. As I was leaving his apartment the next morning, he tossed me a chocolate bar. He referred to my departure as "the liberation."

We never spoke again.

Dave hopped on and off the sidewalk, treating the streets like an obstacle course, swerving around clusters of tourists. I tried to remember if he'd showcased such joint dexterity naked. As he trotted off into the distance, I signaled to Vadis that it was okay to stand. In a way, I was grateful for the Dave Egans of my life and the indifference they triggered, if indifference is, by its nature, triggerable. I did not want Dave Egan to get hit by a truck or lose his job. Nor did I not want him to win the lottery. I didn't want anything for him. Not every breakup is acrimonious. Not every relationship has to end with a stab wound. Most of these things don't work out.

I told Vadis the coast was clear. But her eyes were fixed on Dave. She stood on her toes like she wanted to run after him.

"You don't know Dave Egan, do you?"

Whatever social circles Dave jogged in, they did not intersect with Vadis's.

"No," she said, as he receded into the distance. "Maybe . . ."

"What do you mean, 'maybe'?"

"I think we're Facebook friends."

"How do you even know who you're Facebook friends with at this point?"

"Through you," she said, still craning her neck.

"I don't even think *I'm* friends with Dave Egan on Facebook."

"Why does it matter?"

"Because you can barely pick your actual friends out of a lineup."

Dave made a right onto Chrystie Street and vanished, the neon soles of his sneakers turning into little points of color. Vadis was half-listening, squinting between buildings. A woman in a bandeau top walked by, slurping up a gyro like it was the greatest thing she'd ever put in her mouth, and my stomach rumbled. I suggested we go to a healthy restaurant at the fancy end of Canal, one that had clued in to its patrons' unspoken desires for a few cheese-crusted dishes.

"I need you to come with me," she said, solemnly, "but not to eat."

"Fuck you, not to eat."

She squeezed my arm. Her expression was desperate.

"We're close," she offered, adopting the posture of a bloodhound.

"Are you kidnapping me? Is that your van?"

I nodded at a white delivery van across the street. A man was unloading boxes of cactus leaves, picking up strays and tossing them back into the van like green Frisbees.

"No," she said, as if I were serious.

"You're being annoying. Where are we going?"

"Nowhere. But you have to promise not to freak out."

"Why would I freak out about going nowhere?"

She walked me over to Allen as if I were a perp with whom she had developed a rapport and thus agreed not to handcuff. The shift in environment reset her disposition. Once on calmer shores, her face became composed as if nothing out of the ordinary had just happened. I told her that if she thought it was a funny joke to go back to the same goddamn restaurant for a *third* night, it was not a funny joke. Clive was the only person I knew who treated restaurants as personal cafeterias, who took a daddish amount of pride in requesting off-menu dishes.

Vadis sped up. I trailed behind her when the sidewalk narrowed.

"Do you remember the night, like a hundred years ago, when you told me that I made up names for your lovers so they could never be real and therefore could never take you away from me? We were very high."

"Did you just call them 'lovers'?"

"Yes or no?"

"Yes. You cried."

"I did not *cry*."

"You brought it up."

"Fine, I welled. But do you remember what happened after that?"

I scanned my memory but wasn't sure what criteria I was meant to be using.

"You went home and I left with Clive."

"How very on-brand of you to expect me to remember events of your life I wasn't there for."

"Lola, I'm trying to tell you something important."

"Have you been having an affair with *Clive*?"

"No! Disgusting."

As someone who had, at various points, nearly had an affair with Clive, I took umbrage at this. But as someone who knew what a disaster said affair would have been, I was also pleased by her recoiling.

"Like I said, you went home and then Clive—and Zach actually—and I got another drink. Then Zach peeled off and Clive and I got yet *another* drink and another and so forth and that was the night he told me he couldn't keep making cuts at the magazine, that we could pay freelancers twenty cents a word and it wouldn't matter. We were going under. Then, the next day, he told everyone we were being laid off."

"That was the day the magazine folded? I don't remember that."

"It was."

She gestured at me to jaywalk with her.

"Anyway, so it's last call and Clive orders us champagne. And I was like, champagne is for celebrating, we need martinis. Sad unemployed-people martinis. But he insists because he says there *is* something to celebrate. Which is when he first told me about this."

Vadis held the pussy willows in place with one arm and reached into her back pocket with the other. She extracted a business card on cream-colored paper stock. I took it from her, feeling the weight between my fingers. The grain of the paper had a texture to it. On one side was printed . . . nothing. And on the other side was printed . . . nothing.

"Invisible ink?"

She squeezed the edges of the card so that it split in two. It was a little folder. From the inside, I pinched a piece of translucent carbon paper. There was a black-and-white design

91

within a circle, a black bowler hat set against an oculus, and within it, a sketch of what looked like a stained glass window. There were no words at all. Vadis was waiting for me to be shocked.

"Oh my God."

"Cool, right?"

"You guys are in a cult."

"I am not in a cult. Would a cult have business cards?"

"I wouldn't know. But I do know that no one who's in a cult thinks they're in a cult. Maybe you're in a cult masquerading as a secret society. And Clive is your leader. Are you sure you haven't had sex with him? Maybe he called it something else, like a 'cleansing ceremony'?"

"You're not funny."

"Welp, you're either in a cult or you're a creative director," I said, handing her back the card. "I'm not sure which is worse."

"Keep it, it's yours."

"I can't believe you managed to keep whatever this is from me. It must have been slowly killing you. I can't decide if I'm pissed or impressed."

"Lola! I'm not trying to be cloak-and-daggery. I just need you to come with me. All will be revealed. Why is this so hard? God, you're so punishing."

"What is with that word? I am not punishing."

"Judgmental, maybe. Opinionated. Aren't you at least curious?"

"Not really! You left me out of it for this long. You *and* Clive, apparently. Your new best friend. Also, if I'm being honest? Every time you drag me to some secret location, I wind up taking MDMA and talking to assholes in jumpsuits."

"This isn't that, I promise," she whined. "Come on, I never ask you for anything."

"You ask me for things all the time."

She sighed and flapped her arms. It was unsettling to see her like this. The power balance in our friendship had always been weighted in her direction, not because she courted it but because she took for granted that the world would bend to her will—and so it did. The city was chockablock with genetic winners who still had to pay for their own meals and wait in line at the DMV. But Vadis's conviction that the world would do for her was foregone, not manipulative. If I decided to be the kind of person that forgets to renew her passport but still manages to leave the country, I could be Vadis tomorrow.

We rounded the corner, metal doors in the sidewalk making a racket when we stepped on them. We came to the street with the same bright bodega where I'd purchased my cigarettes the night I saw Amos. The plastic cat was waving from its perch on the register. I remembered those cats were meant to symbolize luck. Good omens.

"Et voilà!" Vadis exclaimed.

It was an anticlimactic sight. Wedged between the bodega and a former tenement building was an old synagogue. I must have passed it a dozen times but had never really noticed it before. It looked uncomfortable, crammed between its modern neighbors, condos on one side and the bodega on the other, as if it had come second. There were turrets on each corner, guarded by a pair of lions, leering downward and frozen mid-roar. Beneath their paws were hooded security cameras. All the windows were boarded up except for a stained glass Star of David in the center, with some of the panes missing. The lower part of the façade was decorated in graffiti, the top in pigeon shit, as if both species had come to an arrangement.

"You're Jewish now?"

I glanced at Vadis, who didn't respond, and then back at the building. Why the city's defunct synagogues, in particular, had failed to morph into co-ops and coworking spaces, I never understood. Maybe there were landmark issues. Maybe they were condemned. Maybe an aging sculptor with a septum piercing lorded over them. Whatever the reason, many of these places were now the domain of rats. And those desperate enough to sneak into them. Which, apparently, included us.

"It's not sneaking," Vadis said. "Watch this."

She took a step back, making sure a surveillance camera got a clear shot of her. A red light blinked dumbly. She marched in place. She hopped up and down. Eventually, she wrapped her sleeve over her fist, knocking on the doors until they shook. I could feel the words form in my mouth: *Maybe we should just go.* I'd never heard anyone say this sentence outside of a horror movie. Nothing gets the mansion gate to creak open quite like "maybe we should just go."

"I really don't need to go to some secret place."

I imagined how annoyed Boots would be if he were here, dealing with the whims of Vadis, whose snobberies outperformed mine (she who always had to leave one party for another, she who simply *had* to find the hidden beach town only to declare it dead upon her arrival). He once said, apropos of nothing, "I can't imagine Vadis using an airport bathroom" and I knew just what he meant.

"Let's get pizza," I suggested.

She ignored me, focusing her efforts on composing a rapid-fire text. Before she could finish, I heard a click. The door unlocked.

"Or that," she said, rolling her eyes.

We entered a musty area that looked as I suspected it would, only worse, and smelled as I suspected it would, only worse. Unidentified particles floated through strips of light. A fire had blown through the roof at some point and the walls were dotted with holes. Some were torn down to the plaster, repaired with yellowing newspaper. Beer bottles, relieved of their labels, congregated in the corners. Cobwebs stretched between the charred beams overhead. Everything seemed wet. Over my shoulder, I caught sight of a few pedestrians on the opposite side of the street, peering at us with the New York–specific envy one has for people who have the authority to enter a place they've only seen from the outside.

Then the door banged shut and everything went dark.

Vadis instructed me to watch my step as we swiped the flashlights on our phones. I followed her, stepping where she stepped. One of the beams above us was illuminated by the missing sections in the window, by the afternoon light coming through. On it was carved a string of Hebrew letters and their English translation: "This is the gate of the Lord, the righteous will enter through it."

"Only the penitent man shall pass," I mumbled.

We reached the back of the room, where there was a second door with yet another corroded knob. But instead of grabbing for it, Vadis smacked a bright green button in the door frame and slid the entire thing to the left, moving it on its tracks like an album in a jukebox.

We were standing in what looked like an antigravity chamber, a hallway no wider than a closet, face-to-face with a steel wall. Vertical seams were stitched together by gleaming silver bolts. The hallway seemed to go on forever in each direction—a function of the mirrors affixed to either end. It was freshly cleaned with something that smelled like citrus.

"You're a spy," I said, trying to muster up a list of skills Vadis might have to offer the CIA.

"Is that what you think?"

She entered a five-digit code into a keypad, which blinked for a heartbeat before emitting a harsh beep and turning red. She pushed the buttons more deliberately this time. They made a tune, which Vadis narrated as she pressed:

"Is. This. What. You. Want."

"Ah-ha," she said, as the keypad chirped in recognition.

"Really, are you a spy?"

"No," she said, a familiar slyness crossing her face. "But you kind of are."

She pushed the walls in opposite directions. My eyes squinted as my brain raced to catch up. We were standing in a marble atrium. Light came from a brass-framed skylight above. More light beamed in from the three open floors. It looked as if someone had squared off the interior of the Guggenheim. Above our heads hung two chandeliers that spread out like stalactites, haphazardly dotted with light. Filing cabinets had replaced the pews on what used to be the women's balcony. In the corner, there was a garden sustained by a honeycomb of solar panels. The panels were frozen waves, as if someone had lifted a sheet and it had never collapsed. Beneath them were ferns and mosses, bamboo, cacti, birds of paradise, a couple cannabis plants. A water fountain gurgled away in the center.

"Garden," I said, as if having just learned the word.

"I know, right?" she said, laughing.

But the real star of the show was neither the garden nor the chandeliers. It was directly across from us: an elegant little elevator where a dais must have once stood. You could see through to the mechanics of it, to the cables and wheels, as if we were in the interior of a watch. It was hard to tell which gears were essential and which were decorative. The cage inside was brass but the exterior was glass, like a ship in a bottle. A long silk cord extended up from the middle. Then I heard a noise, something behind me that sounded like an industrial espresso machine, that broke the spell.

It was, in fact, an industrial espresso machine.

A gangly splotched-faced kid, maybe twenty, stood, tucked behind a counter near the entrance, wearing a wedge cap and a bowtie. Behind him were stacks of cups and saucers, a jar of straws. He smiled at me, drilling his lips into his cheeks, a little placid, a little psychotic.

"Coffee?" Vadis asked.

For some logic-devoid reason, I assumed the espresso kid reduced the likelihood of this being an organ-harvesting facility.

"I'm good, thanks."

The elevator began to move, its wheels spinning in an industrial ballet. Vadis and I stood shoulder to shoulder, watching a pair of human feet sink down on a glass platform. The feet belonged to an impeccably dressed Black man in a navy suit with perfect creases running down each limb. He was tall with a fold of neck skin pushing at his collar. When the elevator doors opened, he bent down to pluck some fibers from his pants before walking swiftly across the atrium, extending his hand too straight and too early for such a greeting. This gave him the disorienting gait of Hitler Youth.

"Hello!" he called, as if he'd been screaming it for hours.

When he reached us, he clasped both my hands in one of his, patting the pile of fingers, moving me in haphazard directions like he was shaking a cocktail. His skin was surprisingly cool. This whole place was surprisingly cool. It probably cost the GDP of a small country to keep it air-conditioned.

"This is Errol," Vadis introduced the man.

"Lola!" Errol exclaimed. "Light of my life, fire of my loins. Well, not *my* loins. Hashtag MeAsWell. Has Vadis given you the tour? Espresso?"

The splotchy-faced coffee kid renewed his smile. I shook my head no.

"She was a showgirl!" he sang from his diaphragm. "*That's* it. With yellow feathers in her hair and a dress cut down to there!"

"Is this an event space?" I asked, my voice sounding not my own.

Errol laughed until he was doubled over and finished with an "Oh, Lola" and the wipe of an invisible tear.

"I haven't told or shown her anything yet," explained Vadis, an apology for my ignorance. "I thought it would be easier to download in person."

"You know my name."

"And you know my name," Errol replied, smiling. "And I know Vadis's name. We all know each other's names. Please, follow me."

"I don't think I should have to keep following people places."

"You never *have* to do anything." He bristled at the suggestion. "We are wholly committed to free will."

"We?"

"It's just there's no conference room on this floor."

"Oh, well, when you put it that way . . ."

Errol smiled again, a pleasingly crooked smile with one front tooth curtseying behind the other.

"You *are* funny," he said.

The three of us crammed into the strange elevator, which I half expected to shoot through the ceiling. Vadis stood in front of me. I could smell her perfume, an expensive mix of fireplace and bergamot. Errol faced forward as well, readjusting his spine. The elevator seemed unnecessary as the whole place couldn't have been more than four floors and it moved extraordinarily slowly. But neither of them acknowledged the slowness. My view of the atrium was intercepted by the whirling of brass gears, but I could still see the barista below us. He was staring into space, eyes unmoved from the spot where we'd been standing, as if having a small stroke.

4

Clive was waiting for us in the glass-walled conference room. A tray of bottled water sat atop a wooden console behind him. He looked both more and less composed since last I'd seen him. More because he wasn't drunk out of his mind, less because he was visibly anxious. He paced around the chairs like a caged animal, jacket flapping, exposing a silk lining. It was creased at the elbows, likely from a long day of maniacal plotting. When we filed in, he stopped pacing and flashed a winning smile. I sensed Vadis and Errol move behind me, trying to hide. Then I realized they weren't hiding, they were *bowing*. Actually bowing. And not to me.

I was too appalled to react.

Behind Clive was the only decoration in the room, a reproduction of a Magritte painting. I knew the one. It was not his most popular but it was his most populated. The painting featured dozens of men wearing suits and bowler hats, scattered against a blue sky, rooftops below them. Clive could be one of them, minus the hat. He stood in front of the painting as if in charge of it. I refused to be dazzled in his presence. Whatever this was, I knew who I was. And I was not a Clive Glenn groupie.

When I'd first met Clive, he was a mid-level editor at a free newspaper. I used to see his byline exploding from kiosks. We went to the same parties, disliked the same people. Before long, we split off from the herd to talk about art and psychology and how technology would ruin us all. His paper was about to open up its online content to comments. *Comments*. From *readers*. Readers with no expertise! He'd heard a rumor from a Silicon Valley friend that Apple was working on combining music and cellular capabilities into one device. Who would want their songs interrupted?! Being around this charismatic older man made me feel established at a time when feeling established seemed important. I liked how Clive presented his opinions, as if with everything he said, he was bringing to bear all his deeply held ideals. And it wasn't just me. He had a natural rapport with everyone. I'd meet him at a bar, and when I walked in, he'd be sharing a joke with the bartender, asking for another round before stepping outside for a cigarette. Were they friends? No, they had always only just met.

We nearly kissed a couple of times, which would have been a gateway to some scarring, useless affair. Clive was still married then, to his college sweetheart, a fact I often forgot because he rarely mentioned her. I was young and so I confused her absence in conversation with an alienation of affection when it was only a compartmentalization of affection. I did not realize that I was being doted on precisely so he *could* stay in his marriage. So we walked it back, calcifying ourselves as friends, analyzing our flirtation in real time. Talking about it served the purpose of scratching the itch without acting on it. We were only flattering ourselves. If our attraction had been that potent, the tension that important, no amount of analysis could have kept it at bay. By the time Clive and his college sweetheart divorced, there was no more itch left to be scratched.

I was Clive's first hire when he became the deputy editor of *Modern Psychology*, a magazine we respected from afar, because of its history, but with which we did not actually engage, as the reading experience so closely resembled eating balsa wood. But Clive gave it energy and style. He made it human without making it dumb, glossy without making it superficial. I was there to witness his lightning ascent to editor in chief. This did not surprise me, given how invested Clive became in the whole field. He couldn't shut it off. He liked to talk about his staff's feelings as if they were data. Or the men I dated as if they were lab rats, the way married people do, as if their life is the control and yours is the experiment. Indulgence disguised as empathy, judgment disguised as friendship. But I spilled every detail because I wanted to stay close to him.

He claimed he didn't like the public face the editor-in-chief role required. He felt like a fraud, attending conferences on behalf of the magazine, appearing on morning shows with lists of ways to "destress before work." What could've gone so wrong with your day that you needed to calm yourself down before 8 a.m.? He used to text us videos of him humping cardboard cutouts of talk show scientists. When he became a regular fixture on those same talk shows, he still joked. At least the designer suits were a tax write-off. No pinstripes, though, Clive said, regurgitating the admonishments of segment producers.

Then Clive got his own show. Just like that. This career for which people jockey all their lives fell into his lap. With the show came his own car service, his own dressing room, and his own shiny new girlfriend, a makeup artist named Chantal who'd been smudging concealer over Clive's pores for months. She had a heart-shaped face and her own line of blush brushes. She got him into Bikram yoga and sage-smudging. Pedicures. When the show was canceled, Clive became a parody of himself. He posted Carl Jung quotes on social media. The bookshelves of his office were now lined with titles like *The Anxiety of Presence* and *Past Life Regression*. A four-hundred-page book called *How to Breathe* sat open in the corner where the DSM had once been. He also started closing his door to meditate, which we thought was bad until he stopped closing the door. We'd walk by and see him, sitting ramrod straight, eyes closed.

"Inner peace as outer performance," Zach said, loud enough for Clive to hear.

"Don't," I said, sensing that ridicule might drive him further away.

"He can't hear me. Can you, Clive?!"

Zach lamented that it was impossible to tell where Old Clive stopped and New Clive began. Still, I defended him. There was no such thing as New Clive. It was all an act on behalf of the magazine, on behalf of this institution we were rebuilding together. We would do the same if we were in his shoes. Sure, Clive would fold in the occasional pat therapy phrase—one had to "set one's boundaries" and "keep one's side of the street clean." But he was still the person to whom I confided during the nights we put the magazine to bed. *I* knew him. I knew him best. But this was before. Before Clive began disappearing just as the magazine was dying, just when we needed him the most, before he began babbling about parallel universes and metaphysics.

And *well* before I'd been dragged to a secret lair on the Lower East Side with a fucking garden in it.

Clive said nothing. He just stood there, waiting for me to speak.

"And to think," I said, "you're not even Jewish."

"Call it a rental," he said, relaxing. "This place used to look like Dresden after the bombs."

"You're flipping synagogues now?"

"Have you had the coffee?"

"Did you guys *drug* the coffee?!"

Errol looked mortally offended. He coughed into his pocket square and excused himself from the room with a bow, the glass door rattling closed behind him.

"Forgive him," Clive said. "The coffee bar is his baby. That's a twenty-one-thousand-dollar machine. Italian. There's usually a line but there's practically no one here right now. Vadis and I didn't want to freak you out."

One thing that had never changed about Clive was that twinkling look in his eyes that said, you're the experiment, I'm the control.

"I can't imagine what you're thinking," he continued. "Will you sit? Please?"

I pulled out a chair across from Vadis, who was pretending to inspect her pussy willows for phantom abnormalities. Overcome with annoyance at her, I reached across the table and chucked them to the floor. Then I sat back. She folded her hands in her lap. There was a knock on the glass. Errol was back, gesticulating at the briefcase by Clive's side.

"I think it's a good idea," Errol shouted, his voice muffled.

"Okay," Clive snapped. "I know."

Clive flicked open the latches of the briefcase and removed a piece of paper and a pen, both of which he slid in my direction, but not quite far enough. I reached for them. The paper had the same bowler hat logo in the corner as I'd seen on the card Vadis gave me. The paragraphs that followed forbade me from divulging "any proprietary information related, but not limited to, development projects to be performed by the Undersigned and those clients, customers, and entities now and in perpetuity."

"An NDA? Are you serious?"

"Just sign it," Vadis snapped. "I did."

"That's a comfort," I said. "Is Errol your lawyer?"

"Errol manages this place," he explained.

"Ah, yes. Someone to do all the work while you piss off to do radio appearances. Old habits die hard, I guess."

Vadis snorted. Clive shot her a look. I scrawled my name.

"Welcome," Clive said, lifting his arms in victory, "to the Golconda."

"The who?"

"It's the name of a very famous impenetrable seventeenth-century citadel in central India."

"Not that famous."

"It also happens to be the name of this . . ."

Clive swiveled and gestured at the painting behind him, at the men in bowler hats, arms at their sides. Dozens of men were spaced equally apart so that the effect was more like wallpaper. The eye had nowhere safe to land and so it was forced to treat the men as a natural phenomenon, like rain or dust. I preferred the one with the pipe.

"Neither floating nor falling," Clive spoke to the painting. "Suspended. Paralyzed. Unable to move forward."

"That's not a print, is it?"

"It's on loan."

"Call it a rental?"

"Exactly. And now I have given the Golconda a third association. It's the name of our little club or society, however you prefer to think of it."

"I don't prefer to think anything."

"It will transcend genre. And no, it's not a 'cult.' And no, you're not being sold into 'sex slavery.'"

"Why are you using air quotes around sex slavery?"

Vadis was beaming, as if Clive's words were confirmation of her existence.

"Really?"

"I don't know why you're being pissy with *me*."

"Well, I'm not joining your cult-non-cult secret rich-person association, so you can forget about initiating me. Or making me sniff quartz or whatever. I don't even belong to a gym. This is a waste of a perfectly good kidnapping."

Clive got up from his seat, strolled over, and put his hand on my shoulder. The comfort of it threw me. I'd seen him put his hand on a lot of people's shoulders, strangers on TV who would break down at a mere "what's this *really* about?" from Clive. They had felt the same weight of the same hand. I hated how effective it was. Boots was the only person I knew who was immune to it. Once, when we were all at dinner, he wondered if Clive had a limp. When I asked what had led him to this conclusion, he said it was because Clive kept leaning on his shoulder every time he got up from the table.

"He's not using you for help," I explained, "he's trying to own you."

I don't know why I never listened to my own advice.

"Do you remember Soren Jørgensen?" Clive asked.

"Another surrealist painter?"

"An elevator repairman who founded a TM-based thought movement. I interviewed him for the magazine. Jørgensen had no formal education but in the early seventies, he began theorizing the human mind was similar to the pulleys and wheels of a traction elevator like the one that brought you up here. When you call for an elevator, it seems as if the cab is being pushed up from below or down from above. Just like when you have a new thought it seems like it's being pushed from the inside out. Even if that thought is triggered by outside stimuli, your brain parses those stimuli and acts accordingly. But according to Jørgensen, our thoughts don't always come from where we think they come from."

"Clive."

"Yes?"

"A Swedish elevator repairman did not discover the subconscious."

"Danish. And we're not talking about the subconscious. We're talking about the assumption that all thought is coming from inside the house. Jørgensen theorized that a percentage of who we are is not just stimulated by external forces but beholden to them."

"It's not a theory; you're talking about mind control."

He shuddered, as if he'd bitten into something rotten.

"You do it every day." He spoke through his teeth. "Your brain waves emit electromagnetic impulses that transfer energy to other people. It's the power of suggestion. You're doing it right now."

"Then what am I thinking?"

"Nothin' good," said Vadis, under her breath.

"We're not psychic, Lola."

"How many people are involved in this?"

"A little over fifty."

"Good God."

"Jørgensen never thought one person could *make* another

person do anything. But the influence we have over the consciousness of our fellow man has been exacerbated by technology. Much as we'd like to think of ourselves as hydraulic elevators, we are traction elevators."

"Okay."

"Okay?"

"Okay, you founded a mind control cult with an espresso machine in it. I'm very happy for you."

"It's *not* mind control," he said, struggling to keep his voice level. "It's ethical persuasion, not coercive persuasion. We're not keeping people here through fear and intimidation. It's a combination of subliminal messaging mixed with meditation."

"Still happy for you. But why am I here?"

He and Vadis exchanged glances. Clive nodded at her to speak.

"Okay, so if we see all of mankind as a single network," Vadis began, grateful to have been passed the conch, "*then* you can inject enough energy into one part of the network and it has an impact on another part. Like pulling a thread. Like when your engagement ring ruins the cashmere sweater I lent you. For instance."

"Some guy left that sweater at your house, you don't even know who."

"Not the point."

"Vadis's saying that we can use a marriage of holistic and technological techniques, positive and negative reinforcement, to encourage certain behaviors. Certain movement."

Clive loosened his tie, as if warming up a studio audience. It was difficult to be around him when he was like this. It felt like being physically shaken.

"Do you need a whiteboard?"

"Imagine," he said, ignoring me, "walking around this city in the hours before you've been told a hurricane is gonna hit. A breeze blows that is in no way different from any other breeze. Trash that is in no way different from any other trash spins in a circle that is in no way different—"

"I get it. Trash."

"And yet!" he shouted. "Because you were *told* something is afoot, you can feel the city turning its many eyes to the same subject. The conversations change, the social media posts change. Collective energy can overpower individual energy, particularly if we can magnetize one specific individual. Which is where you've been coming in."

"One more time?"

"Yes," confirmed Vadis, "have been."

I had a flash of running into Amos on the street. *Hello, Stranger.*

"This has been happening since Friday night," I said.

Clive looked at Vadis, who nodded.

"It's working a bit faster than we'd imagined, which is great."

"And I'm the hurricane?"

"You're the hole," said Vadis, "the eye of the doughnut."

"You're our case study, our model."

I put my head on the table and groaned. I watched the Magritte painting, waiting for all those men to move. Had I sensed them being shooed in my direction? Maybe if I was more in tune with my physiology, one of those people who quit social media because of the dopamine rush, I would've known.

"When did you decide I was the hole?"

"At the reunion dinner before last."

"The jerk-chicken place?"

The memory of hot meat and scotch bonnet turned itself into acid in my throat. I caught sight of my reflection in the glass and forced myself to see beyond it, past the chandeliers, where filing cabinets were arranged like card catalogs. An Indian man in an argyle top and an older white lady with big jewelry walked by. They passed a Korean woman around the same age as the barista, wearing a white tunic and silver sneakers. They all greeted one another with a little bow, though less dramatic than the one Vadis and Errol had given Clive. The Korean woman wore gold-rimmed glasses and wheeled an AV cart with wires peeking out over the edge. None of them looked at us.

"You built this in two months?"

"Oh, no," Clive corrected me. "I signed the lease when the magazine folded, but you try getting building permits for a temple. We were pre-revenue for a long time. Then we started taking on investors and selling memberships, mostly through referrals."

"Who are all these people?"

"I can't tell you that."

"I signed an NDA."

"Doesn't mean you get to know who shot JFK," Vadis scoffed.

Clive and I cocked our heads and squinted at her in unison.

"Fine. Why me?"

"Because we know you," Clive said, as if I should be bowled over by simplistic reasoning. "And you have a bona fide problem that is geographically contained, easily manipulated, and romantic in nature. When it comes to the power of suggestion, we've found that love is the easiest frequency to tap. Every other emotion burns bright and flames out. But love leaves a network of associations. And you, my friend, have been in love *a lot*."

"Infatuated," Vadis corrected him. "A serial monogamist. A people hoarder."

"Where do you source your facts?"

"Romantic emotion," Clive continued, "leaves a neurological footprint. But we needed names. And data about those names. And as your friends, we've watched you lead a corrosive and insurmountably haunting love life for decades. You're a ghoul for the past. You've been very vocal about it."

"Well, fuck you, too. What about Zach?"

Vadis scrunched her nose.

"Who would monogomize with Zach?"

"No, I mean does Zach know about this?"

"Zach doesn't know about any of this," said Clive.

"Yeah, because he already thinks the rich are brainwashing the poor!"

"You have to stop thinking of it as mind control."

"If it's not mind control, I don't *have* to do anything."

"Lola, even if the power of suggestion were mind control, which it is *not*, you're not the one being controlled. We're just encouraging people to congregate around a five-block radius of this exact spot you're sitting in, using the world's first harmonious concentration of spiritual and machine learning. That's all. One of our members is ex-NYPD. If I told you his retainer, you'd pass out. Another used to be a resource specialist at the NSA, another is IDF, another studies advertising algorithms, another is a media studies professor, another was employee number nine at a ubiquitous tech company. Did you know that former paramours are the fourth most popular search field item, below porn but *above* diseases?"

"I did not know that."

"Listen, clearly it's working. We can't be everywhere *you* go, but as long as you come within a reasonable distance of this exact spot in the next two weeks—"

"I'll run into an ex."

"Pretty much."

"Because you brought together a spy supergroup to disrupt my life with . . . vibes?"

"Not to disrupt, to *help*. And not with *vibes*. Energy and social media manipulation. If you want to get conceptually crude about it."

"I really do. Did you guys know that Boots is going out of town?"

Clive shook his head and exhaled.

"You didn't know?"

"We don't keep tabs on your life, Lola," said Vadis.

"Actually," Clive corrected her, "it's the only thing we do. But no, we didn't."

"Okay. Okay, but how did you get Eliza to pick that restaurant?"

"Eliza," Clive repeated, as if having remembered the title of a song. "I didn't even know she existed until Vadis texted me about her on the way over here. She seems to have been more of a meditative product than a technological one."

"A meditative product?"

"We have a big room where people sit around and think about you," Vadis said, as if this were her own life's dream.

"You'll find coincidences pick up naturally," said Clive. "It would have been unlikely for Eliza to pick a restaurant that *wasn't* in this neighborhood. Lola, this is only about you *for now*. If we can get enough people with tangential knowledge of a subject's life to massage that person's circumstances,

imagine what could be prevented. I know I sound like some
melioristic kook, but imagine the long-term implications for
PTSD, for grief, for addiction, for trauma, maybe one day for
climate change and *nuclear war* . . ."

"You're going to make Kim Jong-un confront all his exes?"

"Vadis, will you excuse us?"

Vadis groaned, pushing herself away from the table, low-
ering her head in his direction as she did. She scooped her
pussy willows up off the floor. Once she was gone, Clive hiked
up his pant leg and sat on the edge of the table.

"Lola, think of it as *A Christmas Carol*."

"Yeah, by way of *The Exorcist*."

"I'm sorry you didn't know. I know the whole thing seems
sneaky."

"Sneaky? Am I five? It seems amoral."

"There was no way for you to know. Look how you're reacting. You would've overridden the whole process. We
needed you and the men to just show up."

"Clive. People are supposed to run into their exes, like,
once a year, if that."

"That's only because you assume there's no alternative. But
what if you could prepare for the past instead of having it
sneak up on you at random?"

"I feel like you're playing God. Or like you feel like you're
playing God."

I focused on an arbitrary spot on Clive—a button on his
shirt—and imagined him pushing the button into the hole.

There were years of flirty text exchanges in my pocket
with every man I'd entertained as partner, however fleetingly.
Vadis was right. I was a people hoarder. Sometimes I would
pull up an old exchange and feel myself fall backward as if

through a tunnel, coming out the other end with emotions that were meant to be memories. It was like sticking a pebble in a wound, then getting frustrated the wound wasn't healing faster. It was also falsely communal as I reread these men's words, which weren't theirs anymore but artifacts of their former selves. It was not healthy to binge episodes of a sitcom starring my ex-boyfriend's cousin, but I did this like I smoked, with an acknowledgment of each instance as poisonous and yet only the vaguest of acknowledgment that my body was tallying the bill.

"Here," Clive said, "let me show you something."

We walked across the hall to the filing cabinets, where he opened several drawers and closed them.

"Ah, behind you."

I moved aside as he pushed one of the middle drawers. It snapped out into the air. Inside was a laminated sheet with the word MENU on top.

"It's a prototype," Clive said, handing me one, "for future scenarios."

Light from the chandeliers skittered around the text. My hand was shaking, so I held the sheet with both hands:

Welcome to the Golconda. We are pleased to offer the following packages to our members. Please note that due to safety, legal restrictions, and staff limitations, only one package may be selected per calendar year. Prices available upon request.

"Go on," he said. "Read it out loud so I know where you are."

I cleared my throat.

"Blood in the Streets: You encounter your ex nonfatally

bleeding in the street, having fallen off a bike. Seeing this person in physical danger will cause you to imagine caring for them again, thus providing closure."

I looked up at his face, at the lines springing from the corners of his eyes.

"You're pathological. Like a total sociopath."

"Tomato, potato."

He flicked the corner of the sheet.

"Hell Is Other People: You watch through a two-way mirror as all your exes find themselves stuck in a room together. You see how long it takes for them to figure out it's you they have in common. In Flight: You are seated next to an ex every time you board an airplane. Suitable for business travelers. Please note: we are not responsible for flight durations. Jesus."

"Yeah, that one's a doozy. Can you imagine flying to Tokyo next to someone who broke your heart?"

"No. You're a sadist. Hero Worship: Your ex who thinks you're a terrible person witnesses you yank a child to safety just before a truck comes. Contingent on availability."

"Of the truck?"

"Of the child."

"Clive!"

"Prototype!"

"The Station Agent: Ever wish you could find out what your ex *really* thought of you? We'll make sure they witness a capital crime, are brought into police custody and hooked up to a sodium thiopental drip. Sex on the Beach: TBD. What's that?"

"For now? Vodka and peach schnapps."

"Come on."

"Prototype!"

"And you're going to sell these experiences to people? For how much?"

"You don't want to know."

"And yet I asked."

"Up to two hundred and fifty thousand dollars per experience."

"So you *can* put a price tag on closure."

"We have to keep the lights on! Your package alone has taken months."

"But let's say I'm a rich person and I've already given all the money I'm gonna give to buy my kids into Harvard. Even then, am I going to pay for this?"

"Think about how much people pay for therapy over the course of a lifetime. The answer kept *Modern Psychology* in business for a quarter of a century. We're offering people a chance to confront their demons in the span of minutes."

"Unless one of them boards a flight to Tokyo."

"Prototype!"

My phone vibrated. It was a text from Boots: *ETA?*

It was bizarre, this tendril of reality, this missive from the outside world. I felt as if I'd climbed Everest with my house keys in my pocket. I texted him back, saying I'd be home soon but Vadis was having a personal crisis—so believable a lie, it was probably true.

"What's mine called?"

Clive flipped the sheet for me and pointed: The Classic.

"Because you're the first," he said, "the first monkey in space. The first dollar taped to the wall. Our canary into the coal mine."

"As I understand it, the canary generally dies."

"You'll be the original after we go global."

"Don't you have to wait to see how this goes? Like, don't you need more funding before I'm the first of anything?"

"Let me worry about that. Ideally, you'll report back after each encounter. The more data we have, the better this will work."

"What if I don't do it?"

Clive considered this idea. Rather, he put a showman's effort into making it seem as if he were considering it.

"Then you won't grow."

"You mean this won't grow," I said, swirling my finger. "Your little cult."

"It's *not* a cult."

I saw the lady with the big jewelry again, in the opposite hall. I could see only the top half of her as she passed a hunched man, his cane bobbing alongside him. They were already bent, but still they bowed to each other. I made a face.

"Vadis and I care about you. Whatever comes next, we want you to make the best decision possible."

"There it is! I can't believe we're talking about me getting married."

"There's no desired outcome. This is about figuring out what *you* want."

"Don't do that. You're not a shrink just because you play one on TV."

Clive pried the menu from my hand and shoved it back in the drawer like a cadaver being slid back into the wall. Below, the garden fountain made a plangent sound. He leaned in close. He smelled like the world's most overpriced citronella candle. I thought he might do something truly repellent like kiss me.

"No one gets this, Lola," he whispered, "not in the history of the world."

I stared at his face, searching for motive. Then he nodded to Errol, who had manifested in the hall behind me.

"Have you been here this whole time?" I asked.

"Only the tail end," Errol said.

"Then how'd you know it was the tail end?"

Clive nodded at him once more and I followed him to the elevator. Once inside, all that could be heard were the squeaks of Errol's feet shifting in their leather coffins. He screwed up his brow at a spot on the glass, removed his pocket square, and wiped. I saw a single decapitated pussy willow at my feet, like a furry bug, and picked it up.

"Where'd Vadis get off to?" I asked.

"Juice bar."

"You guys have a juice bar."

"She ran out to Chaste Greens," he corrected me, smiling. "Why would we have a juice bar in here? That's insane."

5

The gum-speckled blocks rushed beneath me as I walked home. I couldn't get back on the train. I couldn't be in a tin can packed with strangers. Above ground was hardly a neutral space either. Like having something stuck in your eye, it hurts to blink, it hurts to not blink. Everywhere were memories encased in glass and concrete. Clive had picked up the globe and shaken it. He had changed my vision to romance, turning everything else into black and white. And now this color, an alchemy of memory and nostalgia was all I could see.

Here is the art gallery where I met a man who would then jerk me around for years, both of us gaslighting the other as if awaiting a third-party verdict. Here is the lingerie store where I spent a fortune on underwear that clipped to other underwear, wasted on the underemployed gentleman of my youth. Here is the bookstore café where my boyfriend broke the news that he'd met someone new. Except I never called him my boyfriend. I just took a disastrous road trip to Montreal with him once. I'd planned poorly for my period that day but I sat there, nodding and bleeding until he left. Then I went to the bathroom, rolled my underwear in paper towels and stuffed it in the trash.

I had not seen this person since. Maybe I would see him tomorrow.

The city was a parade of places shut down, left early from, arrived late to, sat in front of, met to say goodbye at. This is how it was for everyone. If you wait long enough, anyplace will become a barracks of the romantic undead, a sprawling museum of personal bombs. But would all my bombs go off at once? The past is never dead, it's not even the past. Most of the guys I knew detested Faulkner. Self-hating Americans, they preferred the Russians. I could see their worn copies of *The Brothers Karamazov*. I could hear the hum of their refrigerators, smell the stale sweat on their pilled sheets. And here is the stoop where I broke up with one of these men on New Year's Eve, convincing myself this was the humane thing to do. Don't take him with you, I thought. Wound him before the portal shuts. This was before I knew that the timing of a cruel thing does not make it more or less cruel, before I knew the only good way to hurt someone is never.

Something soft absorbed the impact of our front door. The culprit: Boots's overnight bag, gaping open in horror, a dopp kit tucked inside. He was sunk into the sofa, his face illuminated by a laptop screen.

"What's this?" I asked, shutting the door behind me.

"Jess and Adam's wedding."

"I meant like what's it doing in the hall."

I figured it was better to come off as someone suddenly irate about objects on the floor rather than expose myself as having completely forgotten about the wedding of his closest friends. Jess and Adam, the purveyors of every bite of farro salad I'd ever eaten. Judging by his fixation on the flashes of light coming from the screen, Boots was unbothered.

"How's this for a laptop?" I asked, sitting on his lap, my face in front of his.

"Grounds for divorce, that joke."

"We're not married. You don't need grounds. Is this annoying?"

He pressed his lips against mine, popping them off with a smacking sound.

"Yes," he said. "Give me five minutes."

I looked with him, assuming he was watching a show, but he was fulfilling another order, this one for a piece I was sad to see go: a glass hand that was modeled on my hand, if not an actual model (easy with clay, a felony with glass). The fingertips had turned what Boots explained was "sun purple." Certain kinds of glass contain manganese dioxide meant to brighten it, but it turns violet when left out in the sun. Boots was not especially attached to the hand, not when he had two of my real ones around, so he'd kept the inanimate version on the kitchen windowsill of his last apartment until it looked as if it had been dusted for prints.

"Someone bought the hand," I stated the obvious.

"How's Vadis?"

"She's fine."

"I thought she was having a crisis."

Until this moment, I never understood how people in the movies kept their magical powers a secret. But it was because secrets that strain credulity are tricky to jam into conversation. I entertained a partial truth: Clive was starting a new age SoHo House for rich idiots. Simple. But Boots would have questions. He'd wonder who was supplying their glassware, for one thing.

"She just wanted to talk."

"Of course," he said, with an edge he thought I couldn't hear.

I knew he felt as if Vadis were commandeering his future wife. Every hole in the fabric of our relationship was made wider as I aligned myself with someone he knew to be the diametric opposite of him, someone who probably never had the good sense to point out his better qualities. We rarely fought, but if I so much as touched my phone after an argument, I'd get an "Are you telling Vadis how big of an asshole I am?"

"What am I supposed to wear to this wedding?"

"It's casual," he said. "I'm wearing a jacket but that's it."

"Like Donald Duck?"

"Huh?"

I plucked the invitation from the fridge. The reception would be on a goat farm on Long Island, near where Jess grew up. The invitation was bordered with pressed flowers. I liked Jess and Adam in that they were impossible not to like. Our double dates were civilized affairs, planned weeks in advance and just the right amount of drunken. Adam became animated about international affairs and carbon emissions; Jess was tactilely inclined, demanding to know where I got my shirt. The men paid the bill, which I found at once irritating and justified. The four of us had once spent a weekend in the Catskills together. Wanting to be homey, and perhaps accrue some leeway for the occasional cigarette, I made banana bread each morning. At night, as we listened to them have sex, I thought, not incorrectly: I have fueled this noise. Of all Boots's college friends, Jess and Adam were the easiest to be around. But their steady sweetness meant they never said anything outside the range of pleasant. Thus, impossible as I found them not to like, I found them equally as impossible to love.

I slid plastic hangers back and forth in our overstuffed closet. There were dresses I'd bought at sample sales, hovering at the end of the bar, long dresses I thought might make me feel taller but only made me feel sloppy, or structurally complicated dresses I thought might make me feel like the kind of person who owned mid-century furniture. I let my fingers linger on the fabric, on the now-unoccupied places where I'd once been touched. I looked over at Boots and had the same feeling I'd had while watching the man with the backpack reading at the bar the other night. Sometimes choosing the right partner seemed like everything. Sometimes it seemed as deeply irrelevant as deciding what to wear to a wedding.

I made sure to sleep with Boots that night, getting a head start while listening to the sound of his electric toothbrush groaning. Even in the moments I wanted to kill him for being too passive, I could see the headline: "Woman Murders 40-Year-Old Disease-Free Man with 401k: Waste." I thought if I could just feel his hands running down my back, feel him bury his nose in my neck, he could beat back the swell of information in my head. Sex, be it formulaic or exhilarating, could be reductive like that. It tended to complicate relationships when you weren't in them, when you were getting in or getting out, but it simplified things in the middle. Look at us, letting the eagerness of our bodies override the discomfort of our minds. Look at us, in this human bed, doing animal things, blinking from position to position like holograms.

After Boots fell asleep, air whistling through his nostrils, questions raced around my mind. How had Clive managed to renovate a synagogue without anyone noticing? How badly had he brainwashed Vadis in order for her to keep this from me? Were the members also maybe Scientologists? Did Clive really think he was actually doing *good*? And who was responsible for keeping the atrium smelling like lemons? All minor curiosities compared with the biggest one of them all: Did I have it in me to confront the past without getting stuck in it?

If I agreed to this, it would be an advent calendar from hell.

I kicked off the sheets and got up to pour myself a glass of water, leaning forward on our bathroom sink until my nose touched the mirror. I'd always chalked up my devotion to the past as an extension of curiosity. If I found out someone who'd hurt me had gotten married or purchased property, I would google that person. Assumed behavior, but I went beyond the confines of assumption. If they had private social media accounts, I'd send "hang soon?" texts to our mutual friends with some vague fantasy that I'd be able to snatch up their phones while they were in the bathroom. I never did this. But I recognized the impulse as a bad one. I visited the Facebook accounts of the family, the Twitter accounts of the colleagues, the hashtags of the events to which I was not invited. It would've been more efficient to set up alerts for these men, but I never did it for the same reason I never bought a carton of cigarettes—too much of a commitment to bad habits.

If, on top of showing these men *just* the right advertisments and articles, the Golconda was using my search history (the retrieval of which would take negative effort for an NSA specialist), it was a real cheat sheet. Because sometimes, in an effort to repair hours of damaging activity, I'd google people who had wounded me *slightly* less and therefore elicited less of an emotional response. It was a form of croquet, knocking one hurt out for another and another. Sometimes, after I'd knocked all the croquet balls out of sight, there was one left standing—and it had Clive's face painted on it.

Tonight I was filled with rage at Clive for not dating me when he could have. We thought we were so smart, fighting off an inconvenient attraction. It wasn't all his fault. But he was older and, as the one closer to the future, I felt it was his responsibility to see into it. If we had acted back then, maybe we could be together now, be different people now. But the timing was bad. So Clive set me adrift into the dating world, turning me into the perfect candidate for the Golconda. And now he was with Chantal, a woman who posted sexy photos of herself with incongruous captions like "God is in the detours" and "You don't have to act like a man to be a strong woman." As if wearing a bodysuit by a pool were the solution to a problem. She also took a dizzying amount of pictures looking down at her shoes, showcasing the thinness of her ankles. You have to be a certain brand of attractive to take tip-of-the-iceberg photographs of your extremities, safe in the knowledge that anyone will go: "Oh, icebergs—obviously."

Clive never needed a peer, he needed a Chantal.

As I crawled back into bed, Boots was still on his side. Here was a man so at peace with commitment, he became the physical manifestation of it. Each morning, he woke in the first position he'd settled in the night before.

"What am I going to do?" I whispered to the back of his head.

"Whatever you want," he mumbled, half-dreaming. "You always look pretty."

He reached his hand behind him and patted my hip, a gesture that meant both "good night" and "making sure you're there."

6

The next morning, we stood beneath one of the screens at Penn Station, straddling our bags. My eyes were glued to the track assignments. Boots was less competitive in these situations. He reasoned that we had tickets, which meant we had seats, and that was as much thought as boarding a train required. I informed him that this was the approach of a tall white man with no hindrances in his history and no oppression in his genes.

"Does Penn Station have to be about the patriarchy?"

"It was torn down by men and put back up by men," I said. "You tell me."

I primed my muscles to lean in one direction or the other, willing my synapses to transfer the numbers to my brain faster. On cue, I grabbed his hand and made him bolt with me.

"Peconic, first two cars," instructed a conductor. "Only the first two cars will open for Peconic."

He sounded exasperated that we were not born knowing this.

Boots and I sat in a center row, our fingers interlaced in a jigsaw puzzle of bones. I watched as the landscape shifted from apartment complexes to shallow bodies of water, birds bobbing in concert with the telephone wires. Maybe, after we got married, we could live somewhere out here. Find a town the real estate boom hadn't touched. Somewhere safe from memory or coincidence. A place so tiny, *none* of the train cars open, there's just a little chute that spits you out onto the town cushion. I thought of Clive's mother's story, of the lottery and the towns filled with ghosts who would do anything to go back in time. Anything.

I shook the thought out of my head.

"Are you okay?" asked Boots, squeezing my hand.

Adam's brother picked us up at the train station, where we were trailed by a woman who'd been on the train with us, only in a different car. She swallowed her name when introduced so I didn't catch it. She also kept a close watch on her garment bag as it was being loaded into the trunk, showing no compunction about treating the brother like a butler. Boots, in the front seat, turned and widened his eyes at me.

"Everybody in?" asked the brother, even though we had our seatbelts on already.

I always forgot how life outside the city had a completely different texture. The days were easier here, warmer or cooler upon command. Being picked up in a car with no screen or meter affixed to the dashboard reminded me of childhood. But for all the surface comforts, the materials that made up this world were much harsher. Everything was coins in the console, gravel in the shoe, ticks in the grass, ice in the pipes, splinters on the wood. We passed Jess's high school, a stucco palace in beige. It looked like a prison. An electronic sign was having a conniption fit about an impending baseball game.

The woman and I made small talk in the backseat, which smelled of wet dog. She was in the midst of subletting her apartment, which meant she kept asking me questions but getting pulled into an ongoing text exchange about keys. Eventually, we fell into a silence. It was only in the lobby of the hotel, hours later, where guests had congregated in anticipation of a van, that I heard her introduce herself as Georgette. I wondered how I managed not to have heard a name like that. She had the same reaction upon hearing my name, launching into the Kinks song:

"It's a mixed up, muddled up, shook up world except for Loooow-la!"

"Yup, that's it."

"La-la-la-la Loooow-la!"

"It's a good one."

"Now that song's gonna be stuck in my head the whole night," Georgette said, accusatorily.

She sat with us in the van, Boots on one side of me and Georgette on the other. She wore orange lipstick and a silk jumpsuit with a deep V that she could get away with because she had no breasts to speak of. Her hair was up, revealing the parallel lines tattooed on her neck. Sobriety chic. She shook a sandaled foot in my direction. Her toenails were jagged, as if she'd been trimming them with her teeth.

"Do you remember the first wedding you ever went to?" she asked us, tucking a chunk of hair behind her ear that fell right back out. "I was like sixteen, which is disturbing because I remember going to plenty of funerals. I guess my family is better at dying than getting married. Anyway, I think it was in a roadside hotel in Reno, though that can't be right, it was probably just like a hotel with bad carpeting but when you're young you think all weddings should be in magical forests so a Radisson meeting room is a bummer. Have you ever been to

Reno? The bad parts of town are also the sad parts of town, and how many places can you say *that* for?"

She looked at us like we were actually supposed to name some places. Then she changed the subject, talking about Jess and Adam in a gossipy way, deciding this was a safe space to let loose her theories about what the bride and groom saw in each other. She didn't know either of us so this was a risky proposition. She'd dated Adam before he met Jess. Did we know that? We did not. Well, she did. Like right before and kind of *during*. She never really "got" Jess and, furthermore, did not enjoy how righteous Jess probably felt, agreeing to invite a woman Adam used to sleep with.

"Maybe she just likes you," Boots offered.

Georgette snorted and went on, undeterred.

"Then where's my thank-you for training him out of jack-hammering her pussy? He used to jam all his fingers up there like it's 'To Build a Fire' and he's using me for warmth, like he wanted to use my fallopian tubes for mittens. Like there's a fucking game show buzzer up there. Like you know what I want to know? Who are the bitches before me who just let it happen?"

Boots stared out the window, trying to distance himself from the conversation. It was like someone had skimmed off the most offensive parts of Vadis and dropped them into a whole new person. Vadis liked to shock him for sport, not because she couldn't help it. But I stayed with Georgette, sensing that if I broke off as well, it would make things worse. Only once was there a natural pause, when the driver announced that we were approaching the goat farm. We looked out to see clouds rolling over a muted sun. Trees entered the window frame and left just as quickly. On a hill was an ox-blood barn and, behind it, the very tip of a tent.

Georgette was seated at our table for the reception. We discovered that we shared a birthday, though she was two years behind me. She was enchanted by the coincidence, but I had just been told to expect them and thus had no reaction. The DJ probably had our birthday too. She confessed that meeting people with her birthday was jarring if they were younger, because she imagined them coming out of their mothers' vaginas at the same moment she was eating her cake. She tried to will herself to stop imagining it but all she saw was icing and blood.

"Cake, placenta, cake, placenta, cake, placenta."

I was exempt from this imagery because I was older.

"Though," she mused, "if you want to imagine *me* coming out of my mother's vagina, I can't stop you."

"Well, I wouldn't want to ruin cake for myself."

"I wouldn't want to ruin vaginas for myself."

Her collarbone was a speed bump that moved back and forth when she laughed. I couldn't stop looking at her, unsure if I was attracted or repelled.

Then she kissed me. Sudden and efficient. An errand. I scanned the crowd for Boots, who had his back turned. I said nothing, mostly because I knew she did it to get a reaction out of me. Clive used to do this with zits or papercuts, less because he cared to show me, more because he was daring me to be scandalized. I wasn't. Georgette had a similar expression—flirty but smug, like she knew what I was thinking. But what I was thinking was: What if I left Boots for you, Georgette? But then what if it ended and we were stuck in some twisted time loop manned by my former boss? Would I want to be haunted by you then? Would we be with anyone if we knew we could never get rid of each other?

"Go like this," Georgette said, gesturing for me to wipe lipstick from my face.

I put my fingers to my lips but found myself rubbing instead of wiping.

For the first hour of the reception, Boots talked to everyone *but* Georgette. He was in his element and this conversational bully was encroaching on his turf. Though he had to touch down at our table eventually and, a few drinks in, he began to find her amusing. He had the tenor of the wedding on his side. It was from this place of confidence that he asked her questions about her life, taking her side against the landlords and collection agencies that oppressed her, nodding at her tales of friends who'd overdosed as if he'd ever known a single person who'd ever overdosed. In return, we let her in on a few prized private jokes. Like how, when we were first dating, we used to play this game called "How Much Would Someone Have to Pay Me to Kill You?" It was more money with each date.

And so the three of us became one. We danced together, moving our bodies far away from one another and meeting in the middle like we were folding a flag. We became keenly aware when one of us was in a porta-potty or trapped with someone dull. We followed one another on social media. Jess's maid of honor gave a speech about how deserving Jess was of Adam's love. I stifled my giggles as Georgette mimed Adam's fingers, scooping the air. I could sense the night's events unfold before us: Normally, Boots would barely look at another woman—he was puritanical about it, his loyalty wound so tightly around his identity that it choked out every other impulse—but Georgette would be our first threesome. I crossed my legs toward her under the table, bumping my bare calf against the warm silk of her jumpsuit and keeping it there. My abdomen tightened in anticipation of the experience.

"And when is this happening?" Georgette asked with a frozen smile.

She was gesturing at my ring. I could tell she hated it.

"Next fall," Boots said, looking at me to confirm.

"Long time from now," Georgette said.

"Georgette can be our witness!" Boots blurted out. "Or our officiant. Is that the same thing? A celebrant?"

"A priestess," she decided.

"Yes, a priestess!"

I'd known men who became different people, barbarous people, when they drank, and so I knew I was lucky in that Boots became generous. If we owned a house, he would have given away the deed to a stranger in a bar by now. Once inebriated, he became like my parents in this way. All someone would have to do was ask nicely. This was why he was not allowed into a casino unsupervised. And why I sometimes woke at 2 a.m. to the sound of glass blowers or potters in my living room, bragging about the size of their kilns. Of course they could stay over, no problem.

"*If* we ever get married!" he added.

"Ooookay," I muttered, shifting his drink around the centerpiece.

"Let's just do it at city hall," he decided. "We could do it when we get back. The building's there, we're there, the *celebrants* are there."

"Whatever we do," I said, "maybe we should plan further out than Monday."

Georgette circled a spoon inside her coffee cup.

"Hey," she said, "I get it. I'm never getting married."

"There's nothing to get," I said.

"Yeah, there's nothing to get. We're married."

"Well, no," I said, "we're not."

"Why do you have to say 'we're not' like that?"

"I'm not saying it like anything, I'm saying it like facts get said."

"Georgette," he said, turning away from me at a defiant angle, "you just haven't met the right person."

I could sense where this was headed and was frustrated by his delay in picking it up. He was trying to buck up his new friend. But she did not need bucking.

"People aren't for me," Georgette explained, diplomatically, "not like that."

"What does that mean?"

"See that spry-looking woman to the right of Adam's grandma?"

She raised her spoon between her eyes like a hunting dog's paw. A tall Black woman with a tight ponytail was nursing something with a lime in it. Georgette told us how she'd met the woman when they were forced to participate in one of those dumb college orientation activities during which people are split into pairs and told to ask each other the most important question they can think of. The nebulous purpose of the exercise was to illuminate the priorities of the asker. Georgette sat across from the woman and asked her if she thought there was a God. Yes, the woman said, of course there's a God. Then, when it was her turn, the woman asked Georgette to marry her. The woman kept asking every time she saw her for the next year. The proposals became a ceremonial greeting, a joke that was never quite a joke. And Georgette would say no as they continued on with their lopsided friendship.

After four years of this nonsense, Georgette decided to surprise the woman by driving up to Cape Cod over spring break, where her parents were renting a house. Listening to a playlist the woman had given her, Georgette began to think that she *did* want to marry her after all. She saw their lives spread out before them. When she arrived, the driveway was packed with cars so Georgette parked on the street. She checked her face in the visor and walked up to the house. She was about to knock when she heard sounds coming from the back porch. She went around to see the woman, her whole family, and another woman she recognized from her Intro to East Asian Literature seminar and *her* whole family. Mylar balloons spelled out *congratulations*.

As it turned out, the woman with the lime in her drink had been asking "every twat on campus," figuring one of them would say yes eventually. It was an insurance policy for a good story. And all this woman really wanted was a good story. Georgette had gotten wrapped up in someone else's dream. Standing with her at the side of the house, all she could think about was the long drive home and how terrible it would be. But then, as she left, she asked the woman one more time: Do you still think there's a God? The woman said yes, of course.

"Then I got into my car and never had another romantic feeling about her again. Never missed her a day in my life. This is the first time I've seen her since. She looks good."

Boots blinked as Georgette punctuated her story with a bite of cold steak, licking sauce from her fork so that the back of her tongue got the first taste.

"I think we might be missing something," he said.

"There's nothing to miss," she said, shrugging. "It takes people years to learn what I learned in two seconds."

"Which is?"

"Everyone is living separate narratives. Marriage is agreeing to live in someone else's narrative."

"And to think Jess and Adam didn't ask you to officiate," Boots said.

"Listen, she believes a relationship is a good story in the same way she believes in God. People need these fairy tales to function. Let them have them, but I don't have to live in any narrative but my own. It's not that I refuse to participate in this"—she made a gesture that encompassed the stars above the tent—"because I don't want to get *hurt*. It's because there's no such thing as a partner. I'm sorry, but there's not. What a batshit word for the person whose genitalia you see the most often. There are glorified assistants, glorified bosses, and glorified safety blankets and that's all she wrote."

"That's only slightly cynical," Boots said.

He eyed a clump of friends in the corner. They would not hurt his brain.

"Do I sound mad about it?" she asked.

"You sound resigned," I said.

"And bitter," Boots added, "like a bitter person."

I winced. There would be no threesomes tonight. Georgette was talking to the one man in the world who was unsettled by this type of logic, who found a fear of commitment to be a character flaw.

"I just refuse to live my life in response to external pressures and stimuli."

"Do you think that's possible?" I asked, leaning forward and looking into her eyes until I could make out the reflection of tent lights in them.

"Yes," she said, as if she knew what Clive had shown me. "You just have to learn how to fight it."

"Okay, well," Boots said, slapping his knees, "I'm going to stimulate myself at the bar. Lola, while I'm gone maybe you can decide if our life is a narrative sham."

"Don't go," I said.

"I'm not *going*. I'm going to the bar."

He yanked his jacket down. I wondered if I should join him. Was I supposed to join him? I had no interest in being Georgette's accomplice. I, too, was skeptical of the notion that our life together was a "narrative sham." But I was not offended by the questioning. That was the difference. Not only did Boots not want to rock the boat, he refused to acknowledge the boat was on water. Or that we were in it.

Georgette and I were the only ones left at our table. Everyone else was dancing. She fished a weed pen out of a pouch in her jumpsuit and offered it to me. I shook my head. She shrugged and inhaled. Guests ambled around the perimeter of the dance floor, following the scent of butter cream. Bridesmaids adjusted themselves for a photographer, hands on their hips, elbows in the next time zone.

"Actually, yeah," I said. "Sure."

The smoke was stripper-sweet. I preferred the earthy burn of joints, but this was potent enough. At the bar, Boots was ensconced in a conversation with the groom, being recharged by one of the evening's celebrities. I knew how that conversation went, a series of familiar nouns being bandied about, devolving into a language textbook. *Jess and I just came back from Napa. Did you rent a car? It is easier if you rent a car.* I had to pee but the slog to the porta-potties was prohibitive. I wanted to speed up time. How many hours, I wondered, until the post-wedding brunch, which was being held at a nearby antiques store that doubled as a diner, which did not strike me as a hygienic business model.

"*And*," Georgette asked, blowing smoke out the side of her mouth, "where are the motherfucking goats? I mean, have you seen a single goat?"

A caterpillar crawled along the edge of the table, swung once, and fell.

"I have no idea. Asleep."

"You'll be okay, you know. Think of this like Pre-Cana counseling."

"Think of what as Pre-Cana counseling?"

"These kinds of conversations. You can't base your life on fear and guilt. You gotta do what you gotta do because you can't do it twice. You can't go back in time."

"Maybe you can."

"I'm just saying you'll be *fine*, la-la-la-la *Lola*. Here, watch this."

She put the pen on the table and placed one hand on her heart and one on mine, her fingers practically at my neck. She told me to be quiet even though I hadn't said anything.

"I knew it," she said, resuming vaping. "Your heart is bigger than mine because it's been broken so many times."

Was Georgette the Ghost of Christmas Present?

"Did Clive send you?"

"Who?" She laughed and coughed at the same time.

Boots returned, recharged, with two glasses in his hand and a cigarette rocking in his mouth like a loose tooth.

"You don't smoke," I said.

"Ith fur you," he said, in a better mood now.

"My hero, my murderer."

Georgette dug into her pouch once more to produce a few pale pills. She inspected one, bit it in half, and chased it with a glass of tonic water. Evidently, the sobriety only applied to liquids.

"Nice," Boots said, almost meanly.

"Fuck," Georgette said, vigorously rubbing her arms. "Why is it so cold?"

"Because we're on a farm," he said.

Neither of us cared to fight this logic. Boots was still irritable and he and I were no longer an intriguing conversational experiment for Georgette, forget a sexual one. We were pusillanimous and predictable. It was as if we'd all gone to the movies together and Boots and I insisted on staying for the credits and this is how she knew that we were not her people.

"The point is," she said, as if wrapping up a speech, "you guys seem perfect for each other."

Whether this was a dig or sincerity did not matter. What mattered was how I'd allowed myself to feel aligned with this stranger. And how I now felt aligned with neither of them. I had the urge to walk down the road, to keep walking until I came to a bus stop, take the bus as far as it went, transfer to another bus, and just circle the globe like that until I died. Instead, the three of us shifted in place, surveying the gaiety, the grass cold against the arches of my feet. Tomorrow's brunch would bring the dual aroma of bacon grease and mothballs. But, and this I guessed correctly, Georgette would not be there. She'd probably never attended a wedding brunch in her life. Too much of an extension of the day before.

In the moonlight, I could see the glint of a safety pin at the zenith of her jumpsuit, the flimsy mechanism holding it together.

7

I couldn't stop saying goodbye. When Boots got out of the shower, I wrapped my arms around his waist, clinging to his damp skin. It was barely light out but the neon star made it seem later. I watched, hypnotized, as he coiled his phone charger. I followed him into the living room, padding after him, bleating, "How long, again?" Two weeks. Fifteen days, to be exact. And, as he reminded me, San Francisco is not the moon. His enjoyment of this role reversal was apparent. Though not starved for bursts of affection, he was unaccustomed to them for no reason. He welcomed my clinginess without question and did not see it for what it was—an alcoholic's fear of an unlocked liquor cabinet.

"I'll miss you, too," he assured me. "You're my favorite thing."

I didn't cringe at his referring to me as a "thing." I was happy to be put on a shelf like a cake platter and think of nothing. Watching him arrange piles of shirts in his beaten bag, I thought of the last time I'd seen this particular bag.

He'd returned from a camping trip and I was in the bedroom, reading. I greeted him without getting up, which was its own kind of performative romance (he with the "Honey, I'm home," me with the "How was your trip?"). Then he asked, with strained calm, if Rocket was in the bedroom with me.

"Yes?" I said, making eye contact with the cat.

"Can you please get up and shut the door but stay in there?"

"Umm, okay."

I remember feeling that it was too early to propose, that we had not discussed this and, superficially, that whatever ring he'd picked up at a truck stop gift shop might not engender unbridled enthusiasm for the idea. The cat and I sat on the bed, our eyes wide, as Boots rustled around in the living room. I heard the sound of a box being unfolded, followed by a "motherfucker!" Then he whipped open the door.

"I had a stowaway. There was a brown recluse spider in my bag. It was *not* small and I trapped it. I'm getting rid of it and everything is fine."

"Can one of those kill a cat?"

"Better not find out, right? Be right back!"

Then he blew me a kiss and dove back into the living room with a hunter's spring in his step.

Had I ever made him as happy as that venomous spider? I wanted to. I knew how precious it was to have a person love you as Boots loved me. I did not take it for granted that such a person was living in my house. But my efforts to turn stability into desire and familiarity into respect were coming unglued.

"You, too, are also the thing that is my favorite," I told him, "as well."

"I know that," he said.

I kept the door open as I watched him disappear down our steps. The moment he was gone, I issued a correction to the cat.

"Second favorite. Obviously."

She was resting with her chin between her paws. Aware of being addressed but unsure of how she might benefit from this conversation, she looked at me without moving her head. Then my phone vibrated, a skirmish with my desk. It was Vadis, asking me how the wedding was. I did not answer since I knew that's not what she was asking.

I had to go into the office for a day of weekly and annual meetings that had a disturbing amount of thematic crossover. Our directives for two weeks out and six months out had the same tenor, balancing ideas with branding. Our editorial director, a hyper pigeon of a woman in her early thirties, dubbed these "ideas sessions," words my calendar liked to weaponize in **bold**. Even the robots knew *ideas* was a big word for it. It could be disheartening, working at a glorified content aggregator, covering the culture instead of creating it. Our jaws clamped down on prey with clickbaity headlines, only to find we'd caught nothing in our teeth except for the occasional lawsuit. At real media outlets, arts coverage was an art unto itself. But focusing on trends that we had no part in creating or even spotting had a bottom-feeder effect. The younger staffers took it more seriously. *Radio New York* was the only world they'd ever known. Their earnestness made me feel simultaneously jaded and indignant.

At least, at *Modern Psychology*, the publication and the field it covered were locked in a regency dance. Maybe it wasn't *Radio New York*'s fault. Maybe it was New York's fault and Amos has been right all along: There was simply nothing new or unexpected happening on this island. Except for the Golconda.

It was impossible to maintain focus. During lulls in conversation, I piped in with regurgitated ideas that gave the illusion of attention being paid. After the meetings disbanded, I wandered back and forth between my desk and the pantry, getting coffee, forgetting milk, going back to get the milk, forgetting sugar, going back to get the sugar. Stirring it with my finger. I silenced the occasional wail of the phone.

Boots texted to say he'd landed. He got a thumbs-up in return, followed by a *Yay, the plane didn't crash, yay!* This elicited a befuddled: *lol?*

I skipped lunch to sleuth, opting for vending machine pretzels, pushing grains of salt into my mouse pad as I scoured my brain for anyone with whom I'd been on a date ever. A Rolodex of faded faces creaked in my head. Men are the sitting ducks of the internet because none of their names have changed. Every stroke of the return key brought more professional headshots, more neckties, more grinning into the camera like children trying to recall the state capitals. Or else these men were engaged in an industry that required them to lean against a brick wall, arms crossed. Their "about" pages made me feel an almost parental pride, forgetting these were the same people who'd once made me pay for more of the bill because I'd ordered goat cheese on my half of the pizza, the same people who'd exfoliated my face raw with stubble when surely not one of them would appreciate a sandpaper hand job.

My whole life, I'd been telling myself the story of every breakup so that I had more agency in it. Men do not like to entertain the idea that they have destroyed someone and so they behave as if they haven't. I granted them the delusion, forking it over without a fuss. Everyone wins. It's difficult to comfort oneself by shrinking one's emotions without conceding that one has allowed those emotions to expand, unchecked, in the first place. I found it easier to skip this process. In truth, I'd been the victim of a metric ton of rejection. Already I could sense years of psychological work coming unglued as I searched for name after name, subjecting myself to condensed humiliation. I experienced these men as no one is supposed to experience them, as if being propelled from a T-shirt gun. It was like seeing every cigarette I'd ever smoked in One Great Big Pile.

There were men whose dating profiles had read like rules at a public pool: No tattoos. No couch potatoes. No heavy drinkers. No picky eaters. No taking oneself too seriously. NO DRAMA! Men who demanded a woman have a sense of humor but showed no signs of being funny. Men who posted photos alongside striking female acquaintances, as if to say, "just so you have a sense." Men whose insecurities ran so deep, they came out as accusations: "How do you not have a boyfriend? What's wrong with you?" I went out with them anyway, these bouquets of red flags, curious as to how repulsively I'd have to behave in order to trigger a new decree, knowing in advance the answer would be: not very. So many bloodless creatures who wanted all my blood, who offered nothing of themselves in return, who accused me of not "opening up" during the once every two weeks I was permitted to see them. The needle of curiosity goes in, the traits are sent off to the lab, the results never to be shared. There were men who told me they wouldn't sleep with their ex-girlfriends for all the tea in China but who turned out to own an import/export business to Beijing. Men who broke up with me because I was too good for them. Ah, but when do we send our food back to the kitchen because it's too delicious? These were the same men who were always off to the gym. To the studio. The party was lame. The party was boring. You wouldn't have had any fun. Men who didn't think they were misogynists because they defended the actions of famous women. Or famous minority women. Or famous trans women. Men who said I reminded them of the girl who broke their heart in college or the one that cheated on them in grad school, Tuesday afternoon kinda wounds for every woman I knew. Men who told me they would have to be dragged kicking and screaming out of this town but now lived in Idaho. Another woman had dragged them. But how? A blow to the head? Ether and a hand towel? Did she take the back roads? These were the same men who said they'd gone celibate for fear of hurting women, who thought they'd *invented* sadness, who told me I had *no clue* how dark things got in their heads, how dank the basements of their sorrow. Unrequited narcissists, these were men with a delicate sense of injustice when it came to their fellow man. Yes, life's a witch hunt. It will magnify your sins until they are grotesque, canceling you from a program you didn't know you were on. But is that a broomstick between your thighs or are you happy to see me? These men were like tropical fish, easily stressed by too much communication or too little. Some stared into my eyes, attempting tantric meditation over martinis, telling me I was their soul mate after minute ten, some called me their girlfriend after date two, some refused to call me their girlfriend after year one. Some called me someone else's name. There were younger men who were the same age now as I was when they broke up with me—did they feel the burn of shame at having made me feel old, now that they were all caught up? Men who cut lines of powder with a jeweler's precision. A one-time thing. A two-time thing. It's hard to pass off any activity as a sixty-five-time thing. Men who'd hurt me more than once. That was my fault. I wanted to touch the stove, to see if it was still hot: It was still hot. Men who made paper airplanes out of the customer copy while I signed the merchant one. Check's in the mail, hand's on the thigh. Men whose texts I'd shown Vadis, who gamely looked at the time stamps. *Blue, I'm blue, we are all of us blue. Sometimes we are green with inexperience or envy.* Men who preferred missing me to being with me. Men who told me they were falling for me. It felt so good to say it, they'd figure out if they meant it later. But when later came, they were not falling. By God, they had tried. They detailed their efforts to the court. Ladies and gentlemen of the jury, my client has made reasonable attempts. He has gone to great pains. He has texted when he did not feel like it. He has listened when he was bored. He has written down the birthday. Those were the worst of all, worse than the cheaters and the sociopaths. Because, as they stated their cases, they shook loose from the context in which I knew them. They were only people, mired in downy confusion, born a little broken and trying to fix it. In all of history, we had landed in the same city at the same time and, to ladle miracle upon miracle, we had *met*. What were the odds? What were the chances? How could I not love them all just a little? In that moment, they became unanchored from being men at all. They became genderless droplets that floated away before my eyes, drifting into the sea of human fallibility, particles rising toward the surface.

149

By the time I looked up, I could see the reflection of the fluorescent lights in the windows. I could hear cars honking their way into the Holland Tunnel, followed by the sound of the cleaning cart being rolled off the elevator in consecutive thuds. A vacuum cleaner switched on. The cleaning woman jumped when she saw me, holding her hand to her heart.

Near the Second Avenue subway station, children were playing an intense game of soccer under bright lights. They were running back and forth over the yin-yang printed on the Astroturf, intermittently stopping to accuse one another of cheating. The air had grown sharper. I leaned on an iron fence, picking leaves from an azalea bush and folding them between my fingers. They made a satisfying crack. As Clive had explained, I was the magnet (preferable to "hole") within a liminal space and that magnetism was concentric. The Golconda worked *mostly* through the power of suggestion, but Clive also had the members put energy out with the goal of "reeling it back in." Like a tide rising and then receding from the shore, who knew what debris would be dragged my way? I'd spotted Dave Egan, stuck in the sand over on Canal, farther west. I figured I had about the same chance of running into an ex here as I did outside the Golconda's front door, where I would be on camera.

So I stayed put, watching commuters return home, watching tourists get turned around, watching a hunched man carrying a cloud of cans so expansive, it made a mockery of the population's wastefulness. It seemed to me that Clive could accomplish his goal easily enough with a few illusionists on the payroll. Formalizing it all with cult-like rhetoric was preying on people's need for meaning, ethics notwithstanding. Amos had not called Clive a charlatan for nothing. Still, I concentrated on emitting my own vibrations. My own pheromones.

I only managed to make myself sweat.

Clive had said that there might not be a chronology to the next couple of weeks. I'd dated Amos after Willis, and Dave before either of them. What he *did* know was that this would work via emotional impact. That's what the social media monitoring and the meditation had in common. *Love leaves a neurological footprint.* A search history of the soul. It was therefore unlikely that I'd run into any one-night stands, as neither party could be triggered to revisit the other. No amount of planted advertisements for the boysenberry body wash I'd used in 2012 would be effective on such a man. Beyond that? Everyone was fair game.

My pupils stayed vigilant, both fearful of and desperate for recognition. This awareness was draining, reminiscent of spending too long in a museum. Every second of our lives is pressed from two sides—the present and the past—like coal. Mostly we don't notice it. We don't notice we're in a continuum. Other times the pressure gets so intense, it turns all existence into a diamond.

And then I heard a voice call my name.

My shoulders went stiff. I often heard my name in public, or a piece of it, in *slow* or *hola*, words exchanged between people on the street. I'd trained myself not to react. But then I heard it again. This was a woman's voice.

Narrowing the gap between us on the sidewalk was

Adella, a friend of a friend. I was never quite sure what Adella did for a living. What I did know was that she was on the board of a women's folk art museum in Mexico City because I was on the email list despite repeated attempts to unsubscribe. I resigned myself to the fact that Adella would pass through my mind, monthly, for the rest of my life, harmless as a shooting star.

"Lola, I thought that was you," she said, as if my ruse had failed.

I'd never gotten to know Adella because there was no need for me to get to know Adella—I could count our interactions on one hand. We were peripheral people for each other. But even if I'd been desperate to crack her code, she maintained too upbeat a demeanor. Everything was always fabulous. Work? Great. Family? Great. Friends? Manifold. Apartment? Redecorated. Shattered tibia? Healing at record speeds. Only once did she mention the time she'd been held at knifepoint in Buena Vista, blindfolded and forced to make withdrawals from several banks. Then she started talking about an app for haircuts.

But right now, Adella was a gift. I kept losing focus on her, keeping a lookout. Adella soldiered on, releasing information like she was blowing bubbles. She'd had outpatient surgery for endometriosis. She'd hired an assistant she loved. She'd moved back to the city from Chicago, with her boyfriend whom she also loved. (I had not realized she'd left for Chicago in the first place.) Her inquiries about our mutual friends required my participation, but I hadn't seen these people in years. I didn't have much in the way of answers. So she resumed the bubble-blowing: Her boyfriend had inherited "part of a floor" of a building in the East Village. The twinge of real estate jealousy snapped me to attention.

"His great-grandparents ran a canning business out of it," she explained. "Dumb luck, right?"

"Completely stupid."

"His dad lived there but he died. We live on the fourth floor, which is actually—"

"Wait, what did they can?"

"Sorry?"

"The grandparents. What did they can?"

"Oh . . . some kinda fish, I think."

"Herring?"

"Yes! How'd you know?"

There was a clanging of bells in the distance as Adella's boyfriend exited a hardware store across the street. She waved at him with violent cheer as he darted across the street to meet his current girlfriend, her—and his college girlfriend, me.

I struggled to remember the last time I'd seen Jonathan. Was it possible the answer was: Not since the night we broke up? My mental Rolodex began spinning once more. Our breakup would've been about six months after we graduated, and almost twenty years ago. I knew things had not ended well but I could not remember how, which suggested I was the inflictor of pain. One thing I did remember: the apartment. Jonathan's father, an architect, was still living there when we were dating. Jonathan grew up in the neighborhood and was thus doomed to describe the crumbling streets and needle-strewn parks of his youth to a world that refused to absorb the severity of the past. One winter night, his father lent us his Porsche, which made us feel a little like we were in *Ferris Bueller's Day Off* until the taillight got smashed on First Avenue. Then we felt a lot like we were in *Ferris Bueller's Day Off*.

We came back, panting up the stairs, sulking like the teenagers we so recently were. Jonathan's father was hunched over a drafting table, snow settling on the window panes behind him.

Jonathan told him about the car while I hovered around the kitchen area. It was obvious I could hear every word, so eventually I joined them.

"If you can't afford to destroy something," his father said, without raising his face, "you can't afford it."

"But," Jonathan pressed his luck, "I didn't afford it, you did."

"I have insurance."

"It wasn't an accident. The car was too far out into the street."

Jonathan wanted to be punished. This was a stunning realization, one I was too young to transfer to the bedroom. In the early aughts, most of the women I knew still had more business with the twentieth century than the twenty-first, and so much of mainstream sex was defined as "to go along with." It was hard enough, climbing out of this hole of internalized people-pleasing. The idea of then jumping straight into *another* uneven hole, one in which I strung Jonathan up from the ceiling and beat him with a paddle, was too daunting.

"Son," his father said, uninterested in debate, "this world will be hard enough on you without my help."

Would it, though? A well-off white boy with zero college debt?

Life would be hard because everyone's life is hard, but so long as Jonathan remained unmaimed, his challenges would be glaringly internal. What made Jonathan stand out was that he *knew* this and he would not accept a free pass, even if it were foisted on him, even if he were unsuccessful at giving it away. He took pride in trying to step out from his father's shadow. We should've swapped fathers, his nonconformist boomer for my suburban boomer, a man who would happily oblige in chastising Jonathan for minor offenses.

"I like this one's teeth."

It took us both a second for us to realize his father was talking about me. He'd barely looked at me but now he did, setting down his pencil. I grinned nervously.

"See?" he asked Jonathan. "Good teeth."

Later that night, sleeping on a foldout couch more supportive than my own bed, I told Jonathan that I aspired to be like his father.

"Rich?" he asked, on the verge of annoyance.

"Chill," I answered. "Able to let things go."

As Jonathan trotted across the street, holding up his hand to thank a car for not running him over, Adella explained their presence here. They had to have the locks changed after a break-in. Jonathan decided to make keys that could be reproduced only by specific locksmiths. There were three of these locksmiths in Brooklyn, one in Queens, one in Harlem, and one in lower Manhattan, on Forsyth. Which, in Adella's estimation, was why they were here. Not because Clive had conjured her boyfriend using playlists, targeted ads, and modern sorcery. Not because a combination of private investigators and app programmers had put the idea of new house keys into the locked box that was Jonathan's brain.

As I watched him from a distance, I wondered: Had this man been designing my monthly missives about Mexican folk art?

He slowed as he approached. He still had a boy's face. I had difficulty imagining Jonathan paying for goods with cash he earned from a job he held. How would he do these things without using a drawing of a fox as currency?

"What are you doing here?" I asked.

They looked at me in unison. Had we not just been over this?

"I mean now. On Earth. In general."

"Oh," Jonathan said. "I work for the Department of Environmental Protection."

"He's going to save the planet."

I tried to imagine them having sex. Adella was theatrical and confident, the kind of woman who glommed on to her gender as if it would steer her whole personality. And who had done pretty well with this theory. But the Jonathan I knew was uncomfortable in his own skin, rarely thinking of himself as human, forget masculine. He blushed at his own erections. I never saw him crave anything. But we were older now and perhaps Jonathan had learned to funnel his desire for punishment into something satisfying.

"Only mass sterility will save the planet," he deadpanned.

"I love that you guys know each other." Adella changed the topic. "This world is too tiny. I swear, there's just ten people in all of America and the rest is funhouse mirrors."

"Here I was at the end of America," Jonathan recited, "no more land—and now there was nowhere to go but back."

Jonathan had done his senior thesis on the cult of personality surrounding the Beat generation. He interviewed people who made pilgrimages to North Beach, who found the rusted car under the bridge in Big Sur. He tracked them down, recorded their pride and their sadness. He got a tattoo on his shoulder, a line from *Naked Lunch*: "A freight train separates the Prof from the juveniles . . . When the train passes they have fat stomachs and responsible jobs." It was my hand he squeezed when he got the tattoo. How strange, I thought, that I was the first woman to touch it and Adella would probably be the last.

And yet Jonathan had clearly never mentioned any of this to her.

Under normal circumstances, not qualifying for disclosure would've been an insult. But I knew something neither of them did: I mattered enough to him to land him here. And the prophecy of Jonathan's tattoo had come to pass. He *did* have a fat stomach now, an emo gut bloated with years of feelings. And he did have a responsible job. Still, the more he spoke, the more I saw how this was the Jonathan I knew. He told Adella that it might be fun, in case the burglars returned, to tape a thousand different keys to the front door. She looked at him blankly and excused herself to answer a work call.

Branded content? Was it maybe branded content?

Jonathan and I occupied ourselves, wordlessly measuring our current faces against our former ones. I may not have been able to recall how we ended but I could recall how we began— the nights in the basement of our dorm as we waited for a washing machine to free up, searching for each other at parties, writing long emails that continued over summer break. I had an internship in the city and I wrote to him of my adoration for "the vacillating scents of city trash." There were descriptions of New York at the turn of the millennium, during its gimmicky theme bar phase: Korova Milk Bar, Jack Rabbit Slim's, Beauty Bar, Idlewild (which featured real seats from a DC-10). Jonathan was spending the sweltering months volunteering for Habitat for Humanity. He set up an email account for a splinter and sent me a series of missives from the splinter's point of view. The splinter felt stuck. The splinter longed to be removed with my lips.

We were stymied by cuteness, by an inability to speak plainly about our feelings. We'd send each other origami and Polaroids and drugstore birthday cards that said things like "Guess who's 5 today?" Our relationship died for the same reason Jonathan's senior thesis got ripped to shreds: It smothered itself in its own conceptions. Turns out it's a lot harder to write something original about William Burroughs than it is to skewer the people who idolize William Burroughs.

While Adella paced in front of us, fiddling with her earpiece, Jonathan explained how his father had died. Prostate cancer. Stage Four because he hid it, because he wouldn't go to the doctor. Horrific but quick. I felt an unreasonable possession over Jonathan's father, over the apartment I had not seen in years. Never mind the fact that Adella received mail there, kept her toiletries in the bathroom.

"I thought it might be weird to reach out. I should have. He always liked you."

"Really?" I said, my voice going up an uncontrollable octave. "He didn't know me."

"Lola. To not know you is to love you."

"That sounds like an insult."

"I think you know it's not," he said, turning scarlet.

Now I remembered. We were at Zen Palate in Union Square, eating our soy protein balls before they got too cold to consume, and Jonathan got up to go to the bathroom. While he was gone, I held my glass of lukewarm organic wine, contemplating what I knew had to be done. Jonathan had his Polaroid camera on him and on his way back to the table, he took a photo, shaking the picture.

"Look at this composition," he said.

I knew that would be the last picture he would ever take of me, that by this time tomorrow we would not be dating. I wondered if he still had it.

Adella returned to us with a perky "What'd I miss?"

Unlike Willis, Jonathan had not minimized the story of us. He remembered, all right. But like Willis, he also remembered to move on and live his life.

"What's your story these days, Lola?" Adella asked.

"My partner and I are getting married."

I'd never once answered this question like this and considered any unbidden relationship status offensive. Nor had I ever referred to Boots as "my partner." But I enjoyed the ambiguity of it, the pilfered implication of growth, the potential expansion of sexual preference. I didn't need to compete with Adella's completionism, but I wanted to put myself in the ballpark of it. To establish my own ballpark. *I'm self-aware, too. I've evolved into a partnership, too. I don't need to be the boss of someone, nor am I anyone's puppet.*

Even though we were, all three of us, Clive's puppets.

"Congratulations," they said, generously but not too generously.

Our goodbye was an awkward baton pass of hugs. I tried to listen to their conversation as they walked away but their words were unintelligible.

That night, I pulled out the box of old letters that I kept in the back of our closet, wedged between vacuum-sealed sweaters and folded boxes that Boots used for shipping his pieces. I'd probably need to move my secret stash under the bed soon. He'd been selling enough pieces of late, one of my protective walls was thinning.

I had judged Willis for shoving all his experiences into a tidy box, but I had done it literally. I dug until I found one of

Jonathan's old cards. It was dated with a number that made my heart seize. So much time had passed. For a while, any year that began with a "20" felt comfortably contemporary. But now people born in the new millennium were whole people with opinions and degrees, babies even. As such, they were in flagrant violation of this comfort. They were having their own debates, making their own memories, sending their own cards, discovering music with the zeal of the converted. They were walking into parties, hoping their own Jonathans would be there.

The card featured a cartoon of a go-go dancer in white boots, music notes against a rainbow background. It read: *Someone's in the birthday groove!* It still played a tune, a melody like a tiny ambulance.

8

But before I went back to the apartment, back to the box, I dropped by the Golconda. Mostly because I wanted to see if it was open, even as I knew *open* was not quite the word. Clive was too busy laminating prototypes to offer me practical information such as hours of operation. Was it possible the answer was "always," like a 24-hour drugstore that happened to charge $250,000 a prescription? I paced in front of the doors, trying to catch the attention of the security cameras. People were watching and so I pretended to be frustrated with my phone, to be aghast at imaginary incompetence. I found myself unable to stomach the idea of going back to our perpetually bright apartment right away, eating a bag of chips for dinner, testing the limit of the Chip Clip springs. I was midway through composing a text to Clive—*Maybe less with the surrealism and more with the*—when the doors clicked.

I moved quickly, letting the building shroud me in darkness. I nearly fell when a rat decided that the best means of avoiding me was to go directly over my shoe. When I got to the second door, Errol was there to greet me, enveloped in a lemon-scented particle cloud. It was confusing how someone who emitted so much charm had wound up lending his time and talents to Clive. Though I suppose everyone wound up serving Clive eventually, and in ways that broke the boundaries of him signing our paychecks. And that, he didn't always do. At *Modern Psychology*, people were hesitant to badmouth him when he stiffed them. They chalked up an unpaid invoice to a misunderstanding, an accounting delay or Clive's personal economic philosophy bleeding into his professional one. Paychecks were fantastic but surely they only made life better, not livable. And yet those in his orbit kept bringing him *more*—more partnerships, more funding, more cheap labor. They recognized too late that these services were not being offered, they were being extracted.

I doubted his behavior had improved. One look at the chandeliers, those constellations of overpriced incandescence, and it was clear that, if anything, it had gotten worse. I was accustomed to this cycle of Clive-pleasing abuse, having built up a tolerance over the years, escaping only when forced. When the magazine died, the life drained out of Clive's clutches. But Errol was new to the fanaticism. You could see it in his eyes. I had to hand it to Clive: He no longer needed a vehicle for his cult of personality, he *was* the cult.

Errol embraced me with his free arm, holding me to his chest in one fluid motion. He was wearing navy pajamas with white piping. They had a sheen to them.

"Do you sleep here?" I asked, concerned.

"Do I sleep here? Do I sleep here? Such a comedian!"

He escorted me inside, where there were now *two* baristas and still no customers. The new barista was a doe-eyed girl with a messy bun. Blond hairs fell down the nape of her neck.

She looked like she belonged in a field, reaching for a farm-house. She, too, was wearing pajamas as she arranged straws in a jar while the first barista, the boy, offered her smitten words of encouragement.

"Stay here," Errol instructed me.

"Woof."

"Oh my God, *ha*."

He disappeared behind a seamless door in the wall. In my periphery, I saw movement overhead. Several people passed above me, their long shadows extending across the marble floor. Behold, the conductors of my fate, milling about. It was good to see the place more populated, to hear voices. I stood on the tips of my toes. They looked at me, al-most as if by accident, and then quickly looked away. From Clive's description, I'd been expecting a mix of monks and celebrities. Phrases like "pyramid scheme" and "suppressive person" had been scuttling around my brain for days. But these people looked like a cross-section of any subway car. Except, perhaps, for the monochromatic pajamas. And the *bowing*.

There was a Black woman with a face full of freckles tell-ing a story to a younger redheaded man, both of them sipping on coffee. They were laughing quietly. They split to allow a desultory woman with a crown of frizz to pass. She looked like she taught kindergarten. They all bowed to one another. I coughed, trying to get their attention. This achieved noth-ing. The baristas spoke in hushed tones and then the doe-eyed girl offered me an espresso.

"She doesn't want any," the boy whispered sharply.

"Like Jonestown with lattes!" I shouted at them.

The girl started giggling. An anemic woman in a turban was tending to the birds of paradise in the corner. Was it ego to assume these people would take an interest in me? How could they be so incurious about the subject of their own experiment? Perhaps for the same reason no one likes to befriend their food before they cook it.

Vadis materialized from the hallway, an iPad in the crook of her arm.

"Hey," I said, moving my head back in surprise, "I didn't know you were here."

"I had work to do," she said. "We're launching a line of sleep masks."

"Huh?"

"For my *job* job."

"Ah, I almost forgot you had one of those. Is that why everyone is wearing pajamas? Market research?"

"Yeah, those are ours. They're mulberry silk."

I smiled, relieved. When I looked around again, the woman in the turban had vanished along with the other members.

"Where did they go?"

"Where did who go?"

"Please don't make me feel crazier than I already feel."

"They probably went to the meditation room."

"May I see the meditation room?"

"You came back," she said, moving on to the obvious.

"Why can't I just see it?"

"Because it's not *for* you, Nosey Pants."

"I thought this whole shebang was for me."

"It is. Trust us."

"Oh, no, thank you."

"Man," she said, jumping to another train of thought while the first one was still moving, "you're so lucky that Clive selected you. Lola, you've been *chosen*."

"One could argue . . ." I said, motioning to the ceiling, to the sky beyond it.

"It's like a romantic *Minority Report*," Vadis decided. "You know, a SWAT team of cops and robot spiders that show up before you get into a bad relationship."

"Am I in a bad relationship, according to you?"

"That's not up to me."

"But you guys are the cops."

"Nah," she said, taking my arm. "At best, we're the robot spiders. Our members are welcome anytime to concentrate their energy. Between us, that part isn't as effective as the more concrete elements, you know? But it *will* be."

"You really believe in all this?"

"Umm, do I believe in a business model that will make us rich while helping people get over themselves? Do I believe it's possible to apply energy toward spiritual rejuvenation? Umm, yeah. Clive's a genius."

"That's a big word."

"Six letters."

"That's a big word to throw at Clive Glenn. Have you forgotten who we're talking about? Or maybe the blood rushes out of your brain when you *bow* to him like a lovesick geisha."

"You're so crotchety. This is why you need help. So who'd you see?"

Her eyes were like saucers but like flying ones. They darted around my face, searching for a good place to land. When I told her about Jonathan, she didn't remember him. She seemed disappointed not to be able to appreciate the full extent of him.

"He must be from Clive's list, from before I knew you."

"You guys made lists?"

"Obviously."

"Can I see the lists?"

"Do you think you can see the lists?"

She ushered me into an office that once belonged to a rabbi. There were two holes, set at an angle, inside the door frame. On the far wall, you could still make out the outline of framed degrees and in the middle was a matted photo of Clive's *Modern Psychology* spread on Soren Jørgensen. Jørgensen is almost too tall for the page and looking uncomfortable dressed as a bellhop, standing in the elevator of an art deco hotel. The headline read: "Going Up? Connectivity and Higher Consciousness." This is the elevator repairman, the Scandinavian colossus, whose "teachings" Clive had decided to emulate and sell.

On the opposite wall was an old map of the neighborhood featuring a blue stripe from when Canal had been a canal.

"Where?" asked Vadis.

There were three pins already, representing Amos, Willis, and Dave. I pointed. Vadis pressed in a new pin.

"I feel like we're linking a crime spree," I said.

The Korean woman in the white tunic I'd seen the other day was stationed on the far side of the room, wearing headphones around her neck. She was manning a horseshoe configuration of screens, meters, and external drives, a shrunken city of cubes with oblong lights. Beside her was a pile of cassette tapes and a manual. There was also a device that looked like a polygraph test except this one was circular, like a motion-activated toilet seat. Vadis introduced me to the woman, Jin, who asked me to lick a suction cup.

"Just the one," Jin clarified, offering it to me. "Don't worry, we're not going to ply you with electrodes. This is to monitor your biofeedback. Better your spit than mine."

I leaned forward and licked the rubber with my tongue while it was still in her hand, coming to it like a horse. She scrunched up her face.

"I was going to hand it to you."

I granted Jin permission to reach up my shirt. Her hands were cold as she taped wires to my wrists, cutting the tape before it covered too much arm hair. She clipped two pulse monitors to the fingers on my left hand.

"Where's Clive?" I asked, trying to sound casual.

I didn't want to see Clive. But I did want to know if he was leering at us from behind a two-way mirror.

"Chantal emergency," Vadis said.

"What happened, she get an eyebrow pencil stuck up her ass?"

Jin stifled a laugh but gathered herself. Clive was her leader. Best not to trash the boss's girlfriend in his temple.

"Shall we begin?" asked Vadis.

They took turns asking me questions, which were surprising in number and arbitrary in nature. If the objective was to get me exasperated enough to produce uninhibited answers, it worked. Jin turned a few dials. I had to confirm where I was born, my profession, political affiliation, any allergies, the last book I read, aisle or window, right or left side of the bed, an item of clothing I regret purchasing, an item of clothing I regret not purchasing, my astrological sign, my rising sign . . .

"I'm a Virgo too," Jin interjected, which struck me as unprofessional.

That I now thought of this enterprise as professional enough to break its own rules was disconcerting.

"I don't put stock in astrology," said Vadis.

"You always say I'm judgmental because I'm a Virgo."

"No, I don't. Maybe imagined conversations are a Virgo thing."

"Hold still please," instructed Jin. "And when was the first time you called nine-one-one?"

"What does any of this have to do with Jonathan?"

The paper on the circular polygraph was waiting to be scribbled on.

"She's trying to open up your MPs," Vadis explained. "Memory Pathways."

"When I first moved to New York," I relented, "I was going down the escalator to the subway and this kid behind me had one of those black plastic deli bags and it looked like it had batteries in it. And he left it on the escalator and then ran back up. I called nine-one-one but nothing happened."

"What was his nationality?" asked Jin.

"Is punk a nationality?"

"She means what was the color of his skin."

"Oh, is that what she means? Brown. His skin was brown."

"The first time I called nine-one-one," Jin said, "I was eleven. My father stabbed my sister in the thigh with a hunting knife and hanged himself in the garage."

I looked at Vadis, who shook her head. I was starting to sweat off the suction cup. But then the lights on the boxes began to blink, like a modem waking up.

"Here we go," Jin spoke to her machines.

"When was the last time you thought about Jonathan?" Vadis asked.

I sat back in my chair.

"Prior to tonight?"

"Yes," said Vadis, "prior to tonight."

If they'd asked me straightforward questions, I might not have had access to the information. Terrorist suspects experience a version of this kind of inquisition. I knew because I'd interviewed a slew of military psychologists for a *Modern Psychology* feature about how their tactics could be broken down to help people. "Watered Down Water Boarding." People pulled their subscriptions. Former detainees spoke out. Zach was apoplectic at having to take the side of the military and threatened to quit. Clive dedicated his editor's letter to issuing an apology. All this happened before the dawn of Twitter, which could explain why, to this day, people were still willing to give him money.

"I probably think about him all the time without thinking about him."

"How so?" asked Jin.

"I guess it's just the same way if you saw Indiana missing from a map of America, you'd be like, 'That's an incomplete map of America,' without missing Indiana in any real way."

"That makes sense," Jin said, encouragingly. "But have there been any triggers?"

"When I see people with quotes tattooed on their shoulders."

"What about quotes other places?"

"No," I said, "not then."

"What about single words?"

"I think it has to be the whole sentence."

"Hmmm," said Jin, adjusting a knob. "And when was the last time you thought about him in a concentrated way?"

"As in prolonged?"

"More as in voluntary. Without outside stimuli."

"Is there any other kind?"

"Lola," Vadis groaned, "were you listening to a *word* Clive said?"

"No?"

Jin turned her attention to one of her screens and began clicking a mouse. I tried to peer over to see the screen but she angled the monitor toward her.

"I guess never, then. I never think about him on purpose."

"Were you ever in love with this 'Jonathan'?" Vadis asked. She was still irritated that she had never heard of him.

"It was college. I loved ska and wine coolers."

"Did you ever tell him you loved him?"

"No."

"And did he ever tell you he loved you?"

"No."

"But did he love you?"

"Yes."

"And you knew about this discrepancy when you were together?"

"Yes."

"Starting when?"

"Within five minutes of meeting him."

I gulped. My Memory Pathways were bringing me unwelcome feelings.

"But you stayed out of insecurity."

"I stayed out of hope."

The needle moved so fitfully over the paper, I thought it might rip.

"I was scared Jonathan would be it. I sort of always think a guy will be it."

"As in 'the one'?"

"No, as in an endangered species. I'm sorry if that sounds pathetic, I'm sure it does. But it's where monogamy comes from and no one thinks monogamy sounds pathetic."

"Is this a source of shame?" Jin asked. "That you didn't love him but kept dating?"

I thought not of Jonathan, but of other men who'd cared for me. And whom I'd hurt. Especially when none of us had a clue what we were doing. They signed their emails telling me they couldn't wait to hold me, or how they wanted to make me deliriously happy. Not just happy, deliriously so. They sent me sweet texts so I'd have sweet texts to wake up to. None of it meant that I was obliged to love them back. But it did mean I was obliged not to torture them with indecision.

"No," I lied, but quickly surrendered to the needle. "Okay, *yes*. But I would like to address the shame. I didn't throw Jonathan away because he was nice to me. You know, when you're younger, you worry that maybe no one will ever love you and that fear makes you do some dumb shit. What you don't know is that fear has *nothing* on the fear of not being capable of loving someone in return."

"Final question," said Jin, more entranced with her data than with me.

"Great!"

I clapped my hands together. Jin winced at the sound reverberating in her ears.

"At any moment during your interaction with Jonathan this evening, did you sense that you should've tried even harder to make that relationship work?"

"Everyone feels like if only they had been more or less tolerant, if they could commit to a *version* of themselves, they could be with anyone they'd ever dated."

"Umm," Vadis said, "no one thinks that."

"Then they're not thinking about it hard enough. Romance without practicality is a fling. Love is agreeing to live in someone else's narrative."

"Dark," Vadis decided.

"Are you supposed to pipe in this much?"

She raised her palms in the air, unhanding the conversation.

"This is insane. Not *this*. Though yes, *this*. Just this whole line of questioning. We're supposed to think we break up with people because we know who we are and the other person wasn't going to fit. It's why you get all this postmortem feedback after you've been dumped, about how the dumper is incapable of having a relationship. Like literally incapable. As if any of us are in a position to assess someone else's capacity to love. Meanwhile, somewhere across town, that person's therapist and friends and family and whoever are confirming the many ways in which you were wrong for him. A *medical doctor* is telling some bozo that he took the only choice he had. So not only is he not broken or stunted or missing the gene, noooo, he is to be commended for his self-knowledge. How else would he have made the excellent decision to get rid of you? But what happens next, when time passes and he's in a new relationship and he thinks it's going great but then boom: *he's* the one getting dumped? Is it because he's flawed and the other person made an excellent decision?"

"No?" guessed Jin.

"No!" I shouted. "It's because the person who dumped him was incapable. Someone always has to be the broken or immoral one. Maybe we get less terrible about assigning blame as we get older, I don't know. Maybe we learn to retain who we are better instead of giving it all away to a stranger. People do cut their losses, shake hands on it. But no breakup, even an okay one, is complete until you dig like a pair of truffle-sniffing pigs to find out what happened. This is how romantic love keeps itself from going extinct, right? How it *swindles* itself into sentience. Romance may be the world's oldest cult.

It hooks you when you're vulnerable, holds your deepest fears as collateral, renames you something like 'baby,' brainwashes you, then makes you think that your soul will wither and *die* if you let go of a person who loved you. So you better have a good goddamn reason for saying 'nah, not enough.' The love lobby is worse than the gun lobby. More misery, more addiction, more heads on spikes. And for what?"

"Fucking hell, Lola."

"I'm serious. For *what*?"

Jin cleaned her glasses on her pajama sleeve. Vadis bulged her eyes. She was trying to signal that my point had nowhere to land, not in this building, not with this audience. But my point *was* hers. She had eschewed romance the entire time I'd known her, but I was obliged to believe simply because I'd already put in the effort?

"All love is, is the process of deciding on familiarity."

"Oh, yeah?" she huffed, whirling her finger around the map. "Then why is this working?"

"Because I'm not concussed! I remember these guys and they remember me. I didn't make the rules. Maybe Clive should've put me on a plane to Tokyo."

I took a deep breath. I could hear the sound of the needle's tireless scratching. Jin twisted several knobs, clicking them off, and the whirring of the machines came to a halt.

"I don't know," I gave in, "maybe a perfect relationship is just on the tip of my tongue. That's a clinical phenomenon, you know. It's metacognition. You become momentarily conscious of your synapses firing."

"I wrote the metacognition piece," said Vadis.

"You did? That was a good piece."

"Thanks."

"So this is it?" I asked, rubbing my temples. "I come here every night and bludgeon these gentlemen with analysis until I am cured of indecision?"

"That's closure," said Vadis.

I leaned back in my chair and stared at the ceiling. Someone had done a poor job of repainting it. I could see where the roller of fresh paint had bumped against the wall.

"Men," I said, plunking my chair to the floor. "I can never decide if I forgive them too easily or punish them too easily. My whole life, I've never known."

I flicked the monitors from my fingers and tugged off the suction cup.

"Where do I put these?"

"Anywhere you want," said Jin.

9

Because it couldn't hurt, I dressed up before leaving the house. Or, if I was working from the office, before leaving for work. I wore shoes with heels and applied makeup using tips I'd acquired from shame-watching Chantal's YouTube tutorials, her pupils eclipsed by the reflection of a ring light. The trick was to curl your eyelashes firmly and close to the base, right where the robot spiders get in. I tweezed, I scrubbed, I dusted, I blended. I did interesting things with belts. My younger coworkers, with whom I'd never really bonded enough to categorize our small talk as negative or positive, took notice. "You look nice today" expanded to "You look nice this week" which expanded to "What are you eating?" Potato chips and hard liquor, mostly. A surprisingly fast-acting diet if you really put your back into it.

After work, I'd zigzag through the streets of Chinatown, admiring the intersections of lettering I'd never understand, buying beverages significant enough to merit dome tops, then having to sweet-talk my way into salon bathrooms. I'd sit on the benches on concrete islands or on the biscotti-shaped stoops painted municipal red. I'd watch my reflection warp in the stainless steel doors. Or else I'd suggest drinks meetings be held in the area, dragging publicists to me under false pretenses, ostensibly to discuss *Radio New York*'s coverage of their productions and publications. I went in the evenings because I assumed it would increase my chances. Most of my exes were grown-ups now. They had responsibilities from which no amount of subliminal battering could distract them. They were no longer waking up at noon, still drunk, for instance.

I avoided Boots within reason or else I called him before I went (went hunting, went to be hunted), but only *after* a relatively normal day had passed. It was in this window that I could convince myself nothing out of the ordinary was happening and thus convince him, too. This is how people must conduct affairs, I thought, by hitting the "refresh" button each morning, lying to themselves before they lied to anyone else. That was the secret, to put your denial mask on first before helping others. Most of the time, I got voice mail. Sometimes I got sent there on purpose. The time difference put him in afternoon meetings. When Boots and I did speak, I dodged the topic of myself with the kind of balletic skill that gets confused for curiosity, asking such detailed questions about glassware, it prompted him to offer me a job. Or else I interviewed him about the weather.

"You know what Mark Twain said about San Francisco?" I asked.

"'The coldest winter I ever spent was a summer in San Francisco.'"

"Yup, that's it. That's what he said."

"Did we get something for Jess and Adam?"

"I keep forgetting. I'm sure the only thing left on the registry is a sleigh bed."

"Seriously?" he said, annoyed at this symbol of my warped priorities. "What else have you been doing?"

"Taking a shit? I don't know. Can't you just send them a vase?"

"I'm not *The Giving Tree*, Lola."

"They're your friends," I said, eyeing the glassware shelves. "I thought you'd prefer to send them something you made."

"You *just* told me you forgot."

"That's true. But there's really no way I could have predicted this reaction."

"I feel like I'm talking to Vadis."

"Well, you're not."

One night, I got a twofer. At first, I thought there would be no sighting. I tried to conceal my stakeout by luxuriating in the reflections of people in the windows of lighting stores and rubber emporiums, pretending to inspect the merchandise (*If it's in rubber, we have it!*) or else looking out the corner of my eye while examining the panes of glass circles in the pavement. The glass was centuries old, predating the lightbulb. These were vault lights for the downtown factory workers toiling away in the basement. It would only take a few people to stop, their shoes covering the glass, and it would be a blackout below.

Every face I picked out from the crowd looked normal in that it looked unfamiliar. Perhaps Amos, Willis, and Dave had been coincidences and Jonathan had been a fluke, manifesting only because he came as a matched set. Two consciousnesses are better to manipulate than one?

But then I saw Howard, crossing Mott. At first, I couldn't

be sure it was Howard. It was dark out by then. Plus the Howard I knew had a full head of hair and a pear-shape bottom that one rarely sees on a man. This guy had neither of those things. But I could tell by the gait. Howard sashayed, which was unfortunate because Howard very much wished not to sashay. When we met, he was a pudgy adjunct professor of linguistics on Long Island, cloaking his bulges, dreaming of tenure. If Howard were a woman, he would've been categorized as "basic," but as a man, the expectation of surface individuality was lower while the pressure for conformity was higher. Howard's curiosity was limited to whatever happened to physically cross his path. He stopped for every street canvasser, tried every cookie sample and squirt of lotion. If he saw a billboard for a movie, he'd go see that movie. His sister was the most creative person he knew. She was an artist who painted woodland scenes on plaster casts of her own face. He owned a dozen of the masks, hung proudly across one wall, staring down at us with hollow sisterly eyes.

Now here was Howard again. Had I thought about this man? I didn't think I had. Did I miss Howard or compare Boots to him or associate him with a feature of the world? I didn't think so. In fact, if I'd assumed anything about Howard, it was that I'd never see him again. The only remnant of Howard in my possession was a postcard he'd once given me for his sister's art show. On the back, he'd written, "please cum?" which he quite sincerely meant as slang for "attend?"

Not the most cunning of linguists, our Howard.

Howard was talking animatedly into his phone. He looked as if he was in a hurry. This gratified me as, during the months we dated, he was always blinkered by insecurity, jockeying to be needed, creating micro-situations in which I might depend on him, such as safekeeping our tickets or not telling me the letter of our row, even as we searched for it. Or withholding the address of a party so that I'd have to rely on him for navigation. *I'm on it, Lola, don't you worry.* I wasn't worried, I was annoyed. Perhaps Howard no longer needed to do this. Perhaps he was dealing with real problems, eliminating the desire to manufacture his own. Departmental drama. Arguing with a wife. Scheduling a surgery. Whatever the source of the animation, I was glad for it.

I hung back and watched, as if from the inside of one of his sister's masks, trying to put as much distance between us as possible without losing him. I didn't feel the need to interfere with Howard's evening. I waited for him to hail a cab and for the cab to disappear over the Manhattan Bridge.

I was en route to report this sighting to the Golconda, defenses down, quota met, when I ran into Cooper, exiting the subway. Cooper came at me like a dart, cutting through space in that Brancusiesque way he had, the photonegative of a *sashay*. Cooper was deep in the closet when we were together. His father was the first Black reverend at a Baptist Church in Alabama, and his mother managed a Walmart. She wouldn't speak to him for six months after learning he'd applied for financial aid at a college "up north" (UVA). I very much doubted the topic of premarital sex was on the table in that house, never mind with whom. For a while, I told myself that just because these were the *kind* of parents who might not rejoice in the sexual orientation of their only child, that didn't mean there was anything for him to reveal. Maybe whatever elements of himself Cooper was concealing were more *aspects* than elements. More *curiosities* than elements. Maybe he hid himself when he went home because he didn't want to seem too permeated by the northeast, not because he didn't want to seem too gay.

But Cooper only wanted to have sex with the lights out, from behind, with me lying perfectly still. It felt clinical. Or as if we were role-playing a bank heist during which my sole job was to avoid being detected by lasers. In theory, this should've been a flag, but I'd dated Cooper right after Dave and, more important, after I'd spent a lifetime absorbing the idea that women wound up sublimating their sexual needs for men. It was therefore refreshing, relatable even, to be with two men in a row who needed something more narrative than friction to get off, whose sexuality slid like an abacus. This did not last long.

A magnificent knot of contradictions, Cooper had United Colors of Benetton ads framed in his bathroom, a catalog of musical soundtracks in his living room, and a vanity full of specialized products. He also owned a black leather couch, never had any food in the house, and worked in the merchandising department of the NBA. One day, I asked him: Why this sport and not all other sports? And with the straightest of faces, he told me that in other sports, at least the ones with leagues and federations, you couldn't see the exertion of the players' bodies. You couldn't see the way their muscles shifted from the back to the biceps, from the thigh to the knee.

There was really no bouncing back from that one.

Cooper didn't flinch when he saw me. I was a memory for him, enough for the power of suggestion to get him here, but I was not a life event. Not compared with everything that came after me. I was excited to talk to him, as there was no risk of entanglement. I was not going to cry in front of, slap, or grope Cooper.

But Cooper only grinned, pivoted his phone away from his face, and pecked me on the cheek.

"Cute," he mouthed, gesturing at my outfit.

He was gone before I uttered a word.

I didn't think either of these men was significant enough to write home about. But their presence provided the news that they thought about me, however minimally. Their surfaces could be scratched. Perhaps, I thought, closure was not achieved by exhausting oneself with analysis, but via carrot, through the ego's feeble need for confirmation. There is a membrane of pride that surrounds the heart and I found that when that area got damaged, it was hard to figure out what took the hit. Sometimes it was the heart; often it was only the cellophane.

Seeing these people was a reminder that I had not been through all this by myself. This was a frequently employed tactic among men I knew, to knock you down and then ask what you're doing on the floor. The adult iteration of Why Are You Hitting Yourself? Except most of them sincerely wanted to know. Causation was Greek to them. But I was starting to sense that some of them had grasped the truth of what had happened all along. Some of their hands had been extending down this whole time or vice versa as we wiped the dirt from our butts and waited for the nerves to stop throbbing.

Think you'll live? Good. Then back into the game you go.

I made enough noise to scare the rats. We'd come to an understanding: I would not kill them on purpose and they would not kill me by accident, by making me jump and slam my head on a beam. Once folded into Jin's chair, I licked the suction cup and reported on the nothing of my evening, on how the nothing made me feel. I tried not to lie to the needle about my feelings or to manufacture them. I found it a challenge to experience emotions in the moment and hold on to them at the same time. The blank I drew was genuine. It was fine, seeing Howard and Cooper, just fine. Perhaps, I thought, this was why, whenever I had doubts about Boots, I tried to just concentrate on appreciating him instead.

Vadis left the room in a huff when I told her I'd spoken to neither man, that I'd even gone so far as to *avoid* one.

"This is why you can't have nice things!" she shouted.

"I don't even want this nice thing!"

"You're incorrigible."

"Do you know what that word means? Or is your brain too stuffed with adaptogen powders?"

After she slammed the door, I wondered, aloud to Jin, if my biofeedback was really helping. What good was my heart doing anyone, in any sense?

"It's an information continuum," Jin said. "We just want to know how your psyche is faring from every possible angle, and then we present our findings to Clive, who presents them to our investors."

I knew better than to push too hard with her. Jin was all in. Not only was she like Errol, newly enamored of Clive, but people like her, who invested this deeply in spiritualism, had a history of desperation when it came to technology (ladies and gentlemen, I give you the Ouija Board, the Dream Catcher, the Voodoo Doll). It hadn't worked yet. Was Clive Glenn, inventor of a DSM drinking game, really going to crack a code that had stumped humanity dating back to ancient Egypt?

"So what do you think," Jin asked, "that there will never be anything new because it hasn't existed before?"

"That's not what I'm saying. I'm saying *cold fusion* will never be new because it hasn't existed before. The impossible and the inevitable are not the same."

"I hope this doesn't offend you," she said, wrapping a blood pressure monitor snugly around my arm, "because you seem like an aware person and Vadis speaks highly of you—"

"No, she doesn't."

"—but it's crazy to me how you think you're smarter than Clive."

"I don't, actually."

"You question everything, you argue with everything, when everything you see here is *for* you."

"Not everything," I said, pointing through the wall, at the meditation room. "And maybe I have questions because we're sitting in a temple for a religion founded on debate. Why don't you question it?"

"I already did," she said, tightening the hug of the Velcro. "And I understand that you need to go on your own journey. But all these people, coming to this place, it's because of Clive. Clive is the answer. Your package is *working*. Come on, you don't see why people will pay for this? Clive has created a chance for them to fix their lives."

"Jin, what's your day job? If you don't mind me asking."

"I founded an online payment-processing company but I sold it."

"Like a big company?"

"Depends on your definition of *big*," she said, shrugging.

"You ran it?"

"Sure."

"And you quit to do this?"

"This data isn't gonna map itself," she said, stroking her monitor with a trace of the maternal. "Errol quit his job, too.

He used to do advance for a senator. He's very organized. But it sounded off-the-charts soulless. I think everyone here had hit a wall with how we were using our skills, but we didn't know it until Clive. Until Clive found me. Like what's the point in doing research for global markets when you can do it for human emotion?"

"Money?"

"Sure, but follow the trail. People want money so they feel in control, and they want to feel in control so they feel happy. Love makes people happy."

From CEO to "love makes people happy." This man needed to be jailed.

"So Clive, he's paying you guys?"

"No," she said, as if the notion were a bug to be flicked.

"But you're in on the ground floor, then? Like stock options?"

"Oh, no, Lola. This work will change the world. I'd do this for free."

"But you *do* do this for free."

"That's what I said."

Clive was standing in the middle of the atrium when I left the interrogation room, talking on the phone, sipping coffee, speaking rapidly but trying to keep his voice down. He sounded agitated, maybe not for a mogul but certainly for a guiding light. Not to mention the fact that an atrium seemed like a profoundly stupid place for a private call. He must have been caught off guard by it.

I hid behind the garden so that neither he nor the baristas

would see me. Was this what it had come to, me hiding behind potted palms? I picked up a few words: *transfer, funding, projection, scalable, astral projection.* The woman who looked like a kindergarten teacher passed and gave Clive a little bow as she did. So did a man in clear Lucite glasses. He was wearing a fleece vest even though it was summer, as well as an expensive-looking watch. This must have been the single-digit tech company employee. When they were all gone, I emerged, casually, as if having stopped to smell the moss.

"Problem?" I asked, approaching Clive with exaggerated stealth.

He tucked his phone into his pocket like he was getting rid of evidence.

"No, not really. How's it going, Lola?"

"Umm, fine, I guess? You know, standard. You're asking me this like I started a new diet."

"Maybe I'm just calm, knowing you're benefiting already, accessing the depths of your romantic consciousness . . ."

"You know . . ."

"What? Speak."

"We spent the better part of a decade telling people the only way to get over *anything* was to put in elbow grease, that medication alone would never work without therapy. You hated the quick fixes. At least drugs have science behind them."

"You're our drug," he said, as if making a mental note to jot that one down.

The chandeliers were on a slight dim and I could see the reflection of the elevator gears, shrunken and liquidy, in Clive's eyes. No woman, not me, not Chantal, not Clive's first wife, would capture his heart as Soren Jørgensen had. Clive would never get behind a woman the same way, never refashion his world with her in mind. He could give to others, that was true enough. And it kept him from being a sociopath. But he could never *need*.

"Every last one of you sounds the same, you know that? Rather, everyone sounds like you."

He smiled even though he knew he shouldn't.

"It's not a compliment. You're turning smart people into mush-for-brains."

"I am? Me? Do you know that eighty percent of New Yorkers own smartphones? The city itself has become more machine than human. For the first time in history, we are the ones who need to be tested for signs of independent thought, but I'm *brainwashing* people?"

"You're frightening."

"Awww, no, I'm not," he said, ruffling my hair just as Willis had done.

10

Could I be with anyone I'd ever dated if only I'd been just a *hair* less judgmental? If there was an answer to be found, it was to be found the following night, in Oscar, the platonic ideal of the road not taken. Or, well, *a* road. Oscar was not a great love. But I held a firm outline of him in my mind and he was unique enough to skate through my thoughts on a regular basis, without "outside stimuli." Having dated me would probably disqualify Oscar from being a *member* of the Golconda. Which was a shame. He was a prime candidate.

Oscar was a bourgeois bohemian who'd revolted against his suburban upbringing by diving headlong into alternative medicine. Oil diffusers lined his shelves, hand-labeled tinctures and balms hijacked his bathroom. An amateur apothecary, Oscar put bee pollen in places where bee pollen should never go. He used to fixate on my rising sign in a way that seemed thoughtful at first, his love language, but slowly revealed itself as unhealthy. None of my behavior originated with me, it all came from planets moving out of alignment, from atmospheric imbalances. To no one's surprise, he spent most of our time together angling to meet Clive, asking me what I thought of a commencement address Clive had given, retweeting Clive to his two hundred Twitter followers. This compacted the cringe, imagining Clive registering Oscar as a fan.

I tried to be tolerant. I said nothing when Oscar set up a Kickstarter page for his shaman's temple, nothing when he got rid of his phone because technology was a beta blocker, nothing when he slept with crystals the size of pumpkins. Let the man sleep with his crystal pumpkins, I thought. Do. Not. Judge. Once, I let him put one on my naked chest. He asked me if I could feel anything. I looked at the ceiling, feeling only like a cadaver. I thought of Willis's gold medal, of the weight of it on my sternum. Was I a person men put things on? Like coins on the eyes of the dead for their passage across the river Styx. Eventually, I reported that I could feel something, but I wasn't sure if it was the vibration of the crystal above or the rumble of the subway below.

"Okay," Oscar said, "cool."

His placidity was grating. Boots was uptight by comparison. Being with Oscar was like living in a city without seasons. Do not judge, I thought. Do not punish. Neurosis does not necessitate intelligence. The road to acceptance is paved with natural deodorant.

I bumped into Oscar coming out of a Duane Reade on Bowery. It was late in the afternoon and the skies had opened up, dark rivulets running into the gutters. I'd given up on running into someone—even Clive Glenn was no match for the weather—and decided to lean into the grayness, the sheets of summer rain, and buy myself a pack of cigarettes. When Oscar and I left through the automatic doors at the same time, our umbrellas knocked into each other. I pocketed the cigarettes. Oscar was not surprised by the coincidence of seeing me. This is how his world worked—alignment, inertia, destiny. It took an entire secret society working around the clock to put me in the same headspace.

Oscar was carrying a translucent plastic bag with Western medicine inside, the bag twisting around his wrist.

"Rash," he explained without me asking.

He pulled aside his hair, which had grown long in the back, to reveal a topography of red welts. The welts merged into one another to form an archipelago. I got a whiff of comfrey, the scent of a salve defeated.

"Got it in the Amazon," Oscar said. "They have everything down there."

I had no idea if he meant the rash or the remedy.

The pharmacy doors gaped open periodically as customers came in and out. Looks of disgust flashed across their faces, revulsion that anyone would choose to congregate in this inhospitable vestibule. Over Oscar's shoulder, an aisle of tampons and adult diapers framed the beginning and the end of things. Light from the stoplights across the way got trapped in the droplets on the glass.

"And you came here? I thought you lived in Williamsburg."

I knew Oscar lived in Williamsburg; he'd moved in before it was a glimmer in the Apple Store's eye. There was no way he was moving unless he became nomadic.

"All the pharmacies are closed so I meandered over the bridge."

I imagined Oscar looking up the hours of pharmacies and

would you look at that? The closest one open was on the Lower East Side.

We moved out onto the sidewalk, into the humidity, where Oscar told me he had just come from a "religious retreat," mortar-and-pestling an unpronounceable psychedelic drug, the effects of which made ayahuasca sound like cough syrup.

"Since when are you religious?" I asked.

"We're all religious," he said, bemused.

"Sure."

"I always worried your skepticism was isolating for you. Forces larger than ourselves are the most logical thing to believe in. Like peeing before you poop. Have you ever pooped before peeing? Think about it. Never. You gotta give yourself over to what's natural in this world. The cosmos wants you to be happy. Hey, double rainbows!"

He pointed at the sky and, sure enough, two faint arches stretched across the rooftops. People on the street aimed their phones skyward.

How the hell had Oscar not been the first guy I saw? His psyche was such low-hanging fruit.

Oscar and I ended because of his "structural wavelength nonconformity." Oscar was not monogamy-averse in the way Amos was monogamy-averse. Oscar could not commit to another person because he could not commit to his *own* person, to being in his own body, a spirit vessel he was only ever borrowing. To date Oscar was to date a tenant of the world. Air or salt or bark. One cannot expect loyalty from air or salt or bark. I wondered what it was I was supposed to get from Oscar now that I didn't get from dating him then.

"How are you," he asked, cocking his head at me, "truthfully?"

I told him I was fine, just fine, and spun my ring face-down. I didn't want him telling me how great it was that I'd found my "soul partner," which was just the kind of shit he would say, earnestness that I would have no choice but to match unless I wanted to get into a longer conversation. Now I had a hand in each pocket, one holding the cigarettes and one squeezing the ring, as if these were equivalent objects. Somehow everyone from Eliza, whose only ritual was going to Starbucks, to Oscar, who'd never set foot in one, had decided I was a pathological cynic.

Really, the only person who did not list cynicism among my flaws was Boots. Maybe he just didn't know me as well as we'd hoped.

"Well," I said, shrugging, "I'd hug you goodbye but . . ."

I eyed Oscar's neck.

"Yeah, better not. But hey, it's wonderful to see you in alignment."

I remembered how little I cared not only for this language, but also for his particular use of it. As if Oscar were a fully reformed kid from the suburbs, and I was unevolved because I relied on indulgences like separate bars of soap to wash your hands and your body. And my own toothbrush. But perhaps this was why I saw him now, these prickling memories of the kind of person I almost was. If I could be with *anyone* if only I'd commit to a version of myself, then Oscar was both the definition and the limit of that idea. Perhaps the point of Oscar was to show me how unnecessarily irritated I'd been, how I'd inferred his actions were for me, to convert me, when they were barely in conversation with me. Vadis was right: just because something had entered my field of vision did not mean it was *for* me.

"Hey, Oscar!" I shouted as I watched him walk away. "Don't scratch!"

The doors opened and shut behind me once more, chomping at a sloth's pace.

"I wouldn't dream of it!"

One thing this atrium could use was chairs. Maybe something cute, like a banquette upholstered with the pubes of my former lovers. Clive took the stairs down to meet me. The Golconda was the reverse of every other building on the planet in that the stairs were for efficiency and the elevator was for theatrics. Also, the elevator was being tended to by one of the members, practically a teenager, on a ladder, rubbing metal polish onto the wheels from the inside. He had a single black braid over his shoulder and was concentrating so hard on his task, for which he appeared unqualified, I worried he might fall!. It was liking watching a marionette, working another marionette.

Clive had a manila folder pressed tightly to his ribs as he strolled in my direction. Errol sidled up next to me, bowing in Clive's direction and then burping loudly into his fist. He looked mortified.

"Are you okay?"

"Fit as a fiddle."

His eyes were bloodshot, his forehead slick with sweat.

"I'm fine," he insisted. "Clive took me to that restaurant he likes."

"You had the General Tso soufflé."

"Yes!" he said, gripping my forearm. "It's mostly picked one direction and stuck with it, but for a while there . . . it was like 'you don't have to go home, but you can't stay here.'"

Clive opened the folder as he neared us and began thumbing through pages. I could make out blocks of passport-size photos, clipped to the corner of each page like homicide files. I caught sight of Willis. Even pressed into one dimension, one could not miss Willis. Meanwhile, Clive was glowing.

"Are you wearing glitter on your face?" I asked, narrowing my eyes.

"What? Oh," he said, swiping at his cheeks, "Chantal was testing out new pigments this morning."

"On your face?"

"They're vegan."

"Are they for children? I'm asking."

"Lola, sometimes love is letting the other person put glitter on your face."

"Wonderful. Lesson learned."

"Crap," he said to the folder, "I forgot Vadis's list in the meditation room."

My ears perked up.

"Okay. What exactly goes on in the meditation room?"

"Isn't that self-explanatory?" asked Clive, the little scar on his chin shifting as he smirked.

"Not particularly, no. I mean, *I* think meditation is the process of clearing your mind, but you seem to have assigned it some freakish meaning. Because the minds in that room aren't clear, are they? They've got my disembodied head floating through them. One woman's 'meditation' is another man's 'let's drive Lola insane for sport.'"

"Not for sport," Errol grumbled.

"Sorry, as a *business model.*"

"It's just a room, Lola. But it's in use at the moment. It was originally built as the women's entrance and then, I think, used for Torah study? We thought it a fitting place to focus on your Memory Pathways. Don't look at me like that, it's not sacrilege."

"You're the one who put a coffee bar in a shul."

"And a crystalarium closet!" Errol piped in. "With a hundred-pound crystal!"

"Oh, where's that?"

"Off the conference room."

"What kind of crystal is it?"

"It's an amethyst geode."

"An amethyst geode!"

"Don't be a jerk," scolded Clive.

"She's not being a jerk," Errol said, defending my honor.

"See?" I said. "Not a jerk."

Clive changed the subject, pulling out his phone.

"Check this out," he said.

He pointed at an app on his screen with a little bowler hat in the middle. I wondered at what point this was a copyright issue or, at minimum, an overcommitment to symbolism. I also wondered if an app wasn't jumping the gun for a start-up cult. Clive pressed on the cube. While it gathered its programming wares, a little elevator glided up and down the screen. Clive explained how members could match with other members interested in concentrating on the same packages, exploring the same relationship terrain, how this would deepen the exclusivity of the Golconda by registering if a user had screenshotted the menu, how it would use biofeedback to track emotion. But the best part would be the location services.

"There'll be a map," he continued, "akin to the one you're sticking pins in, that we're gonna design over the automated one, ideally something more localized."

"You mean like what every car service and food delivery app on the planet already does?"

"It's also a means of generating user data."

"You really are the crown prince of print journalism."

"Mock it all you want but my Silicon Valley friends are into it. We'll do Chinatown first, then the rest of Manhattan, then the whole city, then the whole world."

"Where are you getting all this money?"

"Lola, I'm not having the stock options conversation with you."

"I'm not asking you for money, you demon. I'm not even part of this."

"Aren't you?"

I blinked. I *was* part of the machinery that had turned this place into a new age funhouse. Not that I expected to be compensated, not when the people who actually worked here didn't expect it. As far as everyone was concerned, I was being given the gift of a lifetime.

The kid on the ladder was cleaning the elevator cable, making a slow, adoring, sensual motion like he was milking it. He, too, was probably doing this for purpose, not payment.

"Hey!" I shouted, my voice echoing. "Hey!"

"Please don't do that," pleaded Errol.

"Why won't they ever look at me? It's like they feel guilty."

"They don't feel guilty," Clive assured me, amused by the suggestion. "They have to maintain focus."

"Right. On me."

"Speaking of which, who did you see this evening?"

"Oscar," I said, still staring at the kid. "I saw Oscar."

"Oscar!"

Clive seemed overjoyed. The reason I'd never introduced the two of them had less to do with protecting Clive from a superfan and more to do with protecting Oscar from being turned into an acolyte. Clive was a geyser of questions about how long I'd spoken to Oscar, how I felt parting ways with someone as "plugged in" as Oscar. As far as he was concerned, Oscar was the one that got away. But if I only dated people Clive liked, I'd have sex once a decade.

Jin appeared behind us, leaning on the door frame of the interrogation room, arms crossed. She had on expensive-looking sneakers with puffy tongues.

"May I borrow her, Mr. Glenn?" asked Jin, with a hint of a curtsey, one tongue behind the other.

"You make people call you Mr. Glenn?"

"I don't *make* people do anything, Lola."

"One day, you and I are gonna sit down and have a conversation about the semantics of 'free will.' The bowing is gross."

"The bowing is organic."

"Wow."

"It's a gesture to the Golconda more than me."

"Just wow."

"Barry called me Shepherd Glenn for like a week," he said, playing at embarrassment, "but I asked him to stop. I don't think it was catching on anyway."

"Who the fuck's Barry?"

"The barista," he said, as if I'd forgotten my own mother's name.

"Be right there!" Clive shouted to Jin, and then to me: "It's amazing, isn't it?"

"How you're monetizing my personal failings?"

"Sure, but also how it's actually working. We're united by our shared humanity, but somewhere along the way, we get orphaned by our individual history. The Golconda will fix this by offering personal salvation as well as a new paradigm for larger emotional understanding."

Clive's recapitulative blather was starting to prick at me in new ways, ways in which I found myself more depressed than outraged. I longed for the days when he would've skewered this type of new age word salad, cigarette dangling from his lips, ice still rattling around his first drink as he signaled for a second. Thinking of it made me want to light up right now, in front of him, to blow smoke in his face. Actually, it made me want to put a cigarette *out* in here, to watch the ashes swirl across the pristine marble.

"A new means to personal salvation," I said. "That's the definition of a cult."

"If anything, it's the definition of a religion."

"Let no one accuse you of aiming low."

"Give me some credit, Lola."

"Oh, I would," I said, gesturing around us, "but you're all stocked up."

"It's not a religion and it's not a cult. Not in the traditional sense."

"Why does it have to be a cult in *any* sense?! What do you have against starting a podcast empire like a normal person?"

"Because this is the most important mission I'll ever be a part of. Lola, we were so blind all those years at the magazine. Fumbling around, trying to figure out who was fixing people and how, what was wrong with them to begin with. Like if any of it worked, why put out another issue and another and another? It's indulgent to look inward and find out *nothing* about yourself, but it's groundbreaking to do it and find out *everything*. Using tailored scenarios, we can put your past into a cohesive whole in an abbreviated time frame, thereby setting an actual course correction for closure. And it starts with people like you"—he poked me right between the eyes, pressing the bridge of my nose—"telling us all about people like Oscar."

"Should we not wait until she's hooked up?" asked Errol, as gently as could be.

"Absolutely," Clive agreed. "We wouldn't want valuable data being lost to idle chitchat."

11

Over the next few days, a routine emerged. Each evening, I'd have an interaction and then I'd walk over to the Golconda, where Errol would greet me. Then I'd report to Vadis and Jin, the two of them coming just shy of shoving a thermometer up my ass. Errol began escorting me everywhere I went, which seemed more than a little Pyong-yangy. Each time, I was told the meditation room was off-limits, under construction, or no "chaperone" was available. This, despite the fact that Errol was standing right in front of me. Meanwhile, if Clive was around, he'd breeze through, confer with his staff, and thank me for my participation as if I'd signed up to taste-test gum. Then he'd take his leave, off to some event requiring cuff links.

Soon I knew this stretch of Chinatown better than my own neighborhood. I could draw every street corner, reproduce the font on every window. I knew which buildings were diligent about breaking down their boxes and which weren't, which had window ledges wide enough for me to put drinks on.

But the repetition was chipping away at me. Instead of

dressing up in anticipation of the past, I began dressing down for it. So what if someone I used to sleep with no longer entertained the idea? Who cared what these men thought of me? There would be another one of these jokers along at any minute. I felt like a human Etch-A-Sketch—all I had to do was blink and a new chapter of my past would be waiting for me. They say you only hurt the ones you love, but it turns out you can hurt lots of people you only moderately like. I began to feel like my dating life had been some elaborate logic proof, showing me how to wind up with someone not for the one person he *is* but for all the people he *isn't*. If human partnership was founded more on trait elimination than trait gravitation, what were all those years of heartbreak for?

There's an acceptable degree of slovenly that anyone can attain, the point at which one's sex appeal still shines through and becomes more appealing for the challenge. I blew past this point quickly. I wore different combinations of the same set of clothing, which I did not wash. I stopped tucking, tweezing, or shaving anything. I decided that moisturizer was unnatural. The cavewomen didn't have moisturizer and some of them made it to forty. My scalp began to itch. Ponytails were painful to the touch when released. I gnawed at my cuticles until they bled. When I bathed, I did so poorly. Waxy flakes of soap would lodge themselves in the hair at the base of my neck and I'd still be picking them out at noon, sniffing to confirm they were soap.

Spending this much time in the past, with men as the common denominator, wasn't doing my mental hygiene any favors either. On top of being repulsed by the digestion of romance as identity—the world was on fire and I couldn't pass a Bechdel Test *with myself*—my behavioral borders were disintegrating. Devoting my nights to a parallel world made this one feel like a simulation. I stared at people on the street as if I were wearing sunglasses. A woman sitting next to me on the subway would be shaking her foot, and the urge to bash her knee with a book was so overwhelming, I'd have to get up and move.

On the phone with Boots, I'd drift off or stare at the cat while he was talking until it felt like his voice was the internal monologue of the cat.

In the mornings, I'd brush my teeth and stare at the tube of toothpaste, cowed by the mental feat it would take to buy another one when this one ran out, by the repetition of all existence. I imagined some corner of a museum, piled high with empty toothpaste tubes.

At work, people followed up about emails they'd sent and I looked at them as if through a scrim. They were addressing old me, daytime Lola, before my world was flipped over, chunks of the past falling into the well. They'd ask about my weekend plans, which was how I knew it was Friday. I'd stare at my monitor, brightness cranked up, as if trying to blind myself. Oh, how much easier it is for the sane to imitate the insane than the other way around. Who could understand me now? Recently revived coma patients, that's who. Those were my people. People stuck in the past and flung, without their consent, into the present.

Fernando was the son of a prominent commercial director who told him that all women would be after his money. Brush your teeth, go to sleep, don't dream of gold diggers. He eschewed any behavior that teetered on generous. We always split the bill. "Since I got" was a common refrain. *Since I got*

the tickets, you can get the snacks. Since I got the car, you can get the gas. Since I got myself out of my mother's womb, you can get your ass to Queens. Fernando was supposed to help me move apartments, which I'd told myself would be a cementing experience. I had visions of U-Hauls and "Do you really need this many cookbooks?" But he never showed. At first, my texts contained photos of overstuffed garbage bags, accompanied by captions like "thinking of leaving it like this." Then they escalated to "REALLY?!" until, eight hours later, settled in my new apartment, I dug out a cedar stick Oscar had given me and smudged every room.

I saw Fernando through a restaurant window on Hester Street. He was on a date. He had ghosted me in my hour of need, but he *had* thought of me again after that day. Feeling emboldened by my new role as the Night Mayor of Chinatown, I walked into the restaurant, gave the maître d' a twenty-dollar bill, and nodded at Fernando's table. I told him that if two credit cards were presented, the money was to go toward the woman's half of the bill only, but if only one credit card was presented, the maître d' was to keep the money. Then I took a gratified step back out into the night.

Phillip I met in the nascent days of online dating, which meant I half expected him to burst into pixels. The idea that we had plucked each other off a shelf and could just return each other with no consequences was distracting—though quaintly inhuman compared with the swiping of faces that would become muscle memory years later. *This is my online boyfriend* ran like a news crawl across the back of my eyelids.

Phillip, on the other hand, had no reservations about how we met. He opened up. He shared. He was getting his PhD in plant genetics, he wet the bed until he was fifteen, and he carried an EpiPen. I was inconsistent, divulging my deepest fears one moment, neglecting to tell him my office was a block away from his lab the next. Three months in, we were still seeing each other only once a week. In the most polite breakup of its generation, he suggested perhaps it would be easier for all parties to bring that number down to zero rather than up to two.

We should've left it there, but we got back together a month later when I ran into him on a crowded crosstown bus. Having had an IRL breakup animated the relationship for me for the first time. I no longer knew Phillip from online. I knew him from no longer knowing him. Now I wanted to see him all the time.

Phillip's defining moment came during this second chapter of our relationship, when he punched me in the face.

Surpassed only by the time, ten minutes later, when he dumped me. Again.

We were asleep and he was dreaming that he was in a boxing ring, taking swings at the air. He rolled over in the middle of the night and clocked me awake. He bolted to the kitchen and came back with a dish towel and a pint of ice cream, handing me these items like a child hands an adult a broken toy. As I ice-creamed my eye, he sat sheepishly at the end of the bed and informed me that "this" wasn't going to work. I still wasn't "letting my guard down." This was rich, coming from someone who'd just hit me in the face.

What had always interested me about that breakup, in addition to the fact that I had to look as bad as I felt for a week, was that Phillip refused to share any further details of the dream. He was fighting someone or something . . . but what? The obligation to stay with me? The fear of wetting the bed? Was he punching through my barriers? Maybe it was the eight-year relationship from which he'd recently extricated himself, which we never discussed. His attempts to not talk about her were painful to witness.

I watched Phillip through the window of a men's clothing store, examining strips of houndstooth, and was tempted to march in there and ask him about the dream. I wondered if he remembered that night as well as I did. Phillip had sent back a sweater of mine a few weeks after the breakup, accompanied by a note, which I kept. It was my only evidence of him. The note, written on a piece of scrap paper, hoped I was well, which I found to be a grievous glossing-over of events. But seeing Phillip again inspired me to think of the note in a softer light. They were just words, written by someone who didn't know what to say. Prior to the note, I'd never seen Phillip's handwriting. How badly can you be hurt by someone whose handwriting you've never seen?

I followed Phillip as he exited the store, trying not to be seen. He arrived at a bus stop just as a bus pulled up. Then my phone started ringing. It was Boots. We hadn't spoken in a couple of days, kept just missing each other. I sent it to voice mail but it was too late. I was too close to Phillip, who turned and spotted me. I had a flash of worry that he wouldn't be able to place me. I was out of context, a time traveler. And I felt so haggard, part of me felt recognition would be an insult. But as he boarded the bus, he pointed into the open door, and yelled "Bus!" Phillip had places to go, people to see, plants to graft. And it was as if all the feelings I'd ever had about our relationship drove off on the M22 with him.

Aaron was wheeling a baby carriage down Mott Street. He wheeled right past me but I could tell it was him. All these men had lost or gained weight, changed their style, become estranged from their hairline, but their mannerisms were as indelible as fingerprints. I followed him to a bakery famous for its bear claws. There was still a line out the door at 6 p.m. He greeted a petite woman with bluntly cropped hair who handed him a beverage from a cup holder in a second stroller. They looked like they had come downtown for the express purpose of obtaining bear claws. One or both of them had been issued images of pastry by the Golconda.

Aaron was a relic. The summer before high school began, I was hopelessly infatuated with him. He was a lifeguard at our local summer camp, where he was a senior counselor and I was a junior counselor. He used to twirl a lanyard with keys to the equipment shack around his fingers, moving in controlled circles. I spent all summer thinking of ways to get those fingers inside me. I hiked up my shorts, pulled down my V-neck. I had a well-fabricated nightlife. I casually dropped Jerky Boys references in front of him and rented the action movies he liked from Blockbuster. I paid a king's ransom for a vintage Bruce Lee *Fist of Fury* T-shirt. When he complimented it, I pretended to have fished it out of a second-hand bin.

As the summer wore on and Aaron made no overtures of affection, I didn't give up on my forced metamorphosis into cool. I wanted to seem like I had good taste and so I accidentally became someone with good taste. I wanted to seem elusive and so I accidentally became elusive. Aaron took notice on the last day of camp. Men, even boys, are very good at knowing when a woman's heart has left the building. By the time Aaron asked me to help him collect the kickboards, I was inconvenienced.

The walls inside the equipment shack were covered in cheap panels with the manufacturer's logo on them: Beaver Lumber. Aaron had me up against one of the panels, his tongue exploring my ear. This guy wanted to eat my brains. He dug his hand over the waistband of my shorts and under the spandex of my bathing suit, his forearm cut off by two types of elastic. I'll never forget the look of concern on Aaron's face, that I might be unimpressed with his putting his fingers in me. I wanted to tell him there was no need to question if it felt good because *of course* it didn't feel good. I had not expected it to. But I was suddenly responsible for this creature who noticed I wasn't reacting how women reacted in the movies. Neither of us knew how to fix this so Aaron freed his hand and kissed me. He left the shed first.

"See you next summer," he said, even though I'd already told him this was my last summer at the camp.

I watched him through a crack in the door, moving up the slope of a path. Another counselor came up behind him, a girl his age, and punched him affectionately in the arm. I reached my hand down to smell myself. As suspected: chlorine.

Out of everyone, I least wanted to see Knox. I was hoping that Clive had overlooked him, but if the Golconda's net had caught the likes of Howard and Dave, there was no way it was letting Knox slide.

Knox was an emotionally distant librettist and latent sadist from Detroit who looked like a young Daniel Day Lewis. I interviewed him for a *Modern Psychology* feature on prodigies and we had drinks after the story ran. Knox seemed cultured, confident, and unassuming about both, the kind of man who extended himself as much as he retreated, a function of being an in-demand artist who must answer email eventually. The kind of man I thought I *should* be dating. In this way, I was perpetrating the same crime against Knox as Dave had perpetrated against me. Whenever Dave assumed I'd like to go cliff diving with him, I thought: Do I even need to be here for this relationship?

I blamed Knox for why I'd later fall for Amos, because I was hoping to date an artist who was also an intellectual. Boots didn't count because Boots was too practical about his art to risk insufferability. I'd never managed to strike the right balance with creative types. Either I tiptoed around these men, letting them stop me mid-sentence to point out a cloud, letting them expect to be rewarded for banal observations, or I felt self-conscious about my own creative limitations and transformed myself into whatever they wanted me to be.

That's why I was scared of seeing Knox. Because of the monster I became around him.

Knox's concern for my physical well-being was the entry point of his affection. At first, I thought his compulsion to nurse stemmed from his immersion in an older art form and, by extension, an older world. He insisted on walking closest to the curb. Or sending cars to pick me up. He would nonchalantly move our café table away from foot traffic and glare at anyone who jostled me, as if prepared to draw his sword. I had a sharp sense of my own body whenever I was around him. I found myself doing things like blowing into my already-gloved fingers, announcing that it was cold. I'd touch the glass of an airplane window, knowing he was beside me, appreciating the silhouette of my ladylike fingers, speculating about the soft field of my thoughts. I was a fragile product of this big bad world. If I stubbed my toe, I'd say something like, "I don't *think* it's broken." In bed, Knox was adamant about cradling my head to keep it from banging against the wall, even though our sex presented no danger. I'd sigh as I fell asleep, like a baby bear, with a little whistle out the nose and a nuzzle into the pillow, while Knox stroked my hair.

It made him so happy to do these things, it seemed like no sacrifice to pretend to want them.

One morning, our bodies skimmed by the sheets, Knox confessed the reason he taught himself to play the piano was so he could make something beautiful while his father beat his mother. On multiple occasions, the father tried to choke her to death. It fell to Knox to comfort her and then, when he was older, to call the police. The whole neighborhood knew how bad things were in that house, but they did nothing. They had their own problems.

After some prodding, I discovered that *every* woman Knox had ever been with had been assaulted, abandoned, neglected, or sexually abused, often by a relative. Knox's broken-bird complex was not a tic, his aspirational Munchausen by proxy ran right up to the edge of *causing* trauma before backing away. The heavier the topic, the more Knox engaged with it. When I tried to move on from my own insufficient wounds, I could practically hear the cord of his attention being snipped. A hero without a damsel is a mere man. I found I could capture Knox's attention *only* if I was upset. I'd leave parties in a huff, indulging in momentary emotion. Or I'd imply that

Vadis and I had been discussing dark things, secret woman things when, in reality, we had devoted the better part of breakfast to identifying the color of a celebrity's hair.

As our tolerance grew, we needed bigger hits of narrative pain to achieve the same high. I was running out of material. So I began telling flat-out lies. My dalliance with Aaron in the equipment shed became him cornering me against my will. Plus, I was a virgin. That much was true. But when that incident started running on fumes, I exaggerated a story of bad drunken sex in college. Smooth as silk, the drunken sex turned into assault "or something like it, these things aren't always so cut and dry," a reveal I made almost casually, over a plate of shishito peppers.

"I think of men like these peppers," I said, folding a whole one into my mouth like a complete lunatic. "Sometimes they hurt, but mostly they're sweet."

I was a sane person imitating a broken person imitating a sane person, which did not feel sane, not at all.

"Did you press charges?"

I bowed my head and shook it. There was no end to the shame, the unfathomable, bottomless shame, I felt on behalf of women who *had* been sexually assaulted. I was perpetuating one of the more harmful betrayals of womankind. And yet I felt a perverse sense of vindication on behalf of every woman who is told a nonsense story by a man to get her into bed. Men going through an artistic block, men sad about the death of a distant relative or the closing of a record store, men passed over for a promotion who need pussy to heal. But there was no turning back. Knox lit up only when we discussed my turbulent sexual history, and became disengaged otherwise.

I tried to remember: *Had* something more than a little

unpleasant happened that night in college, something more than stylistic differences? Probably. I did not have a great time, that's why the night stood out. But it was so long ago, I had obliterated the truth of it. And now my fake rapist had set up camp, hanging above our bed like a bat.

No longer in the mood to faux-sodomize myself in order to keep my boyfriend, I knew what I had to do—kill the bat. So one afternoon, I showed up at Knox's apartment. I sat on his settee, demonstrably upset. Knox put his hand on my knee while I stared at the carpet: My rapist, I explained, had died. How? A skiing accident. Where? Canada. How did I know? Google alert?

Guess we can explore the psychological soundness of *that* another time.

"Once a bad person," Knox said, "always a bad person."

"And now not even a person."

"How do you feel?"

"I feel free," I said, the first honest thing I'd uttered in months.

The fake tormentor of my fake nightmares could no longer be tracked down. I had achieved closure by pressing Control-Alt-Delete. The problem was, I had finally told a lie so big, there was no way I could stay with the person I'd told it to. Keeping Knox around would doom me to this narrative, folding it into the couple's counseling that was clearly coming. I could not stomach the idea of paying to lie to a therapist.

After I left his apartment, I told myself that at least I'd never have to see Knox again, never be reminded of my own capacity for manipulation.

When I saw Knox on Centre Street, he was with a woman who was looking intently at her reflection in a store window. The sunset was filling in the glass with the same blazing pink as the rosebuds on her sundress. She had a black surgical boot on her right foot and was fishing something out of her eye. Knox had his hand on her back, soothing her as she manipulated her eyelid.

I ran to the Golconda as if it were an embassy on foreign soil.

12

Clive was somewhere in the building but it was unclear where. This was a problem because he had, for some ungodly reason, brought Chantal with him.

Errol yanked me inside by the collar. He pointed at the coffee bar and, sure enough, there she was, a vision in sustainable fashion. To the delight of the baristas, Chantal was ordering an oat milk chai latte as she chatted with Jin. She stood with one foot turned out, as only former ballet dancers and influencers do. Women who know their angles. Chantal's neck was similar to Willis's thighs in that it was its own jurisdiction. Some people have a mouth full of teeth, this lady had a neck full of vertebrae.

I had the faintest inkling she would be inside. When I shone my flashlight over the treacherous path to the inner sanctum, I noticed an empty little bottle of coconut water. Chantal did not strike me as the littering type, but she did strike me as the type to let things just drop out of her bag without realizing it. Like Oscar, Chantal seemed loose when it came to the physical world, at once obsessed with her body and divorced from it, the kind of person who claimed not to see outer beauty but whose life would be threadbare without it. Unlike Oscar, this was because Chantal used social media as a proxy for her soul.

"Lola!" she exclaimed upon seeing me. "Madame! How killer is this joint?"

She spun in a circle, as if appreciating a first snowfall. Her hair was pressed into beachy waves that fell over an asymmetrical top that looked as if she'd pried it off a gondolier. She also had on false eyelashes, the good ones that looked like they'd been clipped from the tip of a lynx's ears. The only time I dared invite such apparati into my life was on Halloween, when my inability to operate them would pass for drunken application. But I could not compute her presence here. Chantal was in on the Golconda too? *Et tu, Chantal?* I couldn't imagine her keeping this place a secret, holding it all in, signing an NDA. Reading an NDA.

She held one of the Golconda's business cards in her hand, squeezing the edges, making the little folder talk.

"Ho-la, Lo-la," said the folder, in a demonic voice.

I could count my interactions with Chantal on one hand, but both in person and online, she would claim to be "obsessed" with all manner of nouns, including me. How would an obsession with a scented candle or a hairbrush or a pair of socks work? Posters of the socks. Driving past the childhood home of the socks.

"Hi, Chantal," I said. "How've you been?"

That was all I could muster. For one thing, I was self-conscious about the state of my appearance in her presence. For another, seeing Knox had hit me hard. I was unprepared to interact with anyone aside from Vadis or Jin. Plus, I needed to reserve my small-talk allowance. I already felt like I was blowing a "how've you been?" on her.

"Not as great as you!" she said. "Tell me everything. You're such a mini-genius."

It would take a regular-size genius to know if she meant my intelligence or my height.

"Do you have a McCarthy genius grant yet?" she asked.

"Not yet," I said, trying to relax my face. "Still chipping away at that communism."

Jin rolled her eyes, grabbed her tea, and retreated to the interrogation room.

"Later, Jen!" Chantal called.

Jin stiffened but didn't turn around.

"So," I asked her, "how goes the beauty business?"

The times I saw Chantal on my own, I felt like her parent. The times I saw her with Clive, I felt like their child. I suspected this was confusing for everyone involved.

"Oh my God, crazy busy. I need a second one of me. Or to become a literal octopus. One e-commerce site, two newsletters, a blog, endless TikToks, and three Instagram accounts is mental hospital time. I was just bitching about it to Harold."

"Errol," Errol said, not for the first time.

"Anyway, I'm in brand partnership hell. I have, like, no interns lined up for the summer, and I'm going to *murder* Kate Hudson. You don't even want to know."

"Chantal," Errol explained, teeth clenched, "is waiting for Clive. So that they can go to the theater."

I heard whispering in the distance. Two women were walking fluidly overhead, like a pair of doctors making rounds. They were draped in grays and egg-shaped silver jewelry. Finally, I recognized one of them. I'd seen her the night Vadis brought me here but hadn't made the connection until now. Her photo appeared frequently enough in publishing trade magazines: Jeannine Bonner. Amos's book editor. The one who'd suggested the restaurant, a night that seemed strangely distant now. One had to admire the scope of Clive's efforts. I held my breath, wanting to observe Jeannine, an eagerness that proved to be one-way.

"We're seeing *Hamlet*," Chantal piped in, waiting for a reaction, perhaps one that would indicate if she was in for a tragedy or a comedy.

"And," Errol continued, "for some reason, Clive decided to come *here* first and she just had to come in with him. Just had to. Would. Not. Take. No. For. An. Answer."

"I've been dying to tour Clive's wellness center! This is exactly what this neighborhood needs. You would not believe how many clients I have who live around here, who have to go to SoHo just to get cupped."

"The *wellness* center," I said, meeting Errol's pleading eyes.

"Gwyneth Paltrow is going to shoot jade eggs out her eyeballs when she sees this," Chantal continued. "Do you realize how thirsty this city is for a natural integration and intersection of spirituality and creativity? Why should we leave Burning Man in the desert?"

"Because of the sand?" Errol asked.

"Clive's a genius," Chantal decided, no qualifiers for him.

Vadis emerged from the interrogation room, immersed in a text until she saw Chantal. She forced a smile, screwing the corners of her lips into her cheeks. Chantal was to Vadis as Amos was to Zach, a souped-up version of her most cherished powers. In Vadis's case, this was a combination of urban bedouinism and a six-figure follower count across four social media platforms. But right now, it was panic, not jealousy, that I saw flash across Vadis's face. Chantal asked who was going to give her an impromptu tour. She promised not to post any photos.

"Top secret," she said. "Roll out social during the soft open. I *get* it. Clive keeps saying it's a wreck. It doesn't look like a wreck!"

I stared up at the chandeliers long enough for the bulbs to leave imprints behind my eyelids, floaters that drifted up and to the left.

"I'm just concerned about time," said Errol. "What time's the play?"

"That's true," said Vadis. "There's no time."

Her tone was gratingly deferential.

"No worries," Chantal said. "You do your thing, girl. Lola will show me around."

Chantal linked her arm around mine, sliding it in there like an eel. She didn't know I was the subject of an experiment. She also assumed the endgame went something like "clear your pores, stabilize your mood." Vadis tried to crush me with her eyes but I ignored her. Chantal assumed I had the run of the place, and who was I to correct her?

"It would be my honor," I said, walking toward the garden with Errol trailing closely behind us.

"We're not gonna shoplift," I assured him. "Your hundred-pound geode is safe."

"There's a crystalarium in here?" Chantal asked brightly.

"Where did you get that shirt?" I asked, turning my attention to her. "I'm obsessed with it."

Errol skipped ahead of us and offered to take over. His explanation of a garden rang true enough. Here is where the Golconda grew flora with "ayurvedic properties" to be used for everything from "olfactory assists" to, well, garnish. He tacked on that the garden was a physical demonstration of how the natural could be filtered through the man-made and come out natural again. A living demonstration of the laundering of energy. It all sounded very wellness-forward indeed. Chantal must've thought so too because she kept closing her eyes, letting the words refresh her like a hydrating mist.

"Is that true?" I whispered to Errol as Chantal paced around the birds of paradise.

"It's a *garden*," Errol hissed, "with *plants*."

"You're good."

His explanation of the interrogation room was equally convincing. Chantal came from a world of Reiki healers and chakra realignments, so explaining that the equipment was there to achieve some kind of higher physical state was an easy sell. She picked up one of Jin's suction cups and stroked her face with it. I wondered if it had been cleaned since last I'd licked it.

"Sweet map," she said, pointing at the wall and spinning back out the door.

We heard the phrase "chic sculpture" and followed her into the atrium.

"It's an elevator," I said.

"Does it work?"

"No," said Errol, surprising even himself.

I looked at him. He mouthed, "I don't know."

A few more members—two women and a man—exited from behind the garden. No one I recognized this time. They were like Oompa Loompas, these people.

I decided to throw in a few questions of my own, just to make Errol squirm. Like, say, what the fuck was the point of a full coffee bar before the "soft opening"? And was it not wasteful to hire not one but two baristas? Errol deftly pinned this on Clive's attention to detail. Chantal put her hand on her heart as if compulsion and consideration were the same thing.

"And what's the room behind the garden?" she asked, pointing.

"Huh?"

"I heard a door slam behind the garden."

"Supply closet," Errol spat out.

"I have to pee," I said, raising my hand. "May I be excused to pee?"

"No, you may not."

"I have to go too," Chantal said, pressing my arm to her side. "Harold, can we have the hall pass?"

"Oh, can we, Harold? Please?"

She pouted. Then I pouted.

Errol begrudgingly gestured down the hall opposite the meditation room. But he couldn't very well follow us into the stalls. Instead, he watched for as long as he could, like a parent waiting to give his children over to a yellow bus. I heard him dart back into the interrogation room when our backs were turned, presumably to find Vadis. Or hide any open files on my exes. It was sloppy for Clive to have brought Chantal here, having lied to her about what this place was, and then leave her unattended.

I'd never pissed in the Golconda before but I was not surprised to see the bathroom was impeccably designed with tiles artfully splashed on the floor in pomegranate bursts. The wallpaper had zebras floating across it, and a communal sink, a trough framed by vases filled with birds of paradise. Chantal placed her phone on the ledge beneath the mirror. So many followers and invitations, so much fabulous ease, were just a password away. As we washed our hands, I felt the need to scrub harder and longer than her, to lather my fore-arms with soap, thereby subliminally transmitting an air of superiority.

As we left, I suggested a shortcut back and told her to follow me. She tittered with delight. We rounded the hall behind the elevator and scuttled past it. I could still see through the glass, but the brass wheels, frozen in place, impeded my vision. I hoped the same was true for Errol, who I could just make out, pacing in the atrium, waiting for us to return. I took Chantal's hand, crouched down, and rushed past him.

Finally, I thought.

No one seemed to have a problem explaining to me, in unsolicited detail, how the technical portion of the program worked, how the Golconda were delving into my life, moving people around like chess pieces. It was the meditative portion—what the members were actually doing when they came here—that remained a haze. Did all these people really just come here to sit and think about me because Clive had convinced them to? It was time to find out.

But behind the garden was just a curved wall, covered in white wallpaper with a silver bar pattern, like a minimalist interpretation of the Magritte painting. There was no sign of a door. And yet both Chantal and I had heard the sound of a door. This was confounding to me but completely logical to Chantal.

"Ha!" she exclaimed, as if the wallpaper had told her a joke. "Clive really does think of everything."

She pressed on one of the silver bars, which, as it turned out, was the door handle, and pulled the door open.

"We have the same thing in our guest bathroom. It drives the housekeeper insane."

I let Chantal go first while I kept a lookout. She leaned her head in at the same pace Rocket liked to employ while stalking a toy mouse. I could tell it was bright behind the door, because Chantal squinted. I strained to hear oms, but all I caught was the hum of an air-conditioning unit. I did, however, see the edge of a piece of furniture in the corner, what looked like a white duvet cover on the corner of a bed.

That's all I got before Clive pushed the door into our faces and slammed it.

"Babe!" Chantal scolded. "You nearly took my skin off."

Clive and I both flinched at the specificity of the image. Standing beside him was a scowling Vadis. His *heavy*.

Clive apologized for disappearing. He was uncharacteristically unkempt. His bright eyes were bloodshot, half-moons of overworked skin beneath them, his five o'clock shadow looking as if it'd been there since 4 a.m. He clearly thought that he would be at Chantal's side, but something had kept him preoccupied. His expression was familiar. I'd seen it when I caught him on the phone in the atrium the other night and the morning, years ago, when he explained that he could no longer keep the magazine on life support. It would die no matter what he did.

"That's okay," Chantal said, adding, coyly, "So what's behind Door Number One?"

Clive offered a half-coherent explanation about logistics that were causing him grief. Something about how you should never put your fate in other people's hands when they have their wallet in yours. I could tell he was lying about something. But Chantal dropped it. Just like that, she turned a dewy cheek. I could see what it was he saw in her. She knew when to tease him, when to compliment him, how to parse out her own upset so that he listened when a crisis arose but never felt the burden of girlfriend maintenance. I had no faucet like that, not with Clive, not with Boots, not with anyone. It was a point of pride. It had also never gotten me what I wanted, not once.

As we walked back toward the entrance, Vadis feigning interest as Chantal explained how she lost followers every time she appeared to be "taken," Clive hung back with me and whispered.

"Who'd you see?"

"Knox."

"The guy who decked you?"

"That's Phillip."

"I always liked Phillip."

"You would. Knox is the librettist with mommy issues."

"Oh, right. We won an ASME for that issue."

"Clive."

"Anyway, we have a teensy problem. But maybe it's a good problem. And maybe not so teensy. Entirely up to you."

"You say 'free will' and I swear to God, I will slap you in a synagogue."

"I'm getting some pushback from a couple of key investors."

"What's their problem? Aside from a stunning lack of moral instinct."

"I—we—may have bitten off a *tad* more funding than we're prepared to chew on the projected timeline, so we need to press pause before we can explore another round of packages."

"What do you need rounds of funding for?"

He arched his back like he wanted to crack it.

"They just want to see more proof that this is working.

Money people have no vision, you know this. You thought the magazine biz was bad? Try the real world."

"I never thought it was a 'biz.'"

"Anyway. The idea was that the Classic would be like a man blizzard. Like the painting. Your life imitating art. An exquisite corpse of sorts."

"A corpse of sorts?"

"But we gotta step on it a bit. Or step off it, rather. We're gonna have time for exactly one more subject."

"What does that mean?"

"Only one more Lola lovah!"

Clive started to strut down the hall, calling after Chantal. But I lunged for him, grabbing at his jacket. He moved like he was shaking off a beggar, surveying the material for signs of disruption.

"Clive!"

"I thought you'd be relieved. You're not even part of this, remember?"

"I—I am relieved. I just thought the point of this was that I was supposed to have time to come to terms with the past. What if I'm not, like, cooked? What if it, I don't know, *grows back*?"

"I don't know what to tell you. Cook faster? You want to be done before your fiancé gets back. Which is when?"

"Two days from now."

"Well, my advice would be to take a night off anyway. Your package is almost complete. And you don't look so good."

Did I feel the completeness of my package? I planned to tell Boots about approximately none of this, to put it in a box as Willis had done with me and as I had done with the ephemera of every single man I'd ever dated. I could do it. I could lie about these weeks for the rest of my life, about how they'd made my head spin and only managed to confuse me more than I was before I started. I envisioned myself as a ballerina on a stage in the moments after a performance; her chest moves like a hummingbird but she conceals all other evidence of her effort.

"It's not my fault," Clive continued, "that you've dated, like, a billion people."

"Sometimes I think it is."

He looked wounded. Clive's eyes inspired an assumption of soulfulness the same way the weight of his hand on a shoulder gave off an air of empathy. But these were physical traits that had little to do with his actual personality.

"You can be a real piece of shit, you know that?"

"And yet," he said. "And yet."

Chantal stopped ahead of us. She called to Clive, waving her phone in the air like a flare. A car was waiting for them outside so we all filed out, gingerly, through the rotted chamber of the lobby. The atmosphere made it feel like we were a team, but we were a team only from here to the door. Chantal tiptoed past her bottle of coconut water but did not pick it up. Vadis and I watched her fold herself into the car, tucking the light load of her legs inside while Clive went around.

"You can always pull out," he yelled, his head poking over the opposite side of the car. "Free will!"

Then he mimed punching himself in the face.

Vadis and I kept standing there, as if seeing them off on a steamship. Their brake lights stuttered through traffic and disappeared.

Who had I forgotten about? Who was coming? I felt exposed as I had not before. Then I realized it was because I *was* exposed. My left hand was bare. I lifted the hand to examine it, front and back, as if one side would produce a better result than the other. I rubbed my thumb against the base of my ring finger, back and forth like a cricket, trying to wrap my head around what I wasn't seeing. *Whose finger is that?*

"Vadis," I said. "My ring."

My hand was shaking, the adjoining fingers in a state of sympathy shock.

"What? Oh my God."

She grabbed my hand but I pried it away. I wanted an unobstructed view in case the ring magically returned, as if I could make it appear if I concentrated hard enough. Or maybe, if the members of the Golconda concentrated hard enough, they could will it back onto my hand.

"Inside," I mumbled, tourniqueting one hand with the other.

"Okay," Vadis said. "It's okay. Remain calm. We'll look for it when we go back in. God, I hope you didn't lose it in the fucking vestibule."

I visualized us shining our lights over the floor, resting them on some rat with its snout jammed into the band. We probably wouldn't be able to spot it even then, the stone was so dull.

"Don't worry, Lola, we'll find it."

This was the Vadis I loved. Emergency Vadis. Your one phone call from a Thai prison. Much as I appreciated her re-assurances, I knew we would never find it. All of Clive's aco-lytes and all of Clive's investors could not put the ring and me back together again. Because I remembered now: I'd heard the tinkle of the thing going down the drain as I washed my hands. It was all that goddamn soap. Foiled by hygiene. In the moment, I assumed the sound was coming from farther down the trough, from one of Chantal's bracelets banging against the faucet as she shared her thrill at seeing *Hamlet*, a play "translated from the Danish." Shakespeare and Soren Jørgensen could have a grave-rolling contest.

"What do we do?" I asked Vadis, beside myself.

"We call a twenty-four-hour plumber. We see if they can snake the pipes or whatever the reverse of that is. Suck the pipes? Blow the pipes? Maybe it got stuck like Baby Jessica."

"A ring is smaller than a baby," I said, a revelation.

"Here, I'll look one up. See? Here's one with 'lightning fast' response time. What's quicker than lightning?"

"Light."

"Lola, on the off chance we don't find it, it was an accident. He'll forgive you. I mean, I forgive you already! And sorry but . . . must I be the one to say what we're all thinking?"

"What are we all thinking?"

"It wasn't *hideous* hideous, but . . ."

"He's *not* going to mind. That's the problem. He won't mind and it will be easy to say it fell down a sink. The sink at a restaurant, our own sink, it really won't matter. It's insured and he'll never know how strange it is that it fell off *now*, and he won't know that I'm bad and he's good and I'm a liar and he's not and he's healthy in the head and I'm sick in the head. And it wasn't *hideous*."

"Isn't hideous. It's not gone yet."

I leaned against the doors and started to cry. This object that had felt so peculiar on my body for so long seemed, without question, like the most beautiful of its kind.

13

I held my arm above my head in the ceaseless glow of our bedroom, moving my bare hand through the morning air as if through water. I couldn't sleep. I felt numb. A 24-hour plumber did, indeed, arrive at the scene. Not at lightning speed, but within two cigarettes and a whiskey soda from the bar down the street. But our hopes of him unscrewing the pipes were quickly dashed. The building was too old, the pipes too embedded. There was no way to address the problem in isolation; he'd have to rip out half the wall. As Vadis and I escorted him out, tipping him for this late-night evaluation, my legs drifted beneath me. I offered him a coffee. He looked at his watch, then again at me.

In the moment, I was devastated by the loss of the ring. I felt its closeness, like it could so easily not have happened. This was what I kept repeating to Vadis, a broken incantation, a spell that wouldn't cast. But during the long walk home, I accepted the course of events, converting them to memory. The ring had fallen into a time and place marked by surrealness, a time and place that I had difficulty delineating as "the present," so that now the loss of the ring felt as if it had happened to someone else.

Would I have been this numb if Boots were here, lying beside me? I missed him but my brain was too crowded for the missing to take root. He floated through my mind like a disembodied head.

Regardless of his motivations, I *had* hoped that Clive was right this whole time. I thought perhaps seeing these men might cure me of my addiction to them in the same way I suspected chain-smoking a carton of cigarettes might cure me of ever wanting another. Instead, years of unsatisfied curiosity had rotted into further obsession. This is how addiction works, I thought. Like a houseguest. It does not break in; it is invited. There is no announcement of when your old impulses roll over to form new ones. Suitcases are exploded, toilet paper rolls denuded. One day your spatula is put back in the wrong drawer and you think "that's weird" and the next all the paint has been stripped from the walls and you think absolutely nothing at all.

I got up from bed, disturbing the cat, whose look of betrayal was apparent. Then I went to the hall closet and returned with my box of mementos, plopping it down between my legs, a girl showing off her sticker collection to no one. I started unfolding letters, their creases stiff from being pressed for so long. I didn't bother turning on the light, but I also didn't need to read them. I had them memorized, down to the syntax. There were NBA ticket stubs from Cooper and letters from Knox, written on airmail paper. There were drawings of animals meant to represent me and their artist, Jonathan. There were all manner of postcards scrawled from road trips or purloined from restaurants, filched cocktail napkins with flirty word games inked into the grain. There was Howard's "please cum?" and the note from Phillip, still hoping I was well after all these years.

I needed to see these men because I'd kept the evidence and I'd kept the evidence because I needed to see these men.

A conundrum.

I put the letters back delicately, individually, like court documents. But as I did, out slid something thick and square, a curious object. It poked my thigh as it fell. I turned it around in my fingers, pressing at corners to make the folder open. Any denial I might have experienced about its provenance was cleared up when I reached inside and extracted a piece of carbon paper. It drooped as I held it up to the light of the window. The bowler hat. The oculus. I looked at the contents of the box. Then at the carbon paper again. Back and forth, back and forth, an uneasy sensation rising within me.

I tried to work backward. Clive had started the Golconda when the magazine folded. He had a penchant for putting the cart before the horse, which meant he probably printed business cards before he did anything else. Which meant an ex had sent me the card a long time ago, slipped it into an envelope or jacket pocket on purpose or by accident, and I hadn't noticed. Because I wouldn't. Because it looked blank to the naked eye.

One of these men knew this was coming.

"But who?" I asked the tidy pile of my life.

The tidy pile of my life did not respond.

14

And then the shelf came down. Because apparently my physical world was hell-bent on crumbling at pace with my mental one. It was the one with the majority of Boots's creations, his personal island of misfit toys. I don't know what made it come down but it was the middle of the night and I woke to the sound of glass smashing and the sensation of the cat's claws digging into my forearm. I padded out to the hallway, swept up what I could of the glass, and dumped it into the trash. For a moment, when I woke again the next morning, I thought I'd dreamed it. But then I went out to survey the damage. Some of what broke were samples, pitchers with handles too thin for their jugs. But, in addition to the little Medusa sculptures and the vases with the frosty coloring, the shelf had taken two bites out of the wall. I stared at the stillness of the wreckage, those holes like misshapen eyes. I could not guess if the news of the lost ring would soften the blow about the shelf or the other way around. This, too, felt like something I should know. Something a different girlfriend would know.

Either way, this would require more than spackle, more than our super nodding at the problem and never returning. There was only one person for this job—the same one who'd convinced himself that manual labor was an act of social revolution.

"*Bonkers*," Zach said, admiring the craters. "It's like you sat on it."

"Yeah, but I didn't."

"But it looks like you did."

"Can I give you fifty bucks to make it look like I didn't?"

He knocked on the wall, putting his ear to it.

"I think you're supposed to do that to the floor. If you want to hear a heartbeat."

"This is plaster," he said, as if the wall had tried to put one over on him. "If you don't get the right brackets, it will rip out again. It's a wall problem, not a shelf problem."

Zach had to spend the rest of the day running errands that struck me as atrocious (someone had paid him to drive their car to the airport, park it, and come back to the city by subway), but he returned that evening, drill in hand. Meanwhile, I'd gone to a bourgeois décor store on my lunch break. I wanted adult shelves for an adult life. Shelves for people who refer to blankets as "throws." I also had the idea that an upgrade might help when Boots saw what had happened. At the store, a salesgirl in a green apron waited for me to make a decision, tapping her fingers on the display as Vadis did. What research had concluded that all salespeople should appear on the verge of grilling? I sent Zach pictures.

He had warned me he might be late, that I was being squeezed in between more lucrative gigs, but he was right on time. He'd also showered and applied cologne. I felt for him because I knew none of this was for my benefit. I was a transitive property, a messenger meant to report on Zach's busy schedule, on how well he was doing. If Zach ever actually saw Vadis for who she really was, not just as a woman to be conquered or convinced, he would know the way to earn her respect was to not shower at all. Or, better yet, not show up at all.

He would never debase himself by asking me direct questions about her. Instead, standing on my stepladder, eyes on the bubble in his level, he circled the topic of Vadis. We all had such different lives now, huh? Long time, no staff meetings. Long time, no free lunches. Say, while we're on the subject: Did I find Vadis's Instagram feed irritatingly curated? Had I ever asked myself who, exactly, was taking all these photos? It must bother her boyfriend to have to do it.

"She doesn't have a boyfriend."

"Oh, no?"

"No, Zach. She's not a boyfriend person."

"So every photo is taken by a different dude?!"

I did not want to get involved. Even if I did, I did not have a live feed of Vadis's heart. Sensing a dead end, Zach moved on to an even hotter topic: Clive. Since there would be no conflating Zach's criticism of Clive with unrequited desire, he poured all his pent-up Vadis frustration into trashing our former boss. The dilettante. The philistine. The God complex. That age-inappropriate hair.

"Jesus. What did Clive ever do to you but employ you?"

"What did Clive do to *you*? You're my safe space on this matter. Why are you so loyal to him all of a sudden?"

"I'm not. Believe me, I'm not."

"Well, it would take me too long to run you through the *list* of Clive Glenn offenses. I have a lot of grievances. But off the top of my head, he just hired some art company to hang photographs in his apartment after *explicitly* indicating that he would ask me to do it."

"Explicit indication?"

"He practically sent me a check."

"Was this at dinner? He was drunk."

"Irrelevant. He's a fucking turncoat."

I would've thought Zach would be repulsed by the idea of doing manual labor for Clive. But he liked the idea that it would make Clive reflect on how his wealth had forced him to put his ill-gotten spoils in the hands of the proletariat. He liked the idea of Clive being at the mercy of his drill bits.

"I think you're giving him too much credit."

"It's classic Clive," Zach said with a snort. "Trust me, I know *exactly* how that guy works."

I wanted to hug his waist. Or kick him off the stepladder. It wasn't that everything Zach knew about Clive was wrong so much as it was more right than he could ever conceive. But why was I keeping Clive's secrets for him? There was a time when loyalty to Clive was loyalty to myself. That's how it was for Errol and Jin and "Barry" and all of Clive's followers. It was the effect of his charisma, an effect he still had on Vadis. But for Zach and me, it *was* all a very long time ago.

"Zach," I said, turning a screw between my fingers, "I have a thing to tell you."

He removed a pencil from his mouth.

"Vadis *does* have a boyfriend?"

I could hear him swallow. I had a passing thought of the NDA. It covered any set of human ears, but I knew it was meant for journalists. Real journalists. I hadn't been one of those in a long time and neither had Zach.

"No."

"You're pregnant?"

"No."

"I'm pregnant?"

"No."

"Then what?"

"I'm gonna need you to come down first."

The cat, usually skittish with strangers, recognized an immobile slab of flesh in the form of Zach's lap. He hadn't moved in an hour and neither had she. I wondered if she would do this if I ever died on the sofa. Boots would be out of town on business and she would just park it on my lap until I went cold. Zach absentmindedly petted her as I explained everything. He made a couple of faces indicating he'd felt left out, but he swallowed his comments. Then he gazed into the kitchen like he was counting the tiles. On the counter were a couple of Asian pears that I'd been saving, resting in squishy white netting. I wondered if I should offer him a pear.

"How's the coffee?" he asked.

"You know? I've never had the coffee."

"Maybe there's something in it."

"Weirdly, I wish that were true. It would simplify things."

"I feel like you're making this up."

"I'm not."

"It sounds deranged."

"Wine? Should I get wine? It has cork shards in it."

"So these guys, they'll just be going about their lives and feel compelled to visit Chinatown?"

"It's happening," I said. "It's already happened. According to Clive, I have one more."

"It's like *Field of Dreams* except instead of baseball, it's your vagina."

"People will come, Ray."

"People will motherfucking come," he agreed, shaking his head.

"Whiskey?"

"They told you it's social media and meditation?"

"Among other things. Do you know what astral projection is?"

"I know it's not real," he said, puzzling out the situation. "There has to be a practical answer to this. They're probably paying these dudes. Or blackmailing them with spyware. Seems like they're set up for it."

It wasn't out of the realm of possibility, but Clive seemed too committed to the purity of his endeavor. Buried underneath the layers of jargon and superiority was passion. It seemed unlikely that he would cheat with something as pedestrian as a computer hack. I showed Zach one of the cards.

"What a waste of money," he said, holding the carbon paper up to the light.

"That's nothing."

"This is some *Inception* shit."

"Even if the energy stuff is a placebo," I offered, "the subliminal messaging is real. I've watched it happen. The social media. The search engine results. The research. Did I tell you they have a guy working for them who can mess with the algorithms on targeted ads? And private investigators? Like former Mossad, maybe, I have no idea."

"I can't believe how much money that guy has," Zach said.

"Yeah," I said, "Clive's rich."

"Not rich. Wealthy. He doesn't need to start a cult."

"It's not a cult. Not in the traditional sense."

"Are you sure?"

"No, not really."

"I can't believe how much money that guy has!"

Zach slapped the arm of the sofa. I knew the exclusivity would trip him up, that I would have to listen to him poke around about the business model before we could get to the more pressing problem: my sanity.

"How much money they all have," I said, throwing a little gasoline on the fire. "Apparently, he's not paying anyone. And no one seems to think this is a problem. Including your girlfriend. Zach, everyone *bows* to him."

"Everyone?" he asked, a pitchy little ski jump in his throat.

"Everyone."

"Jesus. It's like a new age pyramid scheme. And all this for closure?"

"That's the magic word," I said.

He pulled the zipper up and down over the bent seam of his hoodie.

"Well . . . do you feel closed?"

I shook my head. It was turning dark outside, the contrast between architecture and sky becoming less pronounced as the sun slipped between buildings. The cat jumped off Zach's lap, looked at us as if we were fully aware of our crime, and left the room. I was waiting for Zach to say something else.

"I guess I can see how it would be freeing," he spoke, still zipping, "to think of one's exes without also thinking of them dead."

"That's a lovely sentiment."

"And who knows? Maybe this process can tell you what's wrong with you."

"I'm punishing, judgmental, and indecisive. Oh, and crotchety. Or had you not heard?"

"I mean you as in *anyone*. Everyone has had that inkling, right? Like for some reason you are just not meant to pair. And on your good days, you think, hey, it's because my heart is too big to get through anyone's tunnel. And on your bad days, you think it's because my heart is this tiny petrified piece of shit and it passes through other people like a kidney stone. Like it's either nothing or it causes excruciating pain."

"Zach, I've never heard you be this emotional."

"Depression is an emotion."

"Maybe you just need to get laid."

"So says the town bicycle. Can I come with you tomorrow night?"

He brushed wall dust and cat hair from his pants. This had not occurred to me, the idea of bringing a friend.

"I worry it might throw the whole thing off-balance. Not that you couldn't just be in the neighborhood. It's a free country. And not that I *care*—"

"Oh, I get it," he said. "You want to be alone with this last guy. What if he sucks?"

"He will. Everyone kind of sucks. It's human nature."

Zach nodded. Now I was speaking his language. He touched the faded red splotch on the sofa from when Vadis had sprayed wine on it, walking his fingers along the spots.

"And what are you going to do about that?" he asked, nodding at a Polaroid of me and Boots stuck to the fridge.

It was from last Halloween. Vadis had gotten the camera for parties. Zach is in the background, looking gravely bored, wearing all black, sunglasses, and an "I ♥ Venice" T-shirt. He was a Venetian blind. Vadis said the costume was insensitive, which I agreed with until she tacked on that it was "like blackface for the disabled," which I encouraged her never to say again ever. Boots and I are dressed as Mr. and Mrs. Peanut. Mrs. Peanut is distinguishable from Mr. Peanut because of her synthetic eyelashes and her peanut-can purse.

"Have you told him?"

"Are you out of your mind?"

"I'm still getting over the fact that Vadis is involved. She's too smart for this."

I snorted.

"She's *your* friend," he said.

"Yeah, well. With friends like these—"

"Come on, I really want to see the inside of Clive's cult."

"Zach. *I* can barely see it. There's no easy way in. I get escorted everywhere. There's an alleged meditation room I've never seen, and Clive is extra shady about it. I don't know the code to the door. Neither of us is in any shape to dangle the other from a rooftop."

"Speak for yourself," he said, patting his belly.

When men wanted to cry "fat," they touched their stomachs. When women wanted to cry "fat," they touched their thighs, arms, waists, butts, cheeks, and chins. At least we liked variety. No one could take that away from us.

"Just tell me which shul," he said.

"I don't know the name. Isn't that funny? I don't know the name."

"But you know where it is."

"It's not, like, open. And you're not going to break into a synagogue. You're Jewish."

"It's not a synagogue. Not anymore. And you're Jewish, too."

"Yeah, but you're *Jewish* Jewish. You read Aramaic; I have heard of Aramaic. Barely. Fifty-fifty language/perfume, you know?"

"Clive fucking Glenn is getting *wealthier* off your back and you're not even curious as to how?"

"I was curious," I said, rubbing my eyes, "really curious. Now I'm just, I don't know, benumbed."

My landline rarely rang at work. Our desk phones were vestigial tails, demoted to the world's most cumbersome in-house walkie-talkie system. It was therefore jarring to hear that doctor's-office *brrrring* before 10 a.m., before half the *Radio New York* staff had meandered in. My first thought was: Fire. But it was only the security desk, announcing that "a Zach Goldberg" was here to see me.

"Just the one?"

"Should we send him up?"

"Sure, thanks."

The security guard moved the speaker away from his mouth and asked Zach to show his photo ID. I could faintly hear some kind of back-and-forth.

"He doesn't have any identification."

"Okay," I said. "I'll come down."

I was looking forward to telling Zach he was in league with Vadis with the surprise drop-bys. But when I walked through a turnstile in the lobby, its metal arms saluting me, I could see that Zach did not need his day made. He was already beaming like an idiot.

"Why do you not have ID?"

"You should never carry ID. The Stasi taught me that."

"You, personally?"

"First, you walk around with a license, next thing you know, you think it's normal to be asked for your papers, and

next thing you know, you're spitting in a plastic tube, volunteering your DNA to a government website."

"It's too early for this. To what do I owe this corporate
sojourn?"

He pulled me onto a concrete bench with him.

"I have a present for you," he whispered, as if the security
guards cared.

He opened the flap of his messenger bag, an off-brand
version of the one Amos had. I thought about how much this
detail would piss Zach off. Clive having fancy things made
Zach feel better about himself, but Amos having fancy things
meant that there was a guy out there who had managed to
monetize the same personality without the world thinking
less of him for it.

"Et voilà," he said, handing me a piece of paper.

It was a photocopy, grainy in the middle from where the
bookbinding had sprung away from the glass. At the top were
a series of numbered descriptors: (1) double nave, (2) southern
vestibule, (3) sanctuary, (4) main holy hall, (5) western men's
annex, (6) women's section, (7) women's entrance hall. Beneath these was a floor plan for Congregation Beth Shalom
on the Lower East Side. The stained glass window looked
like a camera shutter.

A few months ago, I had a writer pitch me a story on
"reincarnated New York spaces," on the city's cathedrals-
turned-condos. The most famous was the Limelight, which
had undergone several heart transplants over the years—from
Catholic Church, to Andy Warhol's playground, to purveyor
of cheap gifts, to high-end gym. The writer encouraged me to
imagine barbells resting where empty ketamine bottles once
rolled, the spirit of tinsel in the sauna. That space in particular
would probably turn over yet again, she said, before she pressed

"send." My initial reaction to her pitch went something like: What's so revolutionary about buildings that have been other buildings? But I wound up assigning the story anyway. *Radio New York* was in no position to kick hyperlocal clickbait out of bed.

"Where did you get this?"

"Google."

"Wow."

"No, not *Google*," he said, snatching the paper back, punishment for believing him. "I looked up all shuls below Fourteenth Street, and there were two that had changed hands in the past decade, so then I called up the Department of Buildings to see if either one had applied for construction permits. Then I went to the public domain collections and then the Jewish Museum. They sent me to the Tenement Museum, which keeps records of, like, a ten-block radius. Let me tell you, everyone's incompetent, no one knows who has what, and those who *do* know treat you like you're planning on blowing up whatever you find because why else would you be asking."

"You do kind of have 'anarchist face,'" I said, waving around his head. "Also, you need a real job."

He shrugged.

I looked at the map, turning the paper around to get my bearings. I superimposed the soggy Golconda entrance onto the "main holy hall." It was like a satellite picture of Earth, factual but devoid of spirit, devoid of the idea that a human gaze would fill the map from the inside out with experience, that it would test the map's authority against its own. Or like reading a review of a play written by someone who'd seen it with an entirely different cast. The women's section was now the conference room. The coffee machine was in the men's annex. The elevator blocked a sanctuary.

"Look," said Zach, pointing at a series of narrow lines outside the "women's entrance hall."

"What's that?"

"It's a staircase."

I knew of no such staircase. I knew of the hall and its confounding wallpaper, the bane of housekeepers everywhere. I knew of the *visible* staircase. I knew of no secondary snack staircase.

"Are you sure this is the right spot? Maybe all shuls have the same layout."

"You really are a bad Jew. This is it. What do you think?"

He took a half-eaten granola bar from his pocket and started grinning as he masticated the remains.

"Oh, no," I said, pushing the map away from me. "No way."

"I'll take that as a thank-you," he said, pushing it back. "Thank you, Zach, for helping me find a way to crack this capitalist clique that's clearly holding a bunch of definitely illegal files on me and countless men."

"Not *countless*."

Zach shrugged.

"I'm not doing it. I'm not the B-and-E type."

"You don't even know what type you are," he said. "Isn't that the point? That you don't know what you want? Freud said that a man who doubts his own love must doubt every lesser thing."

"Freud thought women were dickless hysterics."

"Irrelevant. Doubt is healthy until it eclipses knowledge."

"Who said that?"

"Me, I say things."

He wasn't wrong. Religion, love, marriage—was there a single belief system to which I subscribed or submitted? What becomes of a person like that, a social heretic who can't even keep a ring on her finger? One thing I did know was that my life was no surrealist painting. That was Clive's life, Clive's mission to bring the unconscious to the surface, to subvert reality. My life was more like a pointillist painting, distinct dots that formed a single image. None of which were meant to be counted, not one by one. None of which were then meant to be seen this close.

Zach was growing peevish and taking it out on the granola bar. Ever since he left my house last night, he'd been sending me texts. It was wrong for these men to remain ignorant of their participation in what amounted to an unregulated clinical trial. As for me? I was no better than a lab rat flinging herself into a vat of acid for the benefit of a pharmaceutical company.

"I'll tell you what I *do* know," I said. "I know I'm the type who doesn't like jail."

"Fine, suit yourself."

For years, Zach had wanted to dissolve the threesome of me and Clive and Vadis as if we were a big bank. If confronted, he'd say he thrived on the idea of being the ostracized one, the reliable narrator, but at the granular level, he only ever wanted to be included. He only ever wanted to be invited into our cult of three, to dive into a conversation without a "who are we talking about?" I'd tried to break ranks for him on multiple occasions, felt it was my responsibility to do so, but the man couldn't last five minutes without misfiring mating dances for Vadis or taking jabs at Clive.

"You barely care about my personal life," I told him. "You want some convoluted Clive vengeance and you're using me to do it. Or using me to get to Vadis. You don't have to break into a building to show her what a big man you are. Just ask her out and see what happens."

"And to think," he gasped, agog, "I came to an office for you."

"I have to get back to work," I said. "I have one night left at the fair before Clive packs up the tents. Boots is home tomorrow night."

I made a gesture of checking the time, consulting my wrist. My naked wrist, naked as it should be. I followed it to my naked finger, naked as it shouldn't be.

Zach got up, leaving the map on the bench.

"I could have just emailed this to you," he said, walking toward the entrance, raising his voice. "And don't talk to me about legality because we both know Clive wouldn't *arrest* you. He needs you. Maybe I am using you, but they're *definitely* using you. I love you like a second cousin, Lola, but you've always been a deputy for that man's agenda!"

The security guard looked up like a startled wolf cub.

"I've come to terms with it!" I shouted, passing back through the turnstiles.

15

From the start, Clive had said that the more I participated in the experiment, the more effective the Golconda would be. *You'll find coincidences pick up naturally.* He also said the system *itself* would grow stronger. It would train itself to herd cats, to see which bait worked and which did not, thus expanding the scope of the Golconda. *Chinatown first, then the rest of Manhattan, then the whole city, then the whole world.* If I doubted this before, I believed it now. Because for its grand finale, it had gone international.

It took me a moment to register Pierre. He was sitting on a low stoop, a lip of concrete at the weary tip of East Broadway, where the bustle of the preceding blocks petered out. He was reading a book with the jacket removed, sitting with his feet too far out into the sidewalk, disheveled and louche. Like deposed royalty. He was drinking from a lidless coffee as if he were looking out over the Luxembourg Gardens.

You know who gets to drink coffee at nonsense hours? I thought. The French.

An electronic sign flashed above Pierre's head, advertising cell phone repairs. He sat in between rows of cheap luggage wrapped in plastic. I could tell he was smoking, even from a distance, by the clawlike way he turned the pages. More than just casually Parisian, Pierre detested and adored Paris in direct opposition to the way Americans detested and adored Paris. He also pretended never to have heard of major cities in Normandy. I'd quit smoking after Amos, but Pierre got me back at it the night we met.

Which was the same night I met Boots. It was Pierre's surprise party.

Since then, Pierre had moved back to Paris and married a woman he'd just started seeing when we met. I spoke to her in passing at his party, while we were waiting for the bathroom. She was Ethiopian and French, raised in Belgium and London, and she now ran a theater company for at-risk teenagers in the Paris suburbs (it was a long wait for the bathroom). She wore a campaign-style button with a picture of baby Pierre pressed into it, a bowl of which was available at the door. For a while after the party, Pierre and his then-girlfriend had been one of my preferred social media pit stops. They spent a lot of time outdoors, kissing each other's cheeks, angling their phones for optimal sun flare. If Willis's online presence had made me feel alienated, Pierre's had made me feel almost familial. I used to worry when she didn't appear in photos for a prolonged period of time. Had she been written out of his life? Had she fallen out of love or into a canal? Maybe Pierre had cheated on her. After all, there'd been a moment when I felt *I* could've usurped her sun flare.

Halfway through the party, Boots had volunteered to go on an ice run, and I stepped onto the balcony to get some air. Pierre was already out there, looking as if he'd been born on the balcony and was fated to stay on it. But when I slid the door shut, trapping the noise of the festivities behind me, he looked up. He didn't want a surprise party, he said. Like most people, he didn't like surprises, and "like most men, I don't love the attention." He offered me a cigarette as he said this, so I took it instead of arguing. He lit it for me, cupping his hands close to my face. There were other people on the balcony with us, but they were low on wine and so they ducked back inside.

Pierre and I chatted about the obvious differences between New York and Paris, both of us pretending they were more revelatory than they were. He connected himself to the woman I'd met while waiting for the bathroom with a literal flick of the wrist, a hand gesture indicating that no, he had not come here alone but yes, he was still free to go.

He asked me if I was with Boots, and I explained that we'd only met a few hours prior. As I did, I looked over my shoulder to make sure he hadn't come back yet. It was because of the cigarette. I didn't want Boots to see me smoking.

"So we're both taken," Pierre reflected.

"I'm not taken," I said, even though I was eagerly awaiting Boots's return. "I don't know him yet."

"Ah, you see? But you're already *planning* to know him. You can't fool me, I saw you two. You are taken."

He wagged his finger at me like I'd been caught, a romantic unmasked. But I was only hedging because I knew better than to jinx whatever might happen with Boots by agreeing with Pierre. I had fallen in lust with enough men over the years and, by my count, not one of them was standing on this balcony with me right now. Pierre thought he was sharing a joke with a fellow slave to seduction, but he was only engaged with someone who'd had a harder time making relationships stick than a scruffy Frenchman for whom people threw surprise parties.

"It's a shame you're so taken," he said, "because you have my baby."

He smirked and pointed at my lapel. I, too, had baby Pierre pinned to my chest.

"Why do I sense you're trying to get me to kiss you?" I asked.

I wanted to make him uncomfortable right back, to bend the tenor of the conversation. Pierre raised an eyebrow, roused by my directness.

"How do you do that?"

"Kiss women on balconies?"

"No, the one eyebrow thing."

"It's muscle memory," he said. "You must take control of your face."

"You're not going to kiss me on a balcony," I decided. "It's a cliché."

"You're pronouncing that wrong."

"Oh, who cares?" I said, rolling my eyes.

"I care. It's my birthday."

Then he pulled me away from the door and into a breeze-less dark corner, sheltered from view. Sheltered from relevant view. The people in the apartment complex across the way could make up any story they liked about us, just like we could make up any story we liked about each other. Was this not the point of living in New York? He tugged at my lip, pulling my back toward his waist with each audible exhale. We broke away at the same time, cutting the mood with laughter. It's impossible to kiss someone if you're both grinning. Like sneezing with your eyes open.

"Je m'appelle Lola."

"You don't speak French, Lola. But you do have a charming name. Now, shall we go back inside and begin our lives?"

I leaned back and turned my neck as far as it would go until I could see the party, wall to wall. Pierre's girlfriend was dancing, arms in the air, nails grazing the low ceiling, hips pivoting. Boots, meanwhile, had returned with a bag of ice in each fist, choking each one by its neck. I felt my whole body warm upon seeing him. He was talking to people with whom he'd not yet caught up because he'd devoted the first half of his evening to me. Now he was sneaking glances around the living room, searching for me the way Jonathan and I used to do in college. By the time he saw me, Pierre and I had gone our separate ways, into separate pods of conversation. How enchanting it was, to be the transparent source of someone else's relief, of their unmarked joy. *Go back inside and begin our lives.* Why not? Really, why not?

Now I was engaged and Pierre was married.

I approached him slowly, observing his mannerisms. Our conversation and corresponding kiss had meant something to him too. Clearly, it had. When I got within a few feet of him, close enough to see the gray in his stubble, he looked up at me with those massive brown eyes that I'd noticed in the shadows of the balcony. The same nose I'd pressed with mine, gently boxing his cartilage.

But something was off. Pierre's expression was different than all the others. He looked neither mystified nor nervous nor happy to see me. He looked . . . relieved. He held his book to his side, kissed me on both cheeks, and said:

"What took you so long, chérie?"

I felt as though the air were being sucked downward, as if the ground itself was gasping through its grates. The street went silent.

"I knew I would see you today," he went on. "I've been feeling it ever since we landed. My wife, she was invited to a theater festival here and so, last minute, I came too. I have always been a little bit *psychique*."

He grinned, his teeth buttery yellow from smoke. I found myself unable to look at him, not unlike the way one holds up one's fingers to block the sun in order to look at the sun.

"And so I went for a walk," he continued, "and I thought to myself, I will sit here and I will wait and if Lola From My Party does not appear before it gets dark, I will go. But here you are! Phenomenal. Tell me, are you still in love with the tall man?"

"He *is* tall, isn't he?" I asked, laughing a disproportionately long time.

When I was through, I held Pierre's face lightly in my hands. Then I kissed him on the mouth. Is this how I tasted after I smoked only half a cigarette, even after I'd brushed my teeth? Boots never said a word about it. Pierre kissed me back, but the reality of his situation put a stop to it. He pinched his bottom lip, folding it.

"Okay," he said, resuming smiling. "Well, okay. I suppose this is what we do. We have a perfect record!"

"I'm so sorry."

"No, it's nothing."

I squeezed my eyes shut as I hugged him as tightly as I could. He was the wrong one to hug. This relative stranger who thought I was crazy, whose body mass was utterly alien to me. I'd spent more time with Barry the barista. Pierre and I had shared only one moment, albeit a significant one. But it was as if I were hugging everyone I'd seen, as if they'd been freeze-dried into a big pill and Pierre had swallowed it.

"Are you okay?"

I could hear the international tone of "how do I leave this interaction?" I shook my head and rubbed my thumb against my unobstructed ring finger. Pierre patted my back, tentative but soothing pats. I either had to go or explain myself, but I couldn't remain like this, a mad American in his midst. I fought the urge to apologize a third time. It's the guilt, I thought, exiting my body.

"I've just been thinking a lot lately of how we lose people."

This was the same casually philosophical tone I'd employed when we were on the balcony, comparing Paris with New York as if no one in the world had done it before.

"Of course," he said, relieved to be speaking in abstractions. "But don't we find them just as often? I found you."

"You did."

Knox used to say that falling in love was like trying to remember something you never knew. The first time I heard him say it, I told him it was beautiful. But when he said it again, a pat piece of poetry thrown into the evaporating pool of our love, I told him that it sounded sad. It meant that love was always out of reach, happiness forever floating on the tip of one's tongue.

After Pierre took his leave, citing jet lag, flinging his blazer over one shoulder, strolling back to his wife, I started, finally, to feel it—the completeness of my package. Something like peace. But then a realization hit me like a dart: I'd never told anyone about Pierre. Not one soul, not even the soul belonging to Vadis. I'd left him out of the story of the night I met Boots because I wanted her, wanted both of us, to focus on the possibility of permanence. This did not include the distraction of a third party, of a mysterious stranger who, because I knew he would remain a mystery, would clobber the reality of Boots. I'd never written about Pierre in a diary or an email or had so much as a text exchange about the man I'd kissed on the balcony. I had no keepsakes of him because there was nothing to keep. Not even the button with his face on it. I hadn't perused his social media accounts in years. There was no list on which Pierre would appear except perhaps for the one I kept on an invisible scroll, curled in my memory.

So how on earth did he get here?

16

I leaned on a strip of brick between stoops, glaring at the building like I wanted to blow it up. I had my arms crossed, as a couple of my exes had done in their headshots, and one foot flat against the wall, as people did in photographs from the '70s. It was strange to think that positions of bodily comfort could be subject to trend. For centuries, men strolled around, lost in thought, both hands clasped behind their backs. Or one hand, palm out. But it didn't matter how I stood—so long as I was out of sight of the Golconda's security cameras.

I called Vadis, who was somewhere inside, and lied. I hadn't seen anyone. I must've run through all my exes already and whoever Clive thought would come simply didn't show. It was an anticlimactic ending but an ending just the same. That was the goal, right? Closure. Progress. She suggested I come by the Golconda anyway, for their version of an exit interview. It was important for their research; Jin would be disappointed. But I couldn't stand the thought of the suction cup on my skin. I told her that two weeks of nightly vigilance had given me a migraine, not to mention a persistent eyelid twitch (true). Clive had more than enough data for his investors. And to seal the lie, an unavoidable truth: Boots would be home in a matter of hours. His flight was in the air. I needed time to gather myself.

Because, at long last, I had made a decision.

I would end it.

A door was closing all right, but it was closing on Boots. In my pocket was a list of reasons why we shouldn't be together. I wrote it out at the office that morning, on a *Radio New York* notepad, which, in practice, struck me as a gratuitous layer of disrespect. It also felt like an immature activity, like I should have written the thing in magenta ink and folded it into a triangle. I had no intention of showing Boots the list. It existed only to steel my nerves for when he said he couldn't believe that I would blow up our lives like this. But he was steady to a fault; he could never surprise me. He was content to the point of incurious, calm to the point of comatose. He was the person I should be able to talk to the most, not the least. I didn't like his friends or his tastes, and he didn't particularly like those things about me either. I was hiding behind him because I didn't feel like being alone anymore, and this was weak and cruel. To top it all off, I'd begun comparing Boots with every man who came before him. As if they were still there for me to choose. As if I were still a choice for them.

He deserved better than to be with a woman who made lists.

I thought of our apartment, of the empty shelves, of the layers of white paint on the door frames and all the altercations that must have occurred beneath them long before we lived there. The joy and the tedium of so many strangers had been painted over so that new strangers could start fresh. It would be painted over again after we moved out.

My phone vibrated. Zach had taken to sending me diatribes about the wealthy circumnavigating landmark laws. Look what they did to the Bowery! Look what they did to Dumbo! They paved a parking lot and put up an even shittier parking lot!

I hear you, I texted back.

This was too curt a missive and triggered a spate of responses:

Wait

Are

You

There

Now?

Answer ME

I ignored him. I was filled with horror for the phone itself, zizzing like a petulant child, horror for the past buried within it. The graveyard of exchanges at my fingertips. I looked at the shape of Zach's texts. The speech bubble had too recently been the purview of comic books. Not enough time had passed between our association of the bubbles with fiction and their transfer to reality. It turned us all into actors, anticipating their lines, reading between them.

I touched my list, pressing down on the paper's edge. In that same pocket was my lighter. If I lit it now, well, at least I could burn the list, too. But before I self-immolated, I needed to know what was in that room.

Because I wasn't allowed. Because I thought I might never see the inside of the Golconda again otherwise. Because Pierre's presence meant the meditation was not total bullshit after all. Because Clive did not need to get rich (so sorry, *wealthy*) using me as raw material. Because the last thing he'd said to me the other night was "free will!"

And because *who was the one with the map*?

And so I watched, waiting to strike. When it got darker, Vadis and Jin left first. Then Errol and a handful of Golconda members, including Amos's editor, Jeannine, carrying a tote bag over each shoulder. Then the two baristas, who shared a furtive kiss on the corner before rounding it. Ten minutes later, Clive emerged, pushing the door closed behind him, cross-referencing his phone screen with the license plate of a black car.

I waited to be sure no one came out or came back. Customers filed in and out of the bodega next door, looking almost embarrassed by their purchases of water or batteries, as if ashamed of addressing a sudden or lazy need. The plastic cat was still on the register, its paw visible from across the street. Perhaps it had not been indiscriminately waving at people, beckoning at random. Perhaps it had been trying to catch my attention this entire time.

I smoked half a cigarette and put it out. Then I pushed off the wall.

There was a dumpster in the alley next to the bodega. That was the hardest part—not the leap onto the fire escape ladder, which was already rust-stuck in a low position, or what to do when I got onto the roof of the building, but the fear that I'd fall into a dumpster filled with freshly severed human heads. Then I'd have to lean into the open necks of the heads in order to get out. Fortunately, the lip of the dumpster was wide enough to support this feline enterprise without requiring a tetanus shot, and inside was only a pile of splintered wood from a construction site. The rest was easier than I'd expected. From the edge of the dumpster, it was a modest leap onto the corroded ladder. As I climbed, I got high enough so that the people below looked to be the size of large dogs. Their dogs looked to be the size of rabbits.

I was not entirely ignored. In the days before social media, the joke about New Yorkers was that they could see someone walking down Broadway with a grand piano strapped to their back and not flinch. But those who spotted me did more than flinch. They took photos. But then they moved on, presuming bad performance art. Which I found insulting.

The roof was concave, its softer parts covered in tar and dotted with ventilation pipes, the tar still sticky from the day's heat. I could see the top of the Golconda's skylight, a glass pyramid coated in grime. A fan pushed a pigeon feather in circles, stuck to one of the blades. I walked over to the brick façade of the Golconda, which I could now touch with my hands. From here, I had two window ledges at my disposal, which were marked on Zach's map. I tried the first window but it was sealed shut, either locked or closed for so many years that the window and its frame were in a common-law marriage. I yanked until my skin went red and the veins in the backs of my hands puffed. But the second window gave after a few minutes of effort, with the whoosh of the frame sliding up on its tracks.

The map showed a small staircase, leading down from the attic into the hall outside what was now the meditation room. How hard could it be, I thought, to find a whole staircase? I held my breath and crawled inside, one leg at a time.

I put both feet on a foldout table beneath the window and hopped down, my shoes leaving indentations in the dust. This space was untouched by Clive's renovations, most likely untouched by his security cameras. I knew, instantly, that he'd never been up here. Mostly, it looked like an attic: old furniture, defunct lamps, cardboard boxes, mousetraps, piles of books. The only difference was that the books were all the same book. And that being here felt more peaceful than being in any other part of the Golconda. Downstairs reminded me of a past I wasn't living up to or a present that evaluated me. The people who used to worship at Congregation Beth Shalom had not been up here, nor had the people who worshipped Clive. This was purgatory. But the one rule of purgatory is that you don't have to go home, but you can't stay here.

I scanned the room, crouching along the perimeter, my eyes adjusting. Then, in the far corner, I saw what I'd come for—my ticket down. There was a square in the floor with a wooden contraption bolted to it. It was a collapsible set of stairs. I grinned. That's why I'd never seen them before. Because they weren't there. I hooked my finger into the loop, pulled as hard as I could, and the stairs creaked down ahead of me, touching down on the marble. I'd never been inside the Golconda when it wasn't brightly lit and somewhat populated, at least without the hum of the espresso machine.

I climbed down, testing each rung to make sure it was fit for human weight. I could go back up. I could always go back up. The air was still, the chandeliers dimmed to the point where their bulbs appeared to glow. They reminded me of the phosphorescent bays in Puerto Rico. I'd been once, with Boots. He insisted on staying on the beach to watch the sunset, and so I let my feet plow into the sand, surveying sandpipers chasing the tide and then the tide chasing them back, while sand fleas devoured us. I didn't want to seem like a bad girlfriend, an unfun girlfriend. Eventually, we scurried back to the hotel before our bites became too many and too painful.

It was an odd sensation, being on this floor with no one in sight. On the one hand, I shouldn't be here. On the other, I felt like a teenager who'd forgotten the keys to her own house. In the dark, I felt along the curved wall outside the meditation room until my fingers touched cold metal. I paused for a moment, listening, scanning the ceiling for any blinking lights. I felt, for the first time in weeks, truly alone.

Then I pushed.

The reality of an image both expands and narrows the imagination. It breathes, inhaling the new understanding and exhaling the old one.

The meditation room was two floors high and divided into the women's entrance hall and the room for Torah study. Moorish arches delineated the space. They were the first things I noticed, the only shapes I could make out, adumbrated by the meager light coming in through a little row of stained glass windows. Beneath them was a wall lined with black binders. I could see the contrast of white strips on them. Labels from a label maker. Probably with the names of men on them. Or Golconda packages. I felt for a light switch, pawing at the wall, but the lights came on before I pressed anything.

I froze, unsure of what I'd done to trigger this flood of electricity. Had I tripped a silent alarm? I squinted. The lights in here were halogen, far less hospitable than the chandeliers. These ones also buzzed.

Then I heard my name.

"Lola."

I was hallucinating.

"Lola."

I was not hallucinating.

"Lola!"

How can I describe the speed with which I turned around? Did I whip or did I send my eyes sideways as they do in horror movies? My only memory is of a man who appeared in the middle of the room. A man with a size and shape as familiar to me as my own.

"Max?" I whispered.

Boots gave me a single wave, like he was brushing an image off a screen.

17

I used to have a recurring daydream about the night I met
Max. I was the one making it recur, which made its frequency less compelling. Still, it had that same vivid remove
from reality that unconscious dreams have. I saw myself on a
film loop, almost getting hit by that bus before Pierre's party.
Each time, I stepped into the street. Each time a different
man yanked me to safety. Whoosh. Yank. Whoosh. Yank.
The hair blows across the face. Whoosh. Yank. The worried
male expressions come into focus, one after the other, panic
followed by heroism. I had the fantasy while in the shower,
while at work, while at the dentist's office. I was ashamed of
the antiquated scenario of it. I am not some helpless woman
who lives in a tower. Should I not be the one yanking myself
to safety?

It's just that sometimes you really need a bus pointed out
to you.

Max looked even taller than I remembered after only two weeks away. And perhaps because we were in a temple, a place where people had come to learn and recite and be reprimanded by God's law, I could feel myself in trouble. Deep trouble. Principal's office trouble. He looked like he was about to eat me.

"Max?" I repeated.

I tried to will my feet to move. *Modern Psychology* once did a sidebar on the oversimplification of dividing a fear response into "fight or flight." This duality left no room for the most common choice: freeze. Most people react to fear with stillness while the heart races and the mind disassociates. They close their eyes and hope the danger passes. Which is what I did. But when I opened my eyes, I was still in this room. Max, stone-faced, walked over to the far wall and returned with two metal folding chairs, which he kicked open.

"When did you get back?"

He looked tired and tense, like he'd just gotten off a flight. He gestured and I sat in the chair across from him.

"That's your question?" he asked.

"It's *a* question. Did you—were you in San Francisco?"

"You want to know if I lied to you? That's cute."

"Boots—"

"Don't. Do not."

"Max! Did Clive kidnap you? He does that kind of thing now."

"Yes, I went to San Francisco," he said, avoiding eye contact. "For two days. I got the contract, incidentally."

"Congratulations."

"Oh, shut up."

I fought to keep my cheeks down. "Shut up" had a long run as the most scandalous phrase available when we were kids, before the full plumage of curse words were introduced.

Now that the lights were on, I could see a platform at the far end of the room with little cubbies, perhaps once used for Hebrew School, now filled with yoga mats, rolled up like Ho Hos. There was also a perfectly made bed and, on the shelf above it, the sculptures Boots had been selling online.

"What in the fuck is going on? Are you the last one?"

"The last one of what? Of the Mohicans?"

"Max."

"I don't know where to begin."

"Maybe start with why you're here. Or how you know of this place. Or how you got in. I'll go first: Me, I scaled a dumpster."

He looked at me as if he were looking straight through me, out the door, out the building. It was the look of someone who wanted to get on a bus and circle the globe until they died. After what felt like a long time, he resumed focus.

"I've *been* here, you idiot. Every night you've been here, I've been here. Every night you've been out, doing God-knows-what with your ex-boyfriends, I've been here. Sometimes alone, mostly alone. Sometimes I order takeout, which sucks because getting in and out of here is a *thing*. Sometimes I sit with these crazy-ass rich freaks in lotus position. They *really* like to meditate. And don't worry, Jin used a fresh suction cup on you."

"What?"

"After she was done with me."

"I feel like I'm having a stroke. You've been *sleeping* here?"

"Clive said it was better if I sleep here."

"God, he's so insane," I said, trying to pry his anger off me.

"It's not so bad. Honestly, it's nice to give my sinuses a break from the cat. I was about to head back to the apartment to meet you because I know tonight's your last night. According to Vadis, at least. Then I heard a thud and there you were. Here you are. Which is how I knew."

"Knew what?"

"That I'm about to get dumped. That's how it works, right? I see you in here, it's bad news for Max. Max is in the past tense now."

"Well, at bare minimum, he's in the third person. So that's not good."

"Nope!" he said, pulling a stick of gum from his pocket and chewing violently.

"I have so many questions."

"You look like a homeless person, by the way."

I wiped the back of my hand against my forehead. My fingers were black from prying open the window. I had attic dust on my face.

"You don't even *like* Clive. You've never liked Clive."

"Lola," he said, snapping, "keep the fuck up. I *hired* Clive."

I felt as if I were above us, that we both were, watching these versions of ourselves, confused and incensed respectively. My major organs were competing to exit through my throat.

"Come again?" I croaked.

"Clive offered to help me and I took him up on it."

"Help you *with what?!*"

He looked around for a place to put the gum, then decided to jam it underneath his seat.

"Max," I scolded reflexively, and he gave me a look as dirty as I'd ever seen.

"A few months ago," he began, splaying his hands on his knees, "I was cleaning out the hall closet and I moved this shoebox. It was heavy so I opened it and it was packed with all these letters and shit. There was this card that played a song, and I thought, huh, maybe this is where Lola stockpiles cards to give to people. My mother does that. But that's when I started reading the letters. Some of them were breakup notes, some of them were nothing—meet me here, see you at eight, nice shoes, let's bang—but you saved them all. And I know women do that. Sorry to be gendered, don't leap down my throat. But you *printed out* emails *from the 90s.* The box was lined with ticket stubs and scrap paper and it was . . . intense. Like hoarding intense."

"I can't believe you went through my stuff."

"Yeah? Call The Hague. Believe me, I have no interest in reading about how some random douchenozzle thought your eyes were like planets, but *you* do. Once I opened that box, it seemed like splitting hairs to suddenly care about your privacy. I don't know, maybe I felt like I'd earned it. Not looking seemed like a convenient morality."

"Like how Julia Roberts won't kiss Richard Gere in *Pretty Woman.*"

"Don't make jokes."

"I wasn't making a joke, I was making an analogy."

"I know we agreed not to talk about our pasts. I know it was my idea. And it's not the box, the box is not the end of the world. It's what the box *represents.* I'm not the moron you think I am. I could sense you pulling back. You nearly went off with that crazy chick from the wedding. Or you wanted to. If I'm honest with myself, and trust me, I've had lots of time to be honest with myself, I've sensed you were a flight risk since the night we met, when I saw you kissing Pierre on the balcony."

"You saw that?"

"And I feel like I've been trying to show you I'm a good fit for you ever since."

"Why didn't you say anything to me?"

"About Pierre?"

"About everything that came after Pierre."

"Maybe I didn't want to rock the boat or see how easily you'd throw me over. I don't know, it's all just very . . . very . . ."

"Nautical."

He nodded and lowered his head. His watch was too big for him, but he centered the face on his wrist anyway, as if it would stay. I imagined what this room looked like when it was full, with dozens of members sitting there with their eyes closed, maybe some with laptops, googling, coding, cracking, manipulating. Like the call center at Esalen in 1969. Max slept alone in this room after they'd all gone.

"So around the same time as the box," he went on, "I get this email from one of my buyers and he wants me to bring him a couple of pieces in person instead of paying for shipping. He bought three and he's downtown so I say okay. And he has me meet him at this annoying fusion restaurant down the street. And I walk in and there's fucking Clive. Then, out of the bathroom, comes my second-favorite person in all the world—"

"Vadis."

"Honestly, you'd been acting so weird, my first instinct was that you were secretly on pills and they wanted to stage an intervention. But then I was like, well, why wouldn't Clive just use his real name?"

"Because he didn't want you telling me you were going to meet him."

"Winner, winner, chicken dinner. Normally, I don't like to give Vadis ammunition but you're kind of the only thing we have in common. So I said something wasn't right with us because it wasn't. Like you weren't *cheating* on me exactly but you were stuck and I couldn't unstick you. Then she turned to Clive, who said, and I will never forget this: 'What if I can unstick her for you, Maxwell?'"

"The exes' pact is not in blood. You could've talked to me."

"I don't particularly like being reminded of your capacity to end things. Haven't you ever asked yourself why I don't like talking about these people? It's because they're chapters so what does that make me? Chapters end, that's what they do. And you could have talked to me, too. At any time."

"That's not fair."

"Isn't it? What were you going to say tonight? Were you going to confess to being half in love with every asshole in this city but the one you're about to marry? Sounds about right. Clive showed me his 'menu.'"

"I saw it too."

"No, you didn't."

"Yes, I completely did."

"Lola," he sighed at the arches, half smiling. "Okay, imagine a Russian nesting doll. I'm the bigger doll around you and Clive is the bigger doll around me. You're 'The Classic,' yeah?"

I nodded.

"I'm 'The Grand Sweep': The chance to get your partner to get over their exes, once and for all, by having them confront and release their ghosts. *That's* the one Clive is testing. We used me and your box to put a list together. It's not rocket science. I mean, it's not *science* science either."

I puffed out my cheeks, sputtering as I exhaled, driving my fingers through my hair. Was this the most romantic or the most psychotic thing anyone had ever done for me? Was there a difference? Max stood like he was preparing to pace but kicked the leg of his chair instead, which squeaked against the floor. He wanted to be physically away from me. He hopped up on the platform and sat on his bed, which was more of a mattress with a lamp beside it, the kind of setup that wanted for a bachelor. Beneath the lamp was the glass hand. I was taken aback by how glad I was to see it again.

"Why would you torture yourself?"

"Because it wasn't supposed to end like this!" he yelled.

"You can't control other people."

"No shit. You should write that down. Did you fuck any of these guys? Don't tell me."

"I did not."

"I told you not to tell me! There's a world in which you could have said no. You could've said, 'Sorry, Clive, I don't need a victory tour of the past.' Vadis was like, oh, don't worry, Max, oh, she just needs to get these dudes out of her system. And I wanted to believe them because I love you. But as someone who loves you, I know you better than these people. Your hang-ups aren't in your system, they are your system. You think I don't notice how you shut off when my friends tell college stories, like it's *so* pathetic when your *entire brain* is old stories? Why would I torture myself? I don't know, Lola. Why would *you*?"

"You were testing me. This is fucked up."

"Yeah, well, right back at you. You know, I think most people go around praying to not be shaped by the bad things that have ever happened to them, by the people who hurt them. A normal person tries to take responsibility for their own choices. But I don't think you're normal. And I love you and it sucks."

I said nothing, only watched him for a stretch of time as we moved through the dips in the silence, making ourselves at home in it before we ricocheted back into discomfort, talking in circles. It's unfortunate, I thought, how some of the world's most productive conversations are breakup conversations. People think, "If only we could have talked like this the whole time, things would've been different." But you couldn't have. That level of honesty requires a resoluteness achievable only by being within spitting distance of the exit. I didn't know I was being watched. But Max had watched. He had seen me with an authority that I could never access.

I looked at the glass hand, an approximation of my hand. It looked funny on the floor, like it was attached to a glass body, reaching up from the grave. He'd been sleeping next to it this whole time.

"So yeah, sure, I'm the last one. Now what's the answer to my question?"

"Which question?"

"Do you want to end it? Do you just not love me back?"

The lights blinked, giving off a crackle. The building was a hundred years old, okay, but how many gurus does it take to change a lightbulb? Still, the distraction was good. Good for me, who was being presented with a question, good for Max, who could look elsewhere while I took my time answering it. I found myself very badly wanting to touch his face, to pretend I knew where his pressure points were, but I didn't move.

"Of course I love you," I said.

It did not sound great. It sounded like habit.

Soon after we met, when I realized Max had an air of permanence to him, I introduced him to Clive. The three of us went to see a comedy show, which, in retrospect, was a horrible idea. The itinerary included ten minutes of waiting in line in the cold, stomping in place, an hour of Clive monitoring him to see if he laughed too much or not at all, and then twenty minutes' worth of perfunctory martinis, over which no significant information was exchanged, save for the revelation that Clive and Max were both a little color-blind.

"Cool," Max decided.

Not that there was a better response to be had, but I wanted him to shine for Clive. When the truth was that Clive should've been putting in the effort, making Max feel welcome. At work the next day, Clive came into my office, pulled up a chair, and sat there in silence until he could stand it no longer.

"I like him."

"Good."

"It's clear you won't harm each other."

"That's a shitty thing to say. It's a relationship, not a Hippocratic oath."

But he was right. *Do no harm.* That's how we became a couple, grafting onto each other's life until our nights apart became rarities. But somehow, I'd convinced myself this was a *bad* thing, that the stability was turning us into two beige fabric swatches who humped on occasion. But it was never a bad thing. And if I did feel bored? And if I didn't like his friends? All I had to do was tell him. Why hadn't I ever just told him? Most mistakes get made slowly, almost imperceptibly, over time. They do not hinge on a moment of epiphany. But I wanted to be with Max, I had always wanted to be with him. Because this desire had never caused me any grief, I did not know until now how much I wanted it.

"I do love you," I said, this time feeling the weight of the words.

I walked over to the platform and sat on the corner of the bed in case he didn't want me there.

"I mean," I said, correcting myself, "I love you."

There was a pinch of tears in my eyes.

"I love you. I love you. I love you. I love you. I love you. I love you and I don't think you're a fabric swatch."

"What?"

"I'm an asshole and I just really love you. I'm sorry."

I sank into myself and cried, giving myself over to the kind of full-bodied hysterics people rarely "burst" into. Normally there's some kind of emotional on-ramp but this was a flash flood. I could not look at him, knowing the contents of the list in my pocket, detailing his flaws as if I had none. I couldn't seem to close my jaw, which was unhinged in self-pity. My nose was dripping. I may have drooled a little.

"Please don't break up with me," I said, shocked at my own wretchedness.

"Jesus, okay," he said, rubbing my back, trying not to gloat.

"I'm sorry," I said, sniffling, my head on his shoulder. "I'm sorry I shut you out and lied to you and got caught up in a weird expensive cult. That was wrong."

"It's not a cult."

"Are we sure?"

"No." He laughed. "Jin told me that Clive was trying to get everyone to call him 'Shepherd' for a while there."

"That's not how he tells it."

"No shit," Max said, laughing.

For the first time in a long time, I looked at him as you're supposed to look at someone you adore, like at any minute you will be asked to sketch that person's face.

"Lola, I know you love me. But all I've ever wanted was for you to love me more than you're sorry. All I've ever wanted was for you to talk to me instead of about me."

He pressed his finger against a raised mole on the back of my neck. I never see it, I just cart it around on my skin like a barnacle.

"I have a whole relationship with this mole. Sometimes, when you're asleep, I stay up and commune with the mole. Like not molesting the mole. Just sorta talking to it."

"What do you talk about?"

"What do you think we talk about?"

He pulled me closer and kissed me, telling me I tasted like salt and snot. But I could still smell him. The familiarity of it made me want to fall asleep in his armpit. It also, for the first time in months, made me want to fuck him. The room was getting lighter from the outside now, the sun groggy through the arches. I looked at my phone: 5:30 a.m. I'd never seen the Golconda in daylight. I had the sensation of emerging from a matinee.

"Clive needs better lighting in this room," Max said, looking up. "It's like a police station in here."

I took advantage of this exposure of flesh, putting my face against his neck. He held my hand, squeezing it intermittently. Then he turned the hand over as if jiggling a doorknob. The ring. He was looking for the ring. I could sense him doing the calculus: Having the ring was better than having lost the ring, but having lost the ring was less of an insult than purposely not wearing it. He furrowed his brow. His skin was warm on mine.

"Is there any chance we can talk about that later?"

Then, as if they'd taken Max's critique to heart, the lights crackled once more and went out.

And that's when we heard the crash.

18

You were right about one thing, Clive: Much as we like to think of ourselves as hydraulic elevators, we are traction elevators. A traction elevator is beholden to outside forces, like electricity, which the elevator requires to move itself up and down. In a *functioning* elevator, when the power is lost, there is an electromagnetic brake that gets automatically released. The brake stops the cab of the elevator. In a *functioning* elevator, there are inspections. Maintenance checks. Code standards. In a *functioning* elevator, the cab of the elevator has multiple ropes that prevent it from falling should the brake fail as well. It is not, say, an oversized dumbwaiter suspended by a single rope and maintained by a loopy teenager with a dishrag.

I popped my head off Max's shoulder.

We locked eyes and jumped down from the platform in unison.

Once in the atrium, we saw glass everywhere, spilled across the floor as if the building itself had been holding a stack of it and tripped. The elevator door had automatically opened when the cab hit the ground. I gasped. Max put his palm over my face but released it when he realized there was nothing to see. No Wicked Witch shins flopped out on the marble, though two heavy brass pieces had spun out and scratched the marble floor, like it was a car that had been keyed. But there was no blood. No parts, not of you at least. You were inside the wreckage under a jumble of metal and glass.

We all die facing in a final direction, even if we are confined to beds. Perhaps with the exception of certain circus performers, who are afforded the opportunity to die spinning. You died facing east, toward the river. Apparently, it was painless. You hit your head when the elevator dropped, which knocked you unconscious. By the time you were smothered by your own creation, you were already gone. I know all this to be true. Still, it's hard to believe in a painless death. There is pain, it's just that your body doesn't have time to dwell on it.

I don't know why you came back or when. By the time the police retrieved the security tapes, all footage older than forty-eight hours had been automatically erased. Vadis knew I wasn't coming in. Max was headed home and you had no plans to meet. Your army of fanatics didn't convene in the middle of the night. None of us were supposed to be there. Had you forgotten something? Were you fighting with Chantal? Did you know I was there? Maybe you died satisfied that your scheming had been, in some roundabout way, effective. Maybe you just loved what you'd built so much, you woke up in the haze of the city's small hours, desperate to crawl inside.

You ran out of money. That's the other thing that happened. Zach couldn't *believe* how much money you had and he was right. It was not believable. Your investors had cut you off and you'd burned the remnants of your war chest on apps and crystals instead of tedious little details like wiring. You were personally bankrupt, financially overextended. You were in the process of putting your apartment on the market. You'd borrowed money from *Chantal*. You were extorting obscene membership fees to defray increasingly absurd expenses while you held investors at bay with false promises about biofeedback that didn't amount to much. Turns out that, despite all that glorious free labor, cults are a bad business model. In the traditional sense. You'd never in your life had something not work out, not had events break in your favor. Then the Golconda itself broke.

So now, on top of mourning you, I am left to explain the ridiculousness of your death *to* you.

Your official obituary was as dry as the coroner's report. The picture they ran was from an old editor's letter, the somber one of you sitting at your desk behind an actual human skull. It could've been worse—you could've been holding the skull. But for the tabloids, you were a dream: *Guru Glenn Gets the Shaft. Cult the Red Wire. Glenn of Iniquity.* And the saddest one, somehow: *Clive in an Elevator.* Here was the event for which the gossip world had been unconsciously waiting: A privileged dick had gotten what was coming to him after hoodwinking investors and viewing the world's philosophies as his personal tapas bar. Even you have to admit you were an easy mark, a Fitzgeraldian figure with a horrendous carbon footprint. The media had a field day, trying to piece it all together before they lost interest. And yet, vicious as the papers were, you got off easy. I mean, not *easy* easy. You're dead. But I imagine part of you, the old part, would have enjoyed seeing your name in the inky pages of local papers, exploding from sidewalk kiosks once more. That's the part of you I will always miss.

But I missed it when you were here.

Clive 2.0, who died early that morning, should find relief in the fact that the Golconda never went public. Financially or physically. All the Google searches in the world wouldn't reveal anything about *who* the members were or anything about me or Max. Even the business cards didn't have words on them. All anyone knew was that your mutant clubhouse had killed you, *Ex Machina*–style. And they knew that much because of Chantal. She posted two photos within a day of your death. The first was from the night you went to see *Hamlet*, the two of you smiling with your Playbills as if they're college diplomas. So many broken-heart emojis, rippling out as they do when a heavy stone is dropped into shallow waters. Then she added a stealth photo she'd taken during her tour.

I'm in it, actually, but just my elbow.

Errol arrived before the paramedics and the cops. He tried to maintain an air of professionalism, but he was blotting his eyes with a pocket square. Max and I took one look at his face and helped him get everything incriminating out of there. All the binders and folders, all of Jin's equipment, all the tapes. Well, almost everything. Max shoved a laminated menu up his shirt. Errol could not do the same with the coffee machine. That was sold at auction, along with the furniture.

The Golconda would not become a nightclub. It would become an office space—several office spaces, actually, occupied by mid-tier companies, none of which I'd ever heard of. It would be used by people who'd never set foot inside the place when it still resembled a temple. The Magritte painting went back to whoever had lent it to you, to be hung on some private wall where it would no longer be imbued with nefarious meaning, where it would just be a rich person's prize, its men floating, unaware, as they'd done for generations.

And here's what I really wish I could tell you, because I know how much you'd enjoy this part: Amos, Willis, Dave, Jonathan, Howard, Cooper, Oscar, Aaron, Phillip, Knox . . . I heard from every last one after you died, their avatars popping up in little circles on my various screens. None of them called, I didn't know any of them well enough anymore for that. But also, none of them knew me without you. Even if they knew me *before* I knew you, they had an inkling that I'd worked at the magazine, that there might be a connection. They were sorry for my loss.

I thanked them, said you were special, and hoped they were having a good summer thus far. *Xo*. Some of them, the ones with whom I hadn't even interacted, reported that they'd *just* been thinking of me when they heard about what happened to you. Wasn't that strange? They'd seen something that had made them want to reach out again. A song had come up on their playlist, a photo on their feed, or the wrong book had been sent to their home. They'd already forgotten whatever it was that triggered those thoughts, but what were the odds? What were the chances?

Your funeral was Vadis and Zach's first date. Vadis loves her drama and her rituals, Zach his morbidity and solemnity. I suppose they are both living in preparation for tragedy, just in different ways. A funeral might be the only setting in which they thrive as a couple. It's too early to say. Zach put his arm around Vadis, and Vadis smacked it away out of habit before apologizing. She's working on affection. Maybe she got something out of the Golconda too. Maybe it worked on her the most.

And maybe you know all this already because you saw it. Who knows what the dead know? It behooves the living to maintain a one-way street of curiosity. We want to know everything about you, but pray that you are not watching when we're picking at and rubbing ourselves. But I hope you heard Vadis speak. She was eloquent. Zach made a big deal of telling everyone how he had not helped her with the speech, which she had to explain to him was just as bad as telling everyone he'd written it for her. She said that we should try not to think about what we had lost but that we were lucky to have known you at all. Your loyal servant until the end.

I avoided your ex-wife, whom I'd never met. I don't think she knows who any of us are. Over the years, you got very good at dividing your life into quadrants. She brought a friend for moral support, hugged your mother, kissed your coffin, and left. She was beamed in from a different time. Cherubic, good-natured, and collegiate, she represented a former version of you. A black cardigan clung to her ass and she wore lanyard jewelry braided by a child. She pulled her hair back when she kissed your coffin. It made me think of her in college, black-out drunk, holding her own hair back over a toilet. Maybe you helped. What a sight it would've been to see you at twenty! Your first wife fell for baby Clive, who was surely ambitious, even then, but who could've been a congressman or a professor.

Chantal avoided your ex-wife too. She was near catatonic in the corner. Though, I will say, when she could speak, she made sure everyone knew about the beauty conference in Europe that she'd pulled out of to be there. There were other women, too, women I didn't know. In the end, there's one surefire way to pull one's exes into the same spot, one package that never fails. It's free but it's permanent.

Errol distributed packets of tissues to anyone who didn't bring their own. He was obsessed with the tissues. It was his way of maintaining control. He also put "reserved seating" signs on some of the chairs, but no one wanted to sit in the front row, not even the celebrities, who congregated in the back and never took off their sunglasses. Jin is the only one who cried. Really *cried*. She understood that you were gone at a point when no one else seemed to. Maybe because of her own history, because of her dad and the hunting knife and the garage. She cried like she knew what death meant.

I held it together until the reception, where I felt, for the first of what would be many times, supremely paranoid. Like maybe I'd be shoving quiche into my face and a ghost from my past was going to pop out at me on a spring. Anytime someone approached me to talk about how great you were, I found myself looking over their shoulder. It didn't help that you were right there, only a parlor away. Eventually, I told Max that I had to use the bathroom. He nodded and kissed me on the cheek, pinching a strand of hair from my dress.

"Go," he said, watching the hair drift to the ground, "go say goodbye."

I slid the dividing doors closed behind me. There were flowers on top of you, arranged in a long bouquet like a fleur-de-lis. Someone, probably Jin or Errol, had crammed a single bird of paradise in there. I heard your mother and the funeral director talking logistics in the hallway. I pulled up a chair and spoke, at eye level, with your coffin. But I didn't know if I was talking to your head or to your feet, so I moved the chair once more, splitting the difference by addressing your torso.

"Fuck you," I whispered, just to see how it sounded.

I wanted to be like Jin, to understand your death so immediately, but I was not like Jin. I was starring in a play about a girl who goes to a funeral. The velvet curtain would be closing soon and then what? I'd have to leave you at the theater.

"It didn't work," I said.

But this was a lie. The Golconda did work, just not in the way you intended it to. You thought I could be cured by confrontation. But the past is too deep a hole to be crowded out by the present. I think, if closure exists, it's being okay with a lack of it. It's to be found in letting the doors swing open, in trusting that if hinges were meant to be locks, well, then they'd be locks. You brought Max and me together, which is what you wanted, for me to choose the future instead of having it choose me. Somewhere, buried beneath those layers of delusion and capitalism, was a generous thing you did.

So shines a good deed in a weary world.

It's funny, the night before last, I was cleaning the apartment and found a whole pile of *Modern Psychology* back issues. I'd saved them even when I didn't have a byline, just because my name was on the masthead. Vadis's and Zach's names appeared too, farther down the pile. One of the issues was from early in your tenure, when you were still contributing to the magazine, and it included my favorite story you ever wrote, about the sociological implications of island burial practices. Because places like Turks and Caicos aren't getting any wider, the majority of their residents get buried on top of each other with a layer of dirt between the coffins, up to five per plot. Every few decades, a groundskeeper digs up the whole thing, takes out the bottom coffins, and chucks the remains back into the ground. It's Death Tetris.

Do you remember this? The magazine ran a photo of a leathered groundskeeper leaning on a shovel, looking like he couldn't care less about you following him around all day, asking him questions. He explained that most people on the island spend their lives looking at the person next to them at the market or bus shelter, knowing there's a decent chance they'll be buried one on top of the other. But the question the magazine asked—the question you asked—is how would you treat other people, knowing the next person you see could be burrowing holes into the back of your head for eternity? For the most part, it deepened the sense of community. But there was also a "see you in hell" undertone to it all.

The groundskeeper told you about the hurricane that blew through years prior and flooded his burial plots. Coffins got mixed up in the mud, and the old groundskeeper, his incompetent cousin, had managed to put half of them back upside down. Strangers were not just lying on top of each other but facing each other. It was ages before they figured it out.

You called me from your hotel while you were working on this story. I was so excited because there you were, in this pink-sanded paradise with an ocean-view suite, where you could be with anyone, talking to anyone, but you chose me. It was some hour so late, it seems possible they don't make it anymore, and I could hear the sound of the ocean, beating against rocks. At one point, you picked up the hotel phone to order room service. I found it intimate, listening to you ask a stranger for something you wanted, being so regular. That was the height of my romantic feeling for you (it was all downhill from there). But I remember wanting to tell you right then that I loved you, wanting to address the tension. Even if you denied all emotions and nipped all confessions, I would get more out of talking about it than I would by saying nothing.

But the moment never presented itself. You were going on and on about the groundskeeper, about the upside-down coffins, about the unremarkable buzz of death.

"It's just skeletons," you read from your notepad, quoting him, "all skin gone, all muscle gone. All memories gone. It's man skeletons and it's woman skeletons and they almost the same."

Then you flipped the notepad closed.

"And that, my friend," you announced, "is the kicker."

I worried it might be too morbid, even for a piece about death. It might upset advertisers that we could not afford to lose. It might also upset *Modern Psychology* readers, who, let's face it, were already subscribing to a magazine called *Modern Psychology*. They had come for insight and practical tips and perhaps did not want to read about floating bones. This came out harsher than I meant. I was mad at you about a conversation we'd never had and never would have. At first, you didn't say anything. Then I heard you slide the screen door open, walk onto your balcony, and light a cigarette. I listened for the ocean, to know I hadn't lost the connection.

"Lola," you said, as if you were already looking into the future, "sometimes people just need to be told what they want."

ACKNOWLEDGMENTS

Enormous gratitude to my agent, Jay Mandel, who has never heard a filtered thought from me in his life, and to everyone at MCD and Farrar, Straus and Giroux, especially my clear-minded editor, Sean McDonald, Jonathan Galassi, Mitzi Angel, Sheila O'Shea, and Sarita Varma. In the early pages of this novel, a character calculates the percentage of his life he will have spent knowing our heroine. It makes my heart swell, thinking of how significant that number is for many of us. Thanks also to June Park, for the phenomenal cover, and to Stephen Weil, for his tireless efforts on behalf of this book.

Thank you to my family, for their ancient and unbreakable enthusiasm, and to my extraordinary and extraordinarily supportive friends for allowing me in their midst. I adore you. I am also grateful to Yaddo for the sleepover, Scribe for the California dream, and the great city of New York forever.